SECRETS ON THE LEVELS

An addictive crime thriller full of twists

DAVID HODGES

(Detective Kate Hamblin mystery book 5)

Revised edition 2019
Joffe Books, London
www.joffebooks.com

Published in Great Britain 2017 as "Deadly Secrets"

ISBN: 978-1-78931-132-7

This book is dedicated to my wife, Elizabeth,
for all her love, patience and support over so many
wonderful years and to my late mother and father,
whose faith in me to one day achieve my ambition
as a writer remained steadfast throughout their
lifetime and whose tragic passing has left a hole
in my life that will never be filled.

AUTHOR'S NOTE

Although the action of this novel takes place in the Avon & Somerset Police area, the story itself and all the characters in it are entirely fictitious. Similarly, at the time of writing, there is *no* police station in Highbridge. This has been drawn entirely from the author's imagination to ensure no connection is made between any existing police station or personnel in the force and the content of the novel. I would also point out that I have used some poetic licence in relation to the local police structure and some of the specific procedures followed by Avon & Somerset Police in order to meet the requirements of the plot. Nevertheless, the policing background depicted in the novel is broadly in accord with the national picture and these little departures from fact will, hopefully, not spoil the reading enjoyment of serving or retired police officers for whom I have the utmost respect.

David Hodges

BEFORE THE FACT

Darkness. Black. Moonless. All but impenetrable. That was how he liked it. He felt safe in its comforting embrace. Secure in the knowledge that he could move about in his thick, rubber-soled shoes without a soul being aware of his presence. Not that it would have been of any benefit to anyone to have spotted his muscular figure in the black hoodie and tight jeans anyway. The close-fitting hood he always wore on his nocturnal enterprises guaranteed him absolute anonymity. Furthermore, the thin leather gloves ensured that he would leave no incriminating prints behind him for police forensics to lift either.

Lenny Stallard smiled grimly in the darkness and stood there on the edge of the shrubbery for a moment, drawing in deep lungful's of clean night air. He was in no hurry to complete the job he had set himself. He was a professional – had been for around 20 years – and a four-year stretch earlier in his criminal career after a disastrous robbery, or "blagging" as they said in the "trade", he mused cynically, which had dented his pride more than anything else, had taught him the value of caution. 'Don't rush things' the old lag in Wandsworth nick had told him when he had joined him in his cell. 'Take your time or make a cock-up and end up *doing* time!' That advice had come a bit too late in the day then, but he had never forgotten it in the years that followed when he'd given up on robbery and branched out into big country house burglaries.

There was no point in rushing this one anyway, he mused. He had all the info he needed on the house – the location of the bedroom where the old girl kept her jewellery and the dodgy kitchen window at the back which would let him inside. He didn't even have to worry about making a noise. The old geezer who owned the place was apparently away in Monaco for a couple of days with his missus and the house had no burglar alarm fitted. Screwing it was going to be child's play.

He glanced at the luminous dial of his watch. Two minutes to midnight. Time to rock and roll.

He left the cover of the shrubbery and crossed the gravel forecourt with a confident, measured stride, ignoring the white sports car parked in a corner which he had expected to be there. The side gate opened with barely a sound and the masked beam of his torch picked out a long strip of crazy-paving beyond, which ran down the side of the house to an ornamental stone archway festooned with roses at the far end. The scent of the roses was almost overpowering as he slipped through, turning right along the back of the house across a broad patio flanked by an extensive area of lawn.

He found the kitchen window and stopped to listen for a few moments. An owl rose like a ghost from a stone figure gracing a dormant fountain in the middle of the back lawn and something scurried through the low-level shrubbery bordering the patio. Otherwise, there wasn't a sound.

He tested the wooden-framed window in front of him and immediately felt it give. He exerted a little more pressure on it and the window suddenly swung outwards, hitting him in the chest. Pushing it back against the wall, he climbed on to a long, wooden garden seat set beneath it and thrust his head through the opening into a gloom perfumed with the sweet smell of fruit. His torch picked out a wooden bowl laden with apples, oranges and pears on a long farmhouse-style wooden table to his left and kitchen cupboards and appliances fitted to both the right-hand side and facing walls.

Turning round on the seat, with his back to the window, he sat on the sill, bent his head and eased himself through the gap. Then, swinging round again to face into the room, he dropped on to the tiled floor on the other side.

A timber cracked above his head and he froze, but the sound was not repeated and he put it down to the usual expansion and contraction of roof timbers. A glass-panelled door in one corner gave access to a long hallway, with doors opening off on both sides and a thickly carpeted staircase, climbing to the upper floor a few feet from the front door.

The stairs creaked slightly when he was halfway up and he froze again for a second, then grinned again. 'Dickhead,' he breathed. There was no one in the house to hear him, except maybe a mouse or two, so what the hell was he so jumpy about?

At the top of the stairs he found himself in a corridor, no doubt corresponding with the hallway downstairs. A similar number of doors opened off on each side, but he was only interested in one. It was the first on his left and according to his information, it accessed the master bedroom.

He turned the handle slowly and pushed the door open, directing his torch in a cursory sweep around the room beyond as he stepped inside, picking out another internal door – probably leading to a dressing room or en suite bathroom – on his left. The pencil beam passed quickly over a heavily curtained window, a double bed with a rumpled duvet – untidy sods had gone away without making the bed, tut-tut – and a double wardrobe and chest-of-drawers, then swung back to focus on a glass-topped dressing-table to one side of the bed. The large ebony jewellery box was set back against the wall, as if trying to hide behind the collection of cut-glass ornaments arranged in a half-circle in front of it, and his heart began to beat faster.

Almost tripping over himself, he stumbled across the room and bent down to turn on the bedside light, which stood on a corner of the dressing-table before switching off his torch, confident that the light would not be visible outside through the heavy curtains drawn across the window.

The jewellery box had three drawers, each crammed with rings, necklaces and earrings in different-sized compartments. Some of the stuff looked to him like custom jewellery and of little value, but there were other pieces – gold necklaces, strings of pearls and a number of gold rings studded with glittering stones – that seemed massively expensive. But he was no expert – he would leave that side of things to the fence he always used in Taunton – and shaking the haversack off his back, he flicked open the clasps and tipped the contents of each drawer into the hungry gaping neck, closing it up again with a flourish.

He grinned at himself in the dressing-table mirror before straightening up. A good night's work, my boy, he mused, but why stop at just one room? With the house empty, he could afford to go through the whole place and there was no telling what he might find. But he never got the chance.

He heard the sound of the toilet chain being pulled seconds before he sensed the presence behind him and turned quickly, just in time to see the elderly woman in a long nightdress, who had evidently just emerged from the en suite, edging her way along the wall towards the bedroom door. Her face was as white as the sheets on the bed, her blue eyes wide and staring and the pale narrow hands clenched tightly by her sides, locked in a grip of absolute terror.

He got to the door even as she grabbed the handle, jerking her back inside the room and dropping his haversack in the process. At once she collapsed in a heap against the wall, shaking fitfully as the tears rolled down her cheeks.

'Please,' she whispered, 'please don't hurt me.'

Stallard was stocky, but not very tall, yet he seemed to tower over the tiny figure, his own hands now clenched by his sides and the face inside the hood convulsed with rage.

'You shouldn't be here!' he snarled. 'I was told you wouldn't be here!'

'Please,' she whimpered again, 'I won't tell anyone, really I won't.'

As Lenny Stallard glared down at her, however, he knew there was only one way he could be sure of that. Then she began to scream …

CHAPTER 1

Detective Inspector Ted Roscoe was his usual morose-looking self when he strode into the CID office at Highbridge police station, his unshaven face wearing the sort of heavy scowl that might have been stamped into his slab-like features by an industrial press, his boot-button eyes resembling twin pistol barrels as they roved around the room as if looking for a target.

The two detectives sitting facing each other across a paper-strewn double desk seemed to hunch lower in their seats, perhaps sensing a "just" job coming their way and doing their best to be invisible.

Roscoe hesitated when he saw them, but a few paces in their direction he glimpsed the auburn-haired woman detective seated on her own on the far side of the room and made a bee-line for her instead.

'A present for you,' he rapped, dropping a thick blue folder held together by two large rubber bands on to the desk in front of her. 'It might jog a few cogs in the old memory machine.'

Detective Sergeant Kate Lewis grimaced at the interruption and pushing back from her computer screen, stripped off the rubber bands and flicked open the cover of what was obviously a prosecution case-file bulging with reports, charge sheets, witness statements, forensic photographs and a mass of other detail. A much slimmer buff file was clipped to the left-hand cover inside, labelled "descriptive file" – otherwise known as a D/F – which contained the personal record of a convicted criminal, complete with a photograph and a copy of his fingerprints.

Kate was drawn to the mugshot for some reason and studied it for a few seconds. The face staring back at her was lean and mean, with a shaven head, bearing a swastika tattoo on one side, and dark hooded eyes that seemed much too close together. The thin lips were slightly parted and turned down at one corner to effect an arrogant smirk, and the swarthy features carried at least a couple of day's growth of beard.

'Nice!' she commented with heavy sarcasm. 'But what about him?'

Roscoe's boot-button eyes bored into her. 'Recognise the name?'

She shrugged. 'Lenny Stallard. Target villain, if I remember correctly. Suspected of a series of country house break-ins which couldn't be proved. Then, around three years ago, he stepped over the line when his last job culminated in murder and he got sent down.'

'Very good,' he patronised. 'You win the prize. But what you should be asking me is why I've given the file to you.'

Kate sighed, dropped it on the desk and leaned back in her chair, regarding Roscoe with the expression of someone who has tired of the game. 'Okay, Guv,' she said, humouring him, 'why have you given it to me?'

Roscoe's scowl deepened and he popped some chewing gum into his mouth. 'It was nearly three years ago. DCI Austin Jacobs from Bridgwater was the senior investigating officer. I was … er … away at the time—'

'Oh yes, your nasty little op,' she cut in with a grin, remembering the embarrassing haemorrhoidectomy which had laid him up for several months. 'Do you find it easier to sit now, Guv? They say that removing the swollen veins from the back passage does help.'

'Don't be so bloody impertinent,' he snapped, reddening appreciably. 'Anyway, you were away for a few weeks too, on that drug squad attachment, so you probably won't know much about the circumstances of the case.'

'As it happens, I do,' she retorted. 'Stallard broke into a house out on the Levels and murdered an elderly woman in her bedroom – I think her name was Daphne Slater – then made off with her jewellery.'

He grunted and propped himself on the edge of the desk, chewing rapidly. 'He coughed to the burglary. Had to. Daphne Slater's husband, Stephen, and their son, Charles, who were out at the time, heard her screams when they returned home, and clocked the arsehole quitting the scene. They later found Daphne Slater stabbed to death in her bedroom and a load of her jewellery missing. This was found on Stallard when he was nicked, so he could hardly deny breaking into the house, but he always denied the murder and claimed he was set up.'

'I forget the detail, but didn't he blame some woman he was seeing to?'

'Yeah, he maintained that screwing the house had been suggested by a blonde tart he had met in a local pub, who'd told him she'd been sacked by Daphne Slater while working as a cleaner at the house and wanted to get her own back on the family. He claimed she filled him on the layout of the place, insisting the Slaters were abroad and wouldn't be back until after the weekend, which meant the house would be empty—'

'But it wasn't,' Kate finished for him.

He blew a bubble with his gum, apparently unaware of the distaste in her expression as he licked the gum back off the underside of his Stalinist moustache. 'Obviously not.'

'Bum information then?' and she grinned again.

His eyes narrowed at her use of the slang term so soon after her reference to his operation and he stopped chewing for a moment. Then, apparently deciding to give her the benefit of the doubt despite the laughter in her eyes, he said: 'No, just a load of bollocks dreamed up by a nasty little shit. Jury thought so too when he finally got weighed off at crown court and he got life.'

'So what about the blonde cleaner?'

'There never was one according to the Slater family, and the licensee of the pub where Stallard was supposed to have met the woman, while admitting that Stallard occasionally drank there, denied ever seeing him with a customer answering her description. So, as I've just said, the toe-rag's story was a load of bollocks. He stiffed Daphne Slater, no doubt about it; he just didn't fancy a life sentence for murder by admitting it.'

'Certainly a nasty business – she was stabbed several times, wasn't she?'

He nodded. 'A long-bladed knife was used, the pathologist reckoned, but the weapon was never found.'

'And you're now going to tell me that Stallard has hung himself in his cell and the coroner has ordered an inquiry?'

He snorted. 'If only! Fact is, he's out on his toes somewhere. Got into a fight with another prisoner in the nick and was thought to have suffered potentially serious head injuries, which the prison medical team couldn't deal with. Bollocks again as it turned out, and evidently part of a pre-arranged plan. Anyway, he was rushed to hospital in an ambulance after allegedly suffering a fit, but miraculously recovered, smacked the doctor who was checking him over and scarpered through a toilet window while the screws escorting him were waiting outside the examination room.'

'And you reckon he'll turn up again on our turf?'

'He may already be here. Happened yesterday morning—'

'Yesterday? And you're telling me now?'

He grunted. 'Only just heard myself. Seems there was one of those … what do they always call them … unfortunate breakdowns in communication? But it means matey-boy could easily have got here by now, heading across country and thumbing it or picking up a lift at one of the motorway services.'

'What, in prison gear?'

He grunted. 'That's the point – he isn't in prison gear anymore. A man answering his description broke into a house near the hospital and raided their wardrobe, leaving his prison clothes behind. He is now believed to be dressed in the sort of clothes he likes best – a black hoodie, plus jeans and trainers. His escape and description is being broadcast on national TV this afternoon because of the risk he presents to the public, but it's all a bit too late if you ask me.'

Kate flipped open the cover of the file again, then frowned. 'Strange that he chose to do a runner now, though, isn't it? He must have been inside at least two years. Something obviously triggered his actions – especially as his so-called medical emergency has to have been planned well in advance.'

He nodded. 'Yeah, but he'd been a good boy ever since he got sent down – even got religion apparently, which a lot of cons do to get privileges – and helped the resident chaplain with his services in the prison chapel. Naturally, the screws thought he'd settled in and would no longer be a problem.'

'But why come back here? Surely he must know it would be the first place we would look for him?'

He shrugged, chewing furiously now and staring out of the window at a pigeon on the branch of a tree. 'He may not have, but revenge is a strong motive. He probably thinks it's pay-back time, which means any of those whose evidence helped put him away could be at risk: the Slater family; the licensee at the pub; the senior investigating officer – their names are all in the file. He's a violent bastard with previous for robbery and GBH with a blade on a postmistress, so I wouldn't put anything past him – just find him before he gets to anybody, okay?'

She grimaced again, glancing sideways at the pile of paperwork in her "in" tray and wondering how she would ever get through it with yet another job to follow up on.

Seeing the direction of her gaze, he grinned. 'It'll give you a chance to get some fresh air for a change,' he said.

She nodded. 'Very thoughtful of you, Guv,' she retorted.

His grin broadened. 'My pleasure,' he said, easing himself off the desk. 'All his previous haunts are in the case file and as there aren't that many, it shouldn't demand too much legwork. But make sure you warn those prosecution witnesses first – just in case Stallard decides to pay them a visit.'

He half-turned and waved a hand towards the two detectives still sitting at the double desk. 'You can take Sherlock over there with you – if he can stay awake long enough to be of any use to you!'

Then he turned on his heel and strode out of the room with the demeanour of a man who has just shed a great weight from his shoulders.

* * *

'So, what was all that about?'

Kate looked up from her third scrutiny of the descriptive file and treated the man who had plonked his ample behind on the corner of her desk vacated by Roscoe to a critical glance.

Just turned 30 like herself, her colleague could not have looked less like the detective he actually was. Distinctly overweight, with a thatch of unruly blond hair that had obviously not seen a comb in recent memory, he was dressed in a shabby, green-checked sports jacket and brown corduroy trousers, and his loosely knotted green woollen tie failed entirely to conceal the yellowish stain on the button band of his red cotton shirt front.

Kate had been married to Detective Constable Hayden Lewis for what seemed like forever now, even though in reality it was just a few years, and she loved the big, affable eccentric more than she could ever say, but had never managed to come to terms with his untidy appearance and blatant work-shy ethic. A former public schoolboy with a classical education and a first-class analytical brain, he could have been well on his way up the career ladder by now, but with his genial, laid-back approach to life he had not so much as stayed in the slow lane, but headed into in a cul-de-sac where he seemed perfectly happy to remain, despite all the cajoling he received from her.

'Come out of hiding now that Roscoe has gone, have you, Hayd?' she said sarcastically, nodding towards the double desk he had just left and the thin tousle-haired man still sitting on one side of it. 'I don't think you or Jamie Foster there could have sunk any lower in your chairs than you did when Roscoe came in.'

He grinned. 'We didn't want to cramp your style, old girl,' he replied.

She glared at him. 'How many times have I got to tell you not to call me that here?' she snapped. 'I'm your bloody DS when we're at work.'

His grin broadened. 'Sorry, *Sergeant,*' he replied, straightening up sharply as if on parade. 'I stand corrected.'

'And for frig's sake, smarten yourself up,' she went on, ignoring his tom-foolery. 'You look like a bundle of shit.'

He winced. 'Do you have to use that sort of foul language?'

'Don't change the subject, Hayden,' she persisted. 'You've no excuse – I left a clean shirt out for you this morning.'

'Ah,' he acknowledged with a heavy sigh, 'but unfortunately I spilt toothpaste down the front of it. I thought the curry stain on this one would be less obvious.'

She closed her eyes in resignation and pushed the descriptive file she had been reading across the desk towards him. 'On his toes from the nick yesterday morning,' she said. 'In for murder.' She tapped the thicker blue folder. 'Prosecution file. Bit of light reading for insomniacs.'

He glanced at the photograph pinned inside the file and quickly scanned the front page. 'Lenny Stallard?' he queried, his brows wrinkled in thought. 'I remember him. I did some legwork on that inquiry. You were on attachment in Bristol and DCI Austin Jacobs from Bridgwater headed the inquiry,' he chuckled, adding: 'Poor old Roscoe was away having his piles seen to at the time, if I recall.'

'Full marks for memory retrieval,' she replied with a faint smile at mention of their DI's operation. 'Well, from all accounts, Stallard's a nasty piece of work and Mr Roscoe reckons he's likely to turn up on our manor, which means certain people could be at risk.'

'Nice one,' he commented drily. 'And you've been lumbered with the job of trying to find him first?'

She smiled. 'No, Hayden,' she replied, '*We've* been lumbered. Capeesh?'

'But I've already put in for a couple of day's leave from tomorrow to go to that classic car rally, you know that.'

'Tough!'

He frowned heavily, then snorted an angry, 'Oh, Gordon Bennett!'

She chuckled. 'Why can't you ever just say "shit" like any normal person?' she queried mischievously.

'Because, as you well know, I don't use foul language and never have,' he snapped back.

'Then maybe you should start,' she countered. 'It's very cathartic.'

'I'd rather hammer a few nails into an effigy of Roscoe,' he said. 'Now that really would be cathartic!'

CHAPTER 2

Sycamore Lodge was a big Georgian-style house, set back behind a high brick wall in the middle of Mark Moor.

After an hour studying Stallard's prosecution file and enclosed D/F and drawing up a list of Stallard's old haunts and potential targets, Kate and Hayden finally pulled up on a shrubbery-fringed forecourt in front of the place , just feet from the front door. A flashy looking red Jaguar XK coupé and a black Volvo XC90 were parked at the far end of the forecourt and Hayden whistled as they climbed out of their car.

'How the other half live,' he murmured appreciatively.

The elderly man who answered the front door was dressed in tweeds and highly polished brown shoes and leaning on a walking cane. He could easily have been mistaken for the long-since deceased actor, Vincent Price, in his later years. Tall and thin, with swept-back grey hair, a thin moustache and the coldest blue eyes Kate had ever encountered, he studied the two detectives with obvious suspicion.

'Yes?' he snapped, his voice as cold as his gaze.

'Mr Slater?' Kate said, flashing her warrant card.

'*Colonel* Slater, young lady.'

Inwardly, Kate winced. Should have remembered that from the file, she mused, and immediately corrected her mistake. 'Sorry, Colonel. DS Lewis and DC Lewis, Highbridge CID. Could we come inside for a few moments?'

'Why?'

Slater was evidently not over the breach of etiquette.

Before Kate could answer, a young, dark-haired woman appeared at his elbow. 'Daddy,' she said, glancing at the warrant card still visible in Kate's hand, 'for goodness sake, invite the officers in.'

The old man threw her an irritable glance, but made no further comment and stepped awkwardly to one side to allow both detectives to step past him into the hallway.

The young woman opened a door to their left and ushered them into a large sitting room furnished with several armchairs, a two-seater settee under the window and a three-seater facing the door. She waved them towards the two-seater with a whiff of expensive perfume that enveloped Kate for a moment, then seemed to linger on her skin even as she sat down.

'Carol Slater,' the woman said, introducing herself and propping on the edge of an armchair. 'Is there a problem?'

Kate studied her for a moment. In her early 30s, she was short, probably no more than 5ft 4ins, quite stocky and very fit-looking, with brown hair which was back-combed and fashioned into a ponytail. She had a healthy tanned complexion, large brown eyes and a slightly crooked nose which matched the aquiline features she had no doubt inherited from her father. More noticeably, she was barefoot and dressed in miniscule shorts and a skimpy top, exposing a nicely tanned midriff, with some sort of pin in the navel – something, Kate observed out of the corner of her eye and with a tightening of her lips which had certainly not gone unnoticed by Hayden.

'Excuse my dress,' the woman said with a slightly embarrassed smile – no doubt conscious of Hayden's gaping interest – 'but we have a gym out back and on Sundays I like to work out. What's the problem?'

'Nothing to worry about, Miss Slater,' she said. 'We're here on a courtesy visit, that's all.'

'Courtesy visit?' barked the old man, who had remained standing beside his daughter, leaning on his stick. 'What the hell does that mean?'

'It's about Lenny Stallard,' Hayden said helpfully.

'Lenny Stallard?' Carol Slater's eyes widened and she reached out to grip her father's wrist tightly with one hand as he noticeably stiffened. 'Why, what's happened to him?'

Kate silenced further comment from Hayden with a baleful glance. 'Nothing's actually happened to him, Miss Slater,' she replied.

'More's the pity,' the Colonel grated.

'But we thought you should be aware of an unfortunate security breach yesterday morning—'

'You mean he's escaped?' her father cut in harshly. 'The swine is out – is that what you're saying?'

Kate made a face, then nodded. 'He got away from his escort when he was sent to a local hospital after a fight in the prison.'

'Damned fools!' the old man exclaimed. 'Don't know what they're doing. Wouldn't have happened with a prisoner when I was in the military.'

'He'll come back here, won't he?' Carol Slater said tremulously. 'He wants revenge?'

Kate shook her head quickly. 'There is no suggestion of that, Miss Slater. He'll probably try to get out of the country.'

'In that case, why have you come here to tell us he's escaped?' the Colonel put in.

'It's … it's just a formality,' Kate explained. 'Something we always do in this sort of situation. We just want you to be aware of the fact and to take sensible precautions in the very unlikely event that he tries to make contact with you – you know, make sure your windows and doors are kept shut and let us know if you see or hear anything suspicious.'

There was sudden movement and the next instant the old man limped past her across the room with surprising agility despite his gammy leg. Then, reaching into a corner behind the empty three-seater settee, he produced a double-barrelled 12-bore shotgun and turned with difficulty to face Kate, with the weapon gripped in one hand, but pointing at the floor.

'Damned swine turns up here and I'll blow his head off after what he did to poor Daphne!' he shouted. 'And that's a promise!'

'Daddy!' Carol Slater exclaimed, leaving her chair like a jack-in-the-box. 'Don't be so bloody stupid!'

But both Kate and Hayden were already on their feet. 'Put that thing down!' Kate rapped. 'Taking the law into your own hands, Colonel, will solve nothing and make you no better than Lenny Stallard. In any event, that shotgun should be locked away in a proper firearms cabinet.'

'It usually is, Sergeant,' his daughter put in quickly, glaring at her father. 'Daddy got it out to clean it just before you came.'

Kate frowned, unconvinced. 'Then I suggest he locks it away when he has done that,' she warned, or he will risk having it seized and his licence revoked.'

The Colonel scowled at her. 'Law's a bloody ass,' he retorted. 'And gun's not loaded anyway.'

After a moment's hesitation, however, he did as he was told and returned the weapon to the corner, only to stand there with his arms folded across his chest, a thunderous expression on his pale face.

Kate could feel the tension in the room now – it was almost tangible – and she threw a swift glance at Hayden who was standing beside her, looking awkward and embarrassed.

She forced a smile. 'Right, we'll leave you good people in peace,' she said. 'Please don't hesitate to contact us if you have any concerns you wish to discuss. I'll leave you my card.'

The old man snorted as she handed the card to his daughter, but without another word, stalked past them back out into the hallway and moments later they heard the sound of heavy footsteps mounting the stairs.

Carol Slater made a grimace. 'I must apologise for my father,' she said. 'He … he has never got over what happened to mummy.'

Kate followed Hayden in the direction of the hall. 'Hardly surprising under the circumstances,' she commented. 'He saw him fleeing the scene, I believe?'

Carol Slater nodded, showing them to the front door. 'My brother, Chas too. They heard mummy screaming when they returned home from the local pub and Stallard barged through them as they opened the front door. Daddy had a gammy leg – an old army wound – and was bowled over, and though Chas gave chase he wasn't fast enough, so Stallard got away.' She shrugged and her voice trailed off as she wiped both eyes on the back of one hand. 'When they got to Mummy's room, she was already – already, you know …'

'You didn't hear the screams yourself then?'

She shook her head. 'I was out that night with my girls from the salon.'

'Salon?'

She smiled. 'Yes, I run an upmarket hairdressing salon and beauticians in Bridgwater. I take my staff out for a meal every quarter as a thank-you for their hard work.'

'Very generous of you.'

She laughed. 'Believe me, I can afford it – and before you ask, yes, my tan *is* out of a bottle.'

Kate returned her smile with a rather stiff one of her own, embarrassed by the fact that Carol Slater had been able to read her thoughts so accurately and anxious to cover her discomfiture as quickly as possible.

'I … I can't even begin to imagine how traumatic this dreadful business must have been for you,' she said. 'First, having to cope with the awful death of your mother and then having to face the perpetrator in court. I'm just sorry that I've had to rake it all up again.'

Carol Slater shook her head. 'Please don't apologise. The murder was obviously awful, but I was actually spared the court case after suffering a breakdown – the shock I suppose – so

I didn't have to face Stallard during the trial. I wasn't required anyway as Daddy and my brother were the ones who had to give evidence.'

Kate nodded. 'Your brother, he was living with you at the time, was he?'

Carol Slater smiled again. 'Still is – bachelor, you know – though, sods law being what it is, he had taken daddy out for a drink the night Stallard chose to break in.' She opened the front door. 'He's not here very often anyway as he's a financial advisor and dashes about all over the place. In fact, he's actually out on business at the moment.'

But even as she spoke, as if to deliberately contradict her, a low growl announced the arrival of a white, old-fashioned sports car, which raced down the drive and pulled up beside the CID car with a swirl of gravel.

A dark-haired young man of about 25, dressed in casual trousers and a yellow open-necked shirt, sprang from the car with all the exuberance of youth and strode quickly towards them.

'Visitors, Cas?' he exclaimed with an engaging smile, his sharp brown eyes appraising Kate's trim figure quite openly.

Carol Slater made an embarrassed face. 'My brother, Charles,' she said tartly.

But Kate already knew who he was. His resemblance to his sister was uncanny – even down to the aquiline features and crooked nose.

She returned his gaze with a half-amused one of her own. 'Police,' she said and had the satisfaction of seeing his smile abruptly vanish.

'Good Lord,' he exclaimed. 'What on earth have we done?'

'They're here about Lenny Stallard,' Caroline Slater explained. 'He's escaped from prison.'

'Escaped? Bloody hell, when?'

'Yesterday morning.'

'We've just called by to let you know,' Kate added. 'It's unlikely that he'll show up here, but it would be as well to be on your guard, just in case.'

The young man frowned and scratched the lobe of his left ear before staring around the forecourt at the encompassing shrubbery. 'How's father taken it?' he asked, turning his head slightly towards his sister.

She made another face. 'How do you think, Chas? It's brought it all back.'

'Damn, damn, damn!' he said slowly and distinctly. 'It would happen now, wouldn't it?'

Kate raised an eyebrow, her curiosity immediately aroused. 'Why, what is so significant about today?' she queried.

The other shook his head irritably. 'Not precisely today, but this week,' he replied. 'It's taken sis and me over two years to persuade the old feller to consider selling up and moving to a smaller place – away from all the memories – and this could set everything right back to square one.'

Kate nodded. 'Oh, I see. Well, hopefully, we'll pick up Stallard soon and put him back where he belongs.'

'Jolly well hope so. There's a lot riding on this potential sale.'

Carol Slater cleared her throat. 'Thank you for letting us know about Stallard anyway, Sergeant,' she said quickly, glancing at the business card Kate had given her. 'We'll keep our eyes open and contact you if we see anything suspicious.'

It was obvious that she saw the visit as at an end and Kate took the hint, nudging Hayden, who had turned to study the sports car with the rapt attention of someone in love.

'Excellent,' she said, nudging him again. 'Thanks for your time, Miss Slater.'

She shook hands with both sister and brother, drawing her hand away sharply when Charles Slater held on to it a bit longer than was required, then quietly pushed Hayden towards the CID car.

'You pillock!' she snapped at her husband as they drove away. 'Are you so thick that you can't see when it's time to go?'

He gave a low whistle, obviously not listening to her. 'Do you realise that was an MGC?' he exclaimed. 'An MGC! Strewth, it could be getting on for 50 years old – in-line OHV six cylinder engine, just under 3,000cc and 150bhp. First produced 1967-68—'

Kate swore. 'Hayden, we are looking for an escaped murderer. Got it? We are not here to drool over sports cars, however fantastic you might think they are.'

He shook his head excitedly. 'But you don't understand, old girl, it was an MGC. Absolutely beautiful. I wonder whether he'd sell it?'

Kate hit the brakes so hard that he would have slammed into the windscreen but for the seatbelt.

'Hayden!' she shouted. 'Stow it about the sodding MGC, all right? And if you so much as try making him an offer, I'll … I'll not be responsible for my actions.'

He gaped at her. 'Okay, okay,' he exclaimed. 'Keep your hair on, old thing.'

Her eyes practically lasered him and he winced. 'Sorry … I meant Sergeant.'

She took a deep breath, glanced in her rear view mirror and pulled away again. 'That's better. Just get used to saying it, all right?'

''Course,' he replied, grinning. 'Maybe I'll sew three stripes on your pjs to make sure I don't forget.'

'I don't wear any pjs,' she retorted, 'as you well know.'

CHAPTER 3

The Scarlet Dancer sounded like the name of a nightclub, but in fact it was a rundown public house on an isolated backroad of the Somerset Levels, surrounded by marshland. Who could have come up with such an inappropriate exotic name was a mystery, since the present licensee had apparently only been there for around ten years and the cracked faded sign, depicting a flamenco dancer in a traditional red dress, had been swinging above the door long before his arrival.

It had started raining ten minutes after the visit to Sycamore Lodge and by the time Kate and Hayden managed to find the pub after three wrong turns it was absolutely pouring down. They made the public bar at a run and slammed through the door drenched to the skin after splashing through large puddles in the pockmarked car park.

There were no customers in the bar and the bald, heavy-set man behind the counter threw them a sullen, unwelcoming glance and put the pint glass he had been polishing back on the glass shelf behind him. 'Wet out there, is it?' he said unnecessarily in a rough London accent. 'So, what'll you be havin'?'

Kate gave him an old-fashioned look and slid her warrant card across the counter towards him. 'Highbridge

CID,' she said as he bent down to peer at the black leather wallet.

At once his eyes narrowed and when he looked up again, pushing the wallet back to her, his face wore a hostile, suspicious expression. 'And what would Highbridge CID be doin' all the way out here?' he said quietly.

'Are you the licensee, Mr … er—.'

'Dibble,' the man finished for her, 'Ronnie Dibble.'

'No relation to the Officer Dibble, who used to be on TV, I suppose?' Hayden cut in with a chuckle, only to freeze under Kate's glare.

Dibble didn't appear to see the funny side of the remark either. 'What is it you want, Miss,' he said, ignoring Hayden. 'Only, I'm a busy man.'

Kate glanced around the empty bar and gave a faint smile. 'Did you know a man named Lenny Stallard?' she asked.

He stiffened. 'I didn't know him, 'cept as an occasional customer,' he said. 'Got sent down for murdering an elderly lady, the bastard.'

'I'm afraid to have to tell you that he escaped from custody yesterday morning and there's an outside chance he might come back here.'

Dibble seemed unperturbed by the news. 'Why would he come back here?' he said. 'Nothin' for him in these parts. Folks got long memories.'

'We don't know,' Kate replied. 'It's just a possibility. You gave evidence at his trial, didn't you?'

He nodded. 'Geezer said he'd met some tart in here what got him to screw that house. I told 'em, I ain't never seen no blonde in my bar with him, that's all.'

Kate nodded, suddenly feeling a little mischievous at his sullen attitude. 'Fine, but it's possible he might have a grievance against those who gave evidence against him.'

He shrugged. 'Please hisself. Come here and I'll sort the bastard out, you can be sure of it.'

Kate sighed, for some reason suddenly curious. 'Stallard said he met this girl in a backroom.'

He nodded. 'That's right. Through there.' He pointed to a door on the other side of the bar. 'It's a sort of snug. Not many use it. And I never saw him with no woman in there.'

'Can I take a look?'

'Why?'

'Curious, that's all.'

He shrugged again. 'Suit yerself'

With that, he turned his back on the two detectives and disappeared through a door behind the bar.

'Nice chap,' Hayden commented.

Kate ignored him and strode across the room to the door Dibble had indicated, but there was not much to see. The tiny room beyond was furnished with plain round tables set in front of cushioned bench seats in three of the four corners and wooden stools grouped around them on the outside. A door in the fourth corner obviously accessed the car park and a sign above it read "Toilets".

'Satisfied?' Hayden asked as they made their way back to the car.

She turned on him. 'Only when you grow up and stop letting the side down,' she retorted. 'Officer Dibble, I ask you! What a thing to come out with. If you carry on like this, I'm going to drop you back at the nick.'

He looked hurt. 'Sorry, old ... er ... Sergeant. I will be the soul of discretion from now on.'

She threw him a cynical glance. 'I'll believe that when I see it,' she said. 'Now, one more port of call, then back for some lunch.'

He frowned. 'I thought we had seen everyone.'

She shook her head grimly. 'Still one left – ex-DCI, Austin Jacobs, who you said earlier that you worked with on the Stallard case?'

He raised both eyebrows. 'What, Creeper of the Yard? How could I ever forget him?'

'Why do you say that?'

He shrugged. 'Former Met DI, hence the "Yard" bit. Promoted to DCI a few years after transferring here. I think the Met were glad to get rid of him. Fellow was a charlatan and a womaniser; wouldn't have trusted him further than I could have thrown him.'

She gave a short laugh as she climbed back into the CID car and started the engine. Hayden never failed to amuse her with his pompous, old-fashioned terminology. 'Well, since he's now retired, you don't have to anymore.'

'But if he's off the books, why are we bothering with him?'

She checked her rear view mirror as she pulled away. 'Didn't you read the file properly? Jacobs was accused by Stallard of concealing evidence and I've since found out that he had an unfortunate, but never proven, reputation for doing just that in other cases in the Smoke. If Stallard is on the revenge trail, I would have thought Jacobs would be his number one target.'

Hayden looked distinctly unhappy. 'How about lunch and then Creeper?' he suggested.

Kate shook her head. 'Business first, pleasure afterwards.'

He snorted. 'It won't be much pleasure for me if I end up with an ulcer?'

She laughed outright. 'An ulcer couldn't survive in that stomach of yours, Hayden,' she retorted. 'It would be asphyxiated by all the fat that constantly slides down your gullet.'

* * *

Austin Jacobs lived in a small bungalow, close to the village of Cannington, a few miles from Bridgwater, with open fields at the back. He obviously wasn't much of a gardener as the front garden was overgrown with weeds and brambles and going by the peeling paintwork on the window frames and front door, he wasn't into decorating either.

Creeper had become something of a legend in the force. Few had doubted that he had a nose for crime and criminals – a sort of inbuilt sense that could sniff villains out at 500 yards. His unorthodox methods, however, had eventually cost him his job. In the absence of any actual proof of misconduct – despite his alleged, though never admitted, use of what was colloquially referred to in police circles as "The Ways and Means Act" to secure convictions and unsubstantiated rumours that he was "on the take" to feed his obsessive gambling habit – he had been squeezed out by the simple expedient of posting him from CID to the headquarters control room on the grounds of career development. This humiliating move had immediately resulted in his voluntary departure on an ill-health pension.

Kate remembered him from her rookie constable years as a tall, dignified man always impeccably dressed in an expensive suit, with jet black hair, a neat military moustache and a sharp, penetrating gaze. But the man who came the door in answer to their repeated knocking was nothing like that. Incredibly thin and stooped, he had shoulder-length grey hair, an unkempt beard and rheumy eyes that suggested alcohol had been his companion for a lot longer than was advisable. He wore a grubby-looking tartan shirt and rumpled grey flannels and he held a lighted cigarette between two fingers of one hand.

'So, Old Bill, is it?' he queried with a faint smirk before Kate even had time to introduce herself.

She raised an eyebrow in surprise and smiled back. 'You're on the ball, Mr Jacobs,' she replied. 'DS Lewis and DC Lewis, Highbridge CID. Can we have a word?'

There was hostility in his gaze now. 'About what?'

'Lenny Stallard,' she said simply.

It was his turn to look surprised. 'Lenny Stallard?' he repeated, taking a pull on the cigarette. 'Now, there's a blast from the past.'

Stepping to one side, he waved them towards a door opening off the hall behind him. 'In there. Apologies for the mess. You know, bachelor and all that.'

It wasn't the untidy state of the sitting room in which Kate and Hayden found themselves that bothered them, though its stained carpet, worn threadbare furnishings and part-pulled curtains did not exactly provide a welcoming touch. It was the smell – a stale unwashed odour that permeated everything, and hung in the air like a miasma.

They soon discovered the source too. A litre bottle of Famous Grouse whisky and a half-full glass stood on a coffee table beside a tatty armchair which had been turned to face a television on a desk in one corner, and an ashtray piled high with cigarette butts was perched on the chair arm beside an old-fashioned yellow telephone.

The television was on, its grubby screen displaying what looked like a list of racetrack runners and riders, and Kate threw it a curious glance as they entered the room.

Seeing her puzzlement, the former DCI sighed. 'I like to gamble a bit,' he said. 'You know, the gee-gees. It passes the time. I do the dogs too when I feel like it.'

'What, all day?' Hayden queried.

Jacobs shrugged. 'What else is there to do?' he retorted. 'And anyway, I have Mr Grouse for company.'

He indicated the whisky bottle with a flick of one hand. 'Fancy joining me?' he added, more as a cynical throw-away remark than a genuine invitation.

Kate's mouth tightened. 'No thanks,' she said, feeling embarrassed to see what this once sharp-minded, smartly dressed colleague had become. 'We won't be staying long.'

Jacobs emitted a harsh chuckle. 'Don't blame you, DS Lewis. Nor would I if I were in your shoes. This is what you've got to look forward to when you retire, though, just remember that. It's how most ex so-called detectives end up – burned out, alcoholic losers with very little money left and nothing but the next drink to look forward to. The job takes it all, you see; sucks the life out of you, then dumps you in the waste bin when you're no further use to it.'

The bitterness in his tone was raw, almost vicious, and for a few moments Kate was taken aback by it, unable to think of a suitable reply. It was obvious that his gambling and alcohol addiction had taken everything from him, except the shirt on his back, and he was probably just surviving on his police pension. Finally, as Jacobs stubbed out his cigarette on the edge of the coffee table and snatched up his glass of whisky, she found her voice.

'Lenny Stallard is out,' she said simply. 'He slipped his escort yesterday morning while attending hospital after being injured in a fight in the nick.'

He shrugged, downing the whisky and pouring himself another. 'Why should that be of any interest to me?' he said. 'I put that bastard away – must be three years ago.'

'Two, she corrected, but maybe he still nurses a grudge?'

He sank on to the arm of the chair, knocking the ashtray on to the floor, and caressed his newly filled whisky glass with both hands. 'My last case before they banished me to the control room,' he said whimsically. 'Remember it well. He got what he deserved.'

Kate nodded slowly. 'Apparently he doesn't see it that way. He reckons he was set up.'

Jacobs studied her for a moment. 'By whom?' he almost spat. 'He was identified by old man Slater and his son as he fled the scene and when we nicked him, he still had Daphne Slater's jewellery in his haversack.'

'He didn't deny breaking into the house, but he said he never touched Daphne Slater. He claimed she started screaming, which spooked him, so he ran.'

Jacobs gulped some more whisky. 'Just another lying shit,' he replied, then abruptly changed the subject. 'So who's your DI now? Ted Roscoe?'

She nodded and he laughed again. 'Good old Ted,' he said. 'Still chasing skirt, is he?'

Kate grimaced and although well aware of Roscoe's past reputation as a womaniser, chose to ignore the comment. 'You said Stallard was always a liar, Mr Jacobs,' she said. 'That suggests you'd had dealings with him before the Slater case?'

Jacobs did not confirm or deny the fact. 'Ted and me, we worked on several cases together after I transferred from the Met, you know,' he said instead. 'Nice enough bloke, but not one to set the world alight. That's what comes of only having one brain cell, I suppose.'

Kate doggedly stayed on course. 'What about the blonde woman Stallard claimed to have put him up to do the burglary?' she said. 'Why would he have come up with something like that if it wasn't true? It was no help to his defence – he'd still broken into the house.'

Jacobs' eyes narrowed, no doubt resenting her persistence, and he stood up a little unsteadily. 'You re-investigating the crime now then?' he queried sarcastically.

She shook her head. 'No, not at all. We're here simply to make you aware of the fact that Stallard is out and to warn you to be on your guard in case he decides to pay you a visit.'

He snorted. 'You let me worry about Lenny bloody Stallard, love. Now, if you don't mind, I've got some runners and riders to look at.'

Kate didn't argue – she had no desire to stay in the bungalow any longer than she needed to anyway – and for once Hayden seemed to be in total agreement with her, as he was out the door and into the hallway even before she managed to turn around.

'What an awful hole, that was,' he remarked as they both returned to the CID car. 'And to think Jacobs was once a DCI too. Just goes to show you what alcoholism can do to a chap.'

Kate slipped the key into the ignition, but sat there for a moment without starting the engine, her brows furrowed in thought and her gaze fixed on some ethereal thing in front of her that only she could see.

'Hayd,' she said slowly. 'Is it my imagination or does everyone associated with the Slater murder case seem anxious to bury it?'

'Your imagination,' he answered brightly, glancing at his wristwatch. 'Now, how about a spot of lunch?'

She glared at him. 'Do you ever think of anything except lunch, Hayden?' she snapped.

He grinned. 'Well, there's always dinner?' he replied.

CHAPTER 4

Lunch, much to Hayden's annoyance, was a chippie in Highbridge, eaten in the CID car, and he glowered at the battered fish and chips in the newspaper on his lap as if willing it to disappear. 'Nice bit of cold pheasant in the fridge at home,' he complained. 'We could have had that for lunch – sitting at a table like normal civilised people, with a glass of Chardonnay to wash it down.'

'Good for the old brain cells, fish,' Kate pointed out through a mouthful of cod.

'Then maybe you should have bought some for Roscoe,' he retorted. 'Might have developed the one brain cell Creeper said he's got.'

She threw him a mischievous glance as she speared two chips with her plastic fork. 'Maybe I should make Mr Roscoe aware of your suggestion?' she said. 'You'd look great back on the beat, wearing a funny hat.'

He snorted. 'This isn't on, Kate,' he continued, without acknowledging the dig. 'The grease from this lot is likely to ruin my trousers.'

She almost choked, grabbing her tin of lemonade from the dashboard with her free hand and clearing the chip stuck in her throat with a noisy gulp.

'Ruin your trousers, Hayd?' she gasped, her eyes brimming with tears of laughter. 'Hell's bells, man, the way you're turned out, who'd know the difference?'

She was still laughing when the mobile facility on her TETRA police radio activated. It was Roscoe and his terse instruction quickly wiped away the humour. 'Get yourself over to the Slater place pronto,' he said. 'Seems like they've had a visitor.'

* * *

Carol Slater ran out of the front door as the CID car pulled up in front of it, just behind her brother's parked MGC. She was dressed in blue jeans, trainers and a short top. Obviously she was no longer working out, Kate mused. She was wearing an ash-blonde wig, which looked almost like natural hair – the skill of the beautician, Kate thought enviously – but which seemed at odds with her tanned complexion.

'Chas saw Stallard peering in through the French windows of Daddy's study at the side of the house,' she said breathlessly. 'He and Daddy have gone out into the grounds looking for him.'

Kate felt her stomach churn, glancing briefly over her shoulder as a marked police patrol car raced down the driveway, lights flashing, and churned to a stop behind the CID car.

'With or without the shotgun, Miss Slater?' she queried.

Carol Slater didn't answer, but made a grimace instead, her eyes wide with shock.

'Shit!' Kate breathed and turned to the uniformed policeman who had jumped from his car and was standing at her elbow, staring about him uncertainly. 'Get on force radio!' she snapped. 'I want some troops here pdq. We may have a prison escapee loose in the vicinity. A man named Lenny Stallard. Serving life for murder. Control room will have the necessary info on him.'

Even as the policeman turned back to his car, Kate jumped as a heavy gunshot sent a flock of panic-stricken rooks hurtling skywards from somewhere at the back of the house.

'Shit!' she said again and started across the forecourt towards an open gate 20–30ft away, with Hayden close on her heels.

A path composed of crazy-paving ran down the side of the house, disappearing through a stone archway, overgrown with dead roses. Beyond the archway, the path struck off sharply to the right between the rear of the building and an extensive lawn bordered on the far side by mature trees and shrubs. There was no one in sight.

Kate came to an abrupt halt and Hayden stumbled into her with a surprised grunt. Silence but for the muted sound of the police car's radio back on the forecourt.

'We'd best wait for the troops,' Hayden advised.

Kate didn't answer, her narrowed gaze slowly moving along the line of trees and shrubs on the far side of the lawn. Nothing at first. Then she saw some movement and started across the lawn at a run, Hayden's warning shout falling on deaf ears.

Within a few yards she was among the trees, glancing around her into sunlit shadows that seemed to have a life of their own as a newly risen breeze whispered to her through the gently stirring boughs.

'You're a darned fool!' Hayden breathed as he appeared at her elbow. 'If Slater's got his shotgun, he could blast at anything that moves.'

'Shut it!' she snapped back. 'Just listen!'

Still nothing, save for the whisper of the breeze and the distant metallic chatter of the police radio. Then they both tensed as the loud crack of a branch issued from the gloom to their right. The next instant a more definite shadow materialised from the patchwork of sunlight and shadow.

Stephen Slater was dressed in the same tweeds as before, but he was now wearing a matching cap and a pair of wellington boots and he carried a double-barrelled 12-bore shotgun.

'I'll take that, sir!' Kate snapped, stepping forward with one hand outstretched.

The old man glared at her. 'You'll do nothing of the sort, young lady!' he rapped back. 'I am legally entitled to shoot on my own land.'

'Yes,' Hayden chimed in, 'but vermin, not people. I think you'd better hand the gun over for safe keeping.'

Slater drew back from them, but still held on to the shotgun. 'Stallard is vermin,' he retorted, 'and I was only going to frighten him with it anyway.'

'Kate gesticulated with her outstretched hand. 'Please, Colonel,' she encouraged. 'You can have the thing back when this is all over.'

The old soldier muttered an expletive, but the next instant broke the shotgun and ejected a cartridge before holding the shotgun out towards her, stock first and still broken.

'Damned impertinence!' he grated. 'Your superiors will be hearing from me about this.'

Kate took the shotgun, verified that it was empty and handed it to Hayden. 'You only ejected one cartridge there, Colonel,' she said, 'and we heard the sound of a shot earlier on. So who were you shooting at?'

'Pigeons,' he replied with a sneer. 'Lots of the blighters around here. Damned nuisance.'

Kate nodded slowly. 'Fine, but I hope that's all, for if we find Lenny Stallard's body peppered with shot, we'll know where to come, won't we?'

He snorted. 'Would have fired over the bounder's head if I'd seen him anyway,' he retorted, 'which I didn't, so that's that.'

'So, where's Charles?' Hayden queried.

'Gone after him,' Slater replied and tapped his left leg. 'Can't do things like that meself anymore. Can't do much of anything for long without this blasted thing.'

He produced a short metal tube from his jacket pocket, flicked it and scowled as the tube abruptly extended into a long, thin walking stick.

Kate frowned. 'Perhaps that's just as well, Colonel,' she said. 'Now, I think it's best we all return to the house so I can arrange for a search team to check out the grounds properly.'

The ex-army man made no further comment, but with his face set into a tight-lipped mask, he limped past her, out of the trees and across the lawn, exhibiting a surprising turn of speed for a man with a gammy leg.

'He's something else, isn't he?' Hayden said, his admiration showing.

Kate grunted. 'He's something anyway,' she replied with a thoughtful frown.

* * *

More uniform back-up had arrived by the time Kate and Hayden returned to the front of the house, but a cursory search of the grounds – the small number of officers available meant that only a cursory search was possible – produced nothing. Charles Slater turned up, breathless, sweaty and mud-stained, shortly afterwards, but was only able to say that the man he had confronted the night of his mother's murder and had later seen in the dock of the court was the same one he had seen peering through the study window, which at least established the fact that Lenny Stallard had indeed been the intruder. As to where the fugitive had gone, he said he had no idea, having lost him in the immensity of the moor soon after chasing him from the grounds of the house.

'What was Stallard wearing?' Kate queried.

Slater shrugged. 'I didn't really take note; I was concentrating more on his face. Dark clothes, I think.'

'And you're absolutely positive it was him? After all, it's over two years since you would have seen him at his trial.'

He gave a grim laugh. 'He killed my mother. Do you think I would ever forget the face of that swine, however many years have passed?'

Kate nodded. 'I see your point.'

He frowned. 'So what do we do now?'

'His description will be circulated on national TV this afternoon and we shall also circulate his details locally. The chances are he will pop up somewhere before long to give us a lead – after all, he'll need food and shelter.'

'Let's hope he doesn't "pop up" here again. Father is already at 50,000ft and still climbing.'

Kate nodded. 'I know. We have had to seize his shotgun.'

Slater frowned. 'Was that really necessary?'

She gave a wry smile. 'If we don't want to end up with another murder investigation, I think it's essential.'

He sighed. 'Father is all talk – he wouldn't really hurt anyone.'

Kate stared at him levelly. 'Is that why you allowed him to take his shotgun with him when you went after Stallard?'

He gave a rueful grin. 'Touché, but you don't allow or disallow Father doing anything – he's his own man.'

She flicked her eyebrows. 'I rest my case.'

He walked with her to the CID car and grinned again when he saw Hayden a few yards away studying his MGC.

'Bit of an enthusiast, is he?' he asked.

She stared at Hayden's back with a kind of weary resignation. 'Don't go there, Mr Slater. He has a Mk II Jaguar – I think he is more in love with that than he is with me.'

Slater raised an eyebrow. 'You mean you're married – he's your husband?'

He sounded incredulous as well as disappointed and she emitted a dry chuckle. 'The fact that we are both named Lewis should have given you a clue; obviously you'd never make a detective.'

He winced and opened the driver's door courteously for her. 'Ouch! Sorry, I asked for that.'

Kate laughed again. 'You certainly did, Mr Slater.' Then she looked past him and shouted: 'Hayden, we're leaving – like now.'

'So you're his boss as well?' Slater exclaimed as Hayden tore himself away from the MG and ambled towards them.

'Oh yes,' she replied gravely, starting the engine and watching her husband climb into the front passenger seat. 'In a lot more ways than one!'

* * *

The caravan had seen much better days, that fact was obvious. Parts of the bodywork were scarred and fractured in places, the windows were all broken and it had sunk down on its ruptured tyres as if it had once been a living thing which had finally succumbed to the ravages of the elements and the insidious creeping damp of the moor.

It stood in the corner of an unkempt, partially flooded field of knee-height grass and nettles just off a back road to the isolated hamlet of Lower Godney and the tatty wooden sign attached to a tree beside the open gateway proclaimed with a kind of grim humour that this was "Paradise".

Kate and Hayden sat for several minutes in their car studying what Stallard's descriptive file had given as his pre-prison address, both inwardly wondering whether it was actually worth checking at all. In the end, Kate made the decision and throwing open her door, stepped out on to a narrow wooden bridge, which spanned a deep ditch or rhyne, as the lattice-work of man-made drainage ditches criss-crossing the Levels were called. Muttering a protest, Hayden got out of the car after her, squinting at the caravan's broken windows glittering in the afternoon sunlight that had suddenly emerged from the rain clouds and wondering why he had ever decided to join the police as he followed her through the waterlogged field to the half-open door.

The interior of the caravan was not much better than the exterior. It stank of damp and there were large patches of green mould on the walls and furnishings. Local thieves had already taken anything that was of value and some bright spark had even tried to saw through the sprung mattress on the bedroom's double bed, no doubt looking for hidden money or valuables.

There was nothing to indicate that anyone had been in the caravan for a very long time and they were on the point of returning to their car when Hayden spotted the white van through a back window, tangled up in undergrowth.

The van turned out to be an old Ford which had been partially stripped, like the caravan, and was smothered in brambles and other types of parasitic climber. Pulling some of the less lethal varieties away from the bodywork, they saw that the van was badly rusted with several substantial dents in the front end and one wing. It had also been partially stripped and not much of the interior equipment remained, just tangles of wiring and torn seats, but it had retained its registration plates.

Hayden returned to the CID car to do a quick vehicle check via the control room. He got a surprise when the answer came back to him and there was a gleam in his eyes as he strode over to where Kate was examining an empty ruined shed, just past the van.

'Nothing but rubbish in here,' she said over her shoulder. 'No evidence of anyone sleeping rough either.'

'Like the caravan,' he replied, then added: 'You'll never guess who the van belongs to.'

Kate pushed the shed's corrugated iron door closed and turned to face him with an inquiring look. 'Well, I would have thought Lenny Stallard,' she said, 'but I suspect you're going to tell me someone different.'

He grinned. 'The last registered owner is one Ronald Leslie Dibble,' he replied, 'of The Scarlet Dancer public house.'

She raised an eyebrow. 'Now that is a coincidence,' she said softly. 'And there was Ronnie Dibble telling us he hardly knew Lenny Stallard.'

Hayden nodded. 'Which has to be a load of Wally as he must either have lent him the van or sold it to him.'

'Unless Stallard stole the thing and Dibble didn't bother to report it?' Kate went on.

'So why would Dibble not report it?'

Kate studied him for a moment. 'Let's ask him, shall we?' she replied.

CHAPTER 5

Ronnie Dibble was definitely not pleased to see the two detectives again.

'What now?' he said heavily, pausing in the act of wiping the top of the counter with a grubby cloth.

The bar was as empty as before. Kate glanced about her and gave a thin smile.

'You're not doing much business today, Mr Dibble,' she observed drily.

'Been a couple in, but I do most of it later in the evening,' he muttered. 'What's it to you anyhow?'

She shrugged. 'Just an observation, that's all.'

'So, you've come back here again to do some bleedin' marketing survey then?'

Kate smiled again. 'No, Mr Dibble, we're here to ask you about a car – or rather a van, to be more precise.'

'What van?'

'A Ford van, colour white.' She produced her pocket book and glanced inside before giving him the registration number. 'Do you own that vehicle?'

He shook his head. 'No, I got a nice Beamer in me garage.'

'Did you ever own it?'

She studied his face and saw his eyes narrow slightly. 'Might've done once – I've owned lots of cars and vans.'

'DVLC say this one was registered in your name.'

'Must've done then.'

'Where is it now?'

'No idea. Sold it on.'

'When?'

'Dunno – few years ago.'

'Who did you sell it to?'

He made a face. 'Sorry, can't remember.'

'Would it have been Lenny Stallard?'

Kate saw something flicker in his eyes and the fingers of one hand tighten on the cloth he was holding.

He snorted angrily and glared at her. 'Look, what is this?' he prevaricated. 'Some sort of bloody interrogation?'

Kate sighed her exasperation. 'No, just a straightforward inquiry, Mr Dibble. Did you or did you not sell the car to Lenny Stallard?

'Might've done.'

'But when we were in here before, you said you hardly knew him.'

'Yeah, and I didn't. But if some punter comes in and offers to buy one of me motors, I don't have to know him, do I? I just sells it to him, if the price is right.'

'Is that what happened with Lenny Stallard then – he bought the van off you?'

'Yeah, I remember now. He needed wheels for some buildin' job he was going for and he offered me a couple of thou' for the van, so I took him up on it. Never saw it again.'

'Funny thing, the old memory,' Hayden put in. 'Can suddenly recall things you thought you'd forgotten – just like that.'

Dibble ignored him, as he'd done before. 'So, what's this all about?' he said to Kate. 'You come in here earlier to tell me to watch me back, 'cause Stallard is out on his toes and now you turn up again to ask me about a bleedin' van I once owned.'

Kate returned her wallet and notebook to her pocket. 'Nothing to worry about, Mr Dibble. It's just that we found your old van parked in a field next to Lenny Stallard's caravan and when we did a registered owner check, it came up with your name.'

She saw him swallow hard, then, as if it had dawned on him that he wasn't in any real trouble, he forced a grin. 'Yeah, well I must've forgotten to let the DVLC know I'd sold the wagon. Sorry about that.'

Kate smiled and turned for the door. 'No worries, Mr Dibble. Glad we cleared the issue up in the end anyway. You have a nice day.'

'You have a nice day?' Hayden echoed with a disparaging snort as they both climbed back into the CID car. 'The fellow's an out-and-out villain. You can smell it.'

Kate nodded grimly. 'No doubt about that,' she replied. 'Isolated pub? No customers? Into buying and selling motor vehicles? Probably nicking and ringing them too. Has to be on someone's radar – maybe the NCA already know about him.'

'The National Crime Agency?' he snorted. 'If they did, they'd hardly have told us about it, going by their usual form. And where does all this fit in with Lenny Stallard anyway?'

She made a face. 'No idea, Hayd, but I'll tell you one thing – this whole business is beginning to develop a nasty rancid smell.'

* * *

Ted Roscoe was incredulous. 'Can you ever do a straightforward job without turning it into some complicated conspiracy?' he blazed, staring at Kate through the clouds of acrid smoke from his newly lit cigarette. 'Correct me if I'm wrong, but weren't you supposed to nail an escaped con who was menacing vulnerable witnesses?'

She grimaced, wriggling in her chair. 'Yes, Guv, but—'

'No soddin' buts,' he shouted. 'You cocked up, that's about the strength of it – despite having half the district's plods at your disposal.'

He shook his head in disbelief. 'And now … now, after letting a dangerous thug simply piss off into the blue, you have the nerve to waltz into my office with some half-baked conspiracy theory about the very people we're supposed to be protecting!'

She closed her eyes briefly in resignation and simply nodded, knowing it was pointless trying to defend her corner when Roscoe was in this sort of mood. Instead, she waited for him to calm down, glancing around the yellowed walls of the tiny office and at the spot from which the "No Smoking" notice – issued by the chief constable in accordance with the law that now prohibited smoking in the workplace –

had mysteriously disappeared.

'There's something funny going on, Guv,' she ventured eventually, waving his smoke away from her face, more as a hint than anything else. 'Dibble at least was definitely hiding something.'

He snorted. 'Was he now? Well, has it occurred to you that he may not be much of a fan of the police? It will probably come as a shock to you to learn that a lot of people actually don't like us.'

She flushed at the sarcasm 'So why would he say he hardly knew Stallard when he must have done to have sold him the van I told you about?'

'Maybe he didn't want to admit it because of what Stallard is? Not very good for trade if a pub landlord is known to have connections with a cold-blooded killer, I would have thought.'

'I think there's a lot more to it than that.'

'Like what, for instance?' He took down a deep lungful of smoke and Kate waited with a sort of macabre fascination to see how long it would be before the smoke exited from his nostrils. In fact, it took some six to seven seconds and then, instead of answering his question, she grimaced and once again waved the exhaled clouds away from her face.

'Listen to me, young lady,' he said, ignoring her gesture, 'you and I have had this sort of conversation before in other cases, haven't we? I'm talking about meddling in things that don't concern this department – going off at half-cock. Do you savvy?'

She shrugged. 'I've always been proven right in the end.'

His eyes flashed dangerously. 'Maybe you have, *Detective Sergeant*,' he agreed, his tone laced with sarcasm, 'but this time I want you to try – just try – to stick to the brief you've been given, okay?' He leaned forward across the desk and she saw a piece of white chewing gum emerge briefly from the side of his mouth before he sucked it back and began chewing rapidly, his cigarette held between his finger and thumb. 'So, forget conspiracy theories and get yourself out there to do what you should be doing – and that is finding Lenny Stallard before he stiffs someone else. Got it?'

She nodded and climbed to her feet.

'And another thing,' he said. 'Return the shotgun to Colonel Slater.'

She gaped at him. 'Do what?'

'Gone deaf all of a sudden? Give him back his gun.'

'But – but he took a shot at Lenny Stallard.'

'We can't prove that. He says he was shooting at a pheasant.'

She looked bewildered. 'A pheasant? He told me it was a pigeon. You've – you've been speaking to him?'

He took another pull on his cigarette. 'He rang the DCI and I've just got it in the neck – all because of you.'

'Guv,' she protested, 'he's not fit to be in possession of a shotgun at the moment. We can't afford—'

'We can't afford,' he interjected, 'to seize his weapon in the present circumstances.'

'Why?'

He sighed heavily, his discomfort apparent. 'You do know who he is?'

Another shrug. 'Widower, well to do, ex-army—'

'And very well connected. He has the ear of the Defence Secretary and following retirement, was for a time an independent MP who served as a military adviser to the MOD.'

'And that makes him above the law?'

He snorted. 'Don't be so bloody naive, Kate. I don't like it any more than you, but I'm not about to stick my neck out over a bloody shotgun.'

'Even if he ends up killing someone?'

He gave a tight smile and met her angry stare with a fixed one of his own. 'If it happens to be Lenny Stallard, I'm not going to cry about it,' he said. 'Now, it's bloody Sunday, which should have been a day of rest, and seeing as I've had no lunch, I'm going out for a pint. Is that okay with you?'

'I don't care what you do, Guv,' she retorted, climbing to her feet, 'as long as I don't have to put up with the smoke from your bloody cancer sticks.'

'Bother you, does it?' he said, deliberately taking another drag.

'It will bother you a lot more if you're caught flouting the law!' she snapped back. 'But maybe the fags will get you first.'

His face darkened and he half rose from behind his desk. 'You cheeky cow!' he snarled. 'Get out!'

But she was already halfway through the door.

* * *

Daniel Sayers had been a close friend of Lenny Stallard since junior school and they had hung out together all through their teens and into their 20s, chasing skirt and going on benders with the potent Somerset scrumpy after receiving their weekly hand-outs on social security. Neither of them had ever managed to hold down a job, but they had seen little reason to bother when the state was in a position to look after them so well without any effort on their part. Inevitably, indolence and greed had soon become the pathway to crime and minor thieving had graduated to burglary and finally, the robbery of a village post office. It was Stallard who had slashed the postmistress with the blade, but Sayers had been a willing participant in the raid, so he had ended up in prison as well – though on a lesser sentence, which cost him three years of his life in custody before parole for good behaviour.

Now stuck at home with his elderly mother – still on a benefits cheque as no one would risk employing an ex-con – he passed the time in his local, knocking back the cider until his money ran out, while the old lady back home cooked and washed for him in the hope that one day he would see the light and finally get a job. Sayers was certainly not a nice person and Kate need not have been aware of his past to form that opinion when she knocked on the run-down council house in one of Highbridge's backstreets and came face to face with the stocky, crop-haired wastrel, dressed in track-suit bottoms, trainers and a dirty vest which revealed a multitude of tattoos on his arms and muscular biceps.

'Highbridge CID,' she announced, showing him her warrant card.

Sayers scowled, glancing with obvious hostility at Kate and Hayden in turn. 'So?' he queried, taking a pull on the dying stub of a cigarette.

'Can we come in and have a word?' she asked, conscious of the fact that despite apparently smothering himself in some sort of strong deodorant, he still hadn't entirely concealed his BO problem.

'Why?'

'It's about Lenny Stallard.'

He grinned. 'Yeah, heard on the news that he'd scarpered. Bully for him.'

'Who is it, Danny?' The querulous high-pitched voice came from the back of the house and Sayers' grin vanished, to be replaced by a sour grimace. 'Noffink for you, ma,' he replied. 'Just someone to see me.'

'Well, ask them in, boy. Don't leave 'em standing on the doorstep.'

Sayers stood to one side and flicked his head in the direction of the voice. 'You'd better come in then,' he growled. 'But keep shtum about who you are. Me ma will fink I'm in bovver again if she finds out.'

The old lady – a thin stooped figure dressed in a grubby house coat of some sort – appeared as they stepped into the hallway and she eyed them suspiciously. 'And who are you then?'

'Social Services, ma'am,' Kate said promptly. 'Just a routine visit.'

Mrs Sayers grunted and turned towards the back of the house again. 'Bloody useless arseholes,' she muttered and disappeared.

'Lenny ain't here,' Daniel Sayers said in a low voice once he had heard his mother close a door behind her. 'I fought you lot would be round sooner or later.'

'Has he contacted you at all?' Hayden asked.

Sayers shook his head. 'Nah, and he wouldn't anyway. He ain't daft. He knows this is the first place you'd look for him.'

Kate glanced around the hallway at the closed doors. 'Mind if we take a look around?'

'No way! I told you, he ain't here.'

'We could always get a warrant,' Hayden warned.

'Go ahead, squire – you won't get past me 'less you got one.'

Kate treated him to a tight smile. 'Perhaps we should ask your mother?' she said. 'After all, she must be registered as the tenant.'

There was alarm in his eyes now and he glanced quickly behind him. 'Okay, okay, you can look around, but make it quick.'

And they did exactly that. The three-bed house offered almost nowhere for a fugitive to hide. There was little furniture and even the loft – which Hayden searched while Kate was poking her head into the garage and checking the old red Land Rover Defender parked there – contained nothing but a leaking water tank. Fortunately for Danny Sayers, his mother stayed out of the way the whole time – the sound of a television in the kitchen explaining why – and his impatience to see the back of them was obvious when they met him in the downstairs hallway again.

'Well, satisfied?' he sneered and reached past Kate to open the front door.

She smiled. 'For now, yes,' she replied.

His eyes narrowed. 'What do you mean, "for now"?'

'We might have to come back again.'

'Come back? Why?'

She shrugged. 'There's always the chance that he might sneak in here when we've gone, so we might have to take another look around.'

'I told you he ain't been here and he wouldn't look me up anyway. He knows I ain't forgotten he got me extra time in stir after he done the postmistress at that blagging.'

'Forgive us if we have difficulty believing you.'

He swore savagely, his face darkening and his fists clenching in anger. 'This is harassment, this is – I'll get on to me solicitor if you turn up here again.'

Hayden chuckled. 'Like you can afford a solicitor, you mean?' he said. 'And I don't think a legal aid brief would be considered appropriate in this sort of situation.'

Sayers glared at him. 'Then – then I'll go to the papers.'

Kate shook her head. 'Oh I don't think so, Mr Sayers. That sort of publicity would do you no good at all and we're only doing our job anyway.'

She hesitated a second. 'Of course, there is another option. You could always tell us where you think your old mate could be holed up – some little hideaway that no one else knows about?'

He shook his head. 'No way. I ain't no grass.'

She sighed and pulled open the front door. 'Okay, Mr Sayers, then we'll probably be seeing you again in a couple of days.'

'No! Wait!'

She turned and stared hard at the meat-hook gripping her upper arm.

He let go immediately. 'There is a place,' he blurted. 'But you got to swear you'll never let on I told you.'

She smiled her sweetest smile. 'Discretion is my greatest asset, Mr Sayers.'

He glanced quickly over his shoulder, as if he expected the KGB to be listening in to their conversation. 'It's … it's a squat … an old cider farm out on the moor a couple of miles from Edington village. It's … it's called Yardley's.'

'Yardley's?'

'Yeah. Folk say it were a small family run business that went bust years ago. Gypos been in and stripped most of the metal what was left behind and it's been a ruin for as long as I been around.'

'How do you know about the place?'

He moistened dry lips. 'We … we used to use it in the old days as a stash for our stuff and somewhere to hole up if fings got too hot.'

She raised an eyebrow and he swallowed hard. 'I ain't been there for yonks, honest,' he added quickly. 'I been straight ever since I got sent down for that post office blagging – but Lenny could be dossin' there. He's … he's short on mates round here after what he done.'

Kate nodded and nudged Hayden ahead of her over the front door step. 'Thank you for your public-spirited co-operation, Mr Sayers,' she said. 'If you think of anything else that might help us, do give us a call.'

'But you won't tell Lenny I told you, will you?' he called after her, fear evident in his voice. 'Make out like you just checked the place 'cause it looked like a doss.'

Kate turned by the gate. 'Bye, Mr Sayers,' she said without answering his question. 'Do have a nice evening, won't you?'

CHAPTER 6

Yardley's Cider Farm comprised a ramshackle collection of ruined stone buildings and wooden barns, almost buried in the undergrowth that also choked the barely visible orchard of neglected apple trees behind it. As Sayers had claimed, it had obviously been derelict for many years and it looked singularly uninviting in the fast fading light.

Kate parked the CID car in a layby a couple of hundred yards away and she and Hayden approached the property on foot to lessen the risk of spooking Lenny Stallard if it transpired that he had actually gone to ground there. But after Kate's rejection of Hayden's vociferous objections to carrying out a check on the farm without first securing the appropriate back-up, the usually genial detective was not a happy man and the angry frown on his face seemed to become more pronounced the nearer they got to the front of the property.

'This is absolute lunacy,' he breathed, tugging at the arm of Kate's short leather coat in a last-ditch effort to change her mind. 'Stallard has already shown himself to be a violent criminal – he's a murderer, for heaven's sake—'

'Just shut it, Hayd, will you?' Kate cut in, turning on him angrily. 'If you want to go back to the car, then be my guest, but I'm doing this, okay?'

'Go back to the car?' he echoed, hurt in his expression. 'What sort of a man do you think I am? I was merely trying to point out—'

'Well, don't!' she snapped and paused briefly by the open gateway to study the skeletal buildings grouped around the wide concrete hard-standing where the lorries had once loaded up with barrels of golden cider.

Nothing moved, save hordes of bats which erupted from the buildings in the now thickening gloom and disappeared into the immensity of the moor.

Moments later Kate and Hayden were standing in the entrance to one of the barns themselves, inspecting the interior with their torches.

The air held a peculiar mixture of odours – the musty smell produced by the bats nesting in the rafters, the decaying essence released by the building itself and the stagnant earthy smell of the marshland – which encompassed the site. But the distinctive smell of ripe apples, which would have been so prevalent in days gone by, was conspicuous by its absence, though that was hardly surprising since cider had probably not been made at Yardley's for decades, and the beams of their torches revealed that the place was virtually empty. Just a few rusted steel brackets and floor plates remained to mark the spot where machinery had obviously once stood – long since either dismantled or cut up by determined thieves, as Sayers had alleged, or removed and sold by the owners when their business had collapsed – a poignant epitaph to a failed dream.

'This would have been the cider mill,' Hayden remarked with an air of authority as his gaze roved slowly around the barn. 'Sadly, the roller mill they'd have used to crush the apples and the cider press itself seem to have walked.'

Kate frowned at him for a moment. 'So how come you know so much about cider-making?' she queried.

He grinned. 'I know a great many things, old girl,' he replied. 'You'd be surprised.'

She grunted. 'Pity one of them wasn't about how to be a good detective,' she retorted.

Moving further into the barn, they discovered that it was actually split into two halves with the inner part, accessed by a wide door-less opening and housing two enormous wooden vats, just over a shoulder's width between them. The vats were almost as high as the vaulted roof itself, and in their heyday had each probably held several thousand gallons of fermenting cider, though now they were likely to contain nothing more than rainwater from the leaking roof. Careful probing with their torches revealed that the building was untenanted and there was no evidence to suggest that anyone had been there since the farm had been vacated.

The same was true of the adjacent building which Hayden, in his self-appointed role as "tour guide", pompously declared to have once been used as the apple store. The wooden frames used to contain the harvested fruit were still in place on the floor on either side of the doorway and the concrete was badly stained, but the place held nothing of interest save an old broken handcart.

Kate was on the point of giving up on their search of the site when the beam of her torch picked out the imprint of heavy boot-prints in the soft earth by the entrance door of a much larger, rectangular stone building, with a smaller square building on stilts attached to one side of the sloping elevation of its corrugated iron roof.

Her hand closed tightly on Hayden's arm and she pointed quickly at the boot-print before extinguishing her torch. 'You take the back. I'll go in the front,' she whispered close to his ear.

He shook his head firmly. 'Not a chance,' he replied. 'We call for back-up – now!'

She glared at him as the darkness thickened around them and produced a small CS gas spray. 'No time,' she replied, her lips brushing his ear. 'He will have heard us by now anyway. So we have to do it as we are or lose him altogether.'

Before he could argue, she was gone, crunching broken glass underfoot as she disappeared through the half-open doorway. With a grimace, he turned down the side of the building, conscious of a very bad feeling in his gut about what they were doing as he jerked his own torch from his pocket to look for a back entrance.

* * *

Kate could feel her heart thumping with the heavy squishy beat of a well-worn water pump as she crept along what appeared to be some kind of narrow corridor with doors on each side – one-time offices perhaps – her torch beam, which was directed at the floor, just a faint glow partially masked by her cupped hand.

Derelict building searches – how she had always loved this aspect of the job. Only a police officer could appreciate how it felt, understand the intoxicating buzz it generated, the sudden rush of adrenalin, the skin-crawling sense of excitement, the tension and – yes – the element of fear that accompanied the whole thing. It was what police work was all about – not the endless paperwork and form-filling, the boring symposiums on crime prevention, crime reduction, departmental budgetary management and resource allocation – but what she had joined the police force for at the job's own unique "coal face".

Then her focus abruptly returned to the task in hand as a scuffling sound in the gloom froze her into instant immobility, prompting her to cover the torch completely with her hand, her throat dry and constricted, her heartbeat seemingly so loud that she felt sure it would betray her position to whoever was hiding in the building. More scuffling and something brushed against her ankle – something soft and furry. She stifled the gasp of revulsion that rose to her lips and kicked out at what was empty air, for the rat was no longer there. But she was still shaking and disgusted with herself for her reaction. Prepared to tackle a violent criminal yet afraid of a little furry animal – what sort of a copper was she?

She was still wondering about that when the figure suddenly burst from a doorway to her right and slammed her into the wall. Winded, but still on her feet, she lashed out with her torch and heard it connect with something hard. There was a sharp cry and the figure vanished into the gloom towards the rear of the building.

'To you, Hayden!' she shouted at the top of her voice. 'He's coming to you!'

Stumbling in pursuit, her torch now blazing a path along the corridor, she heard the commotion seconds later, followed by a yell, then silence.

'Hayden?' she shouted again, concern for her partner now dominating her emotions. 'Where are you?'

There was no answer. The corridor blossomed into a large square room, much like a reception area, with a long broken desk on one side and an open doorway just beyond it at the far end. On the other side of the doorway she found herself in what seemed to be some sort of massive warehouse or storeroom. The place appeared to contain nothing but a few dismembered barrels and crates and a partially stripped forklift truck, but the far end – maybe a loading bay area – was open to the eerie blaze of an emerging moon, against which the forklift was silhouetted like a black etching on a bright yellow canvas. She saw something else too – what looked like a heavy-set man slumped on the floor with his back against the truck. His body was quivering slightly, as if in the grip of some sort of fit and she knew even before she got to him that it was Hayden!

* * *

'So, you lost our fugitive and put your husband in hospital?' Roscoe grated, glaring at Kate across his desk. 'A brilliant day's work. Press have got hold of the story and somehow tied it in with the TV circulation on Lenny Stallard, so they'll be all over us soon. DCI's doing pirouettes!'

Kate said nothing, but simply stared at the floor, white-faced and tight-lipped, waiting for the expected "why didn't you stick to the rules and call for back-up?" Instead, Roscoe sighed heavily and turning to one side, spat a wad of chewing gum into the wastepaper bin by his desk.

'How is he?' he queried in a softer tone, lighting up a cigarette and proffering the packet across the desk, seemingly as a conciliatory gesture, having obviously conveniently forgotten the run-in they'd had before over his smoking habit.

She shook her head at the cigarettes. 'Nasty head-wound. I spoke to the doctor when I went to the hospital and they're keeping him in for observation, just in case – concussion, you know …'

Her voice trailed off and tears flooded her eyes. 'It … it was all my fault,' she choked. I should have called for back-up.'

'What's done is done,' he growled. 'What we have to do now is find the bastard responsible. Did Hayden get a look at him?'

She shook her head again. 'Only saw a figure in a hoodie lunging at him from behind a forklift truck.'

'So it could have been anyone … a dosser, a junkie, someone he spooked?'

'Bit of a coincidence, the hoodie though, isn't it?'

'Yeah, but that wouldn't hold up on an assault charge in court. Do we know what he hit Hayden with?'

She wiped her eyes on her sleeve. 'Before he lost consciousness, Hayd mumbled about it being something like a wooden pole – maybe the handle of a shovel or a broom.'

Roscoe grunted, blowing smoke rings at the ceiling. 'At least Stallard doesn't appear to be armed with anything more substantial, like a shooter …' he said, '… yet!'

He nodded at the clock on the wall. 'Anyway, it's past nine. About time you went home. Nothing you can do here. I've got every available plod out combing the area as we speak, so maybe they'll feel his collar before too long.'

She climbed unsteadily to her feet. 'And if they don't?'

He stubbed out his unfinished cigarette in a tin lid on the desk. 'Then we're up shit creek without a paddle,' he replied, 'and the press will have us for breakfast.'

* * *

Kate drove home like someone in a hypnotic trance and she had no clear recollections of the short journey across the moor. She was simply aware of leaving Highbridge police station one minute and the next, turning into the gravel driveway of the little thatched cottage which she shared with Hayden in Burtle village, the engine of her Mazda MX5 sports car quietly ticking over like a rapid heartbeat as she sat there for several minutes staring into space.

Big affable Hayden; she loved him to bits, despite his untidiness and his infuriating laissez-faire approach to everything. The pair of them were like chalk and cheese. She was the uptight go-getter who always seemed to be jumping into things feet first, while he took everything in his stride, which was not far removed from snail's pace. Yet the lazy eccentric persona he projected did him a grave disservice and gave no hint of his real worth in terms of the razor-sharp mind he possessed. He was a thinker, rather than an action-man, whose cerebral qualities had played a significant part in bringing a number of the department's crime investigations to a satisfactory conclusion. But of greater personal significance to her was the fact that he was a shrewd counsellor who had on several occasions acted as a brake on her more impulsive inclinations, except this time, and as she turned the key in the front door and stepped into the unwelcoming gloom, she was almost overwhelmed by a gut-wrenching sense of despair when she thought of him lying so pale and still in the hospital bed.

'Come home soon, Hayd,' she whispered as she poured herself a stiff glass of whisky. 'I'm lost without you.'

CHAPTER 7

'Well?' Roscoe demanded through the usual wreathes of smoke when Kate turned in late the following morning, pushing her way through the small knot of reporters and photographers gathered outside the police station and making straight for his office. 'Any news?'

She gave a bright relieved smile. 'He was conscious and seemed reasonably comfortable when I went to see him this morning. Worrying about his stomach again, so that's a good sign.'

'Is he staying in?'

'Another night apparently – they want to do some tests today and he lost a lot of blood from the head wound, so he's very weak.'

The DI grunted and drew on his cigarette. 'Out of circulation for a while then. How do you feel about carrying on with the Stallard inquiry on your tod? I can't spare anyone else to help you at present.'

She nodded. 'It will take my mind off things.'

'Good thinking. Got a message for you an hour ago.' He gave a humourless smile. 'My ex-compatriot, DCI Austin Jacobs, phoned in. Wants to see you again.'

She raised an eyebrow. 'Did he say what it was about?'

He shook his head, then grinned suddenly. 'Wouldn't tell me why, but he sounded a bit agitated. Could be you stirred his juices – and that wouldn't be unusual for old Creeper.'

She gave him an old-fashioned look and climbed to her feet. 'You should give up smoking, Guv,' she threw back at him as she left the office. 'It is seriously stunting your wit.'

* * *

There was no sign of life in the small bungalow when Kate pulled up outside the place in the CID car. Maybe Jacobs was asleep after a skinful, she thought grimly as she pushed open the garden gate, and that possibility seemed even more likely when she tapped loudly on the front door with the rusted brass knocker. There was no response.

Grimacing, she rapped even louder, but after a wait of at least a minute without any result, she went to the sitting room window and peered through. The television screen was illuminated with what looked like another list of runners and riders at one of the horse racing venues and a bottle of whisky and a full glass stood on the coffee table by the armchair Jacobs had been occupying when she and Hayden had last visited him. There was no sign of the former DCI himself, however. She checked the window on the other side of the front door, but the curtains were drawn and she couldn't see into the room at all.

Maybe Jacobs was in the toilet or the shower, she mused – though, having seen the state of the man before, she didn't think the shower was very likely. She knocked again, then pushed in the letterbox flap and shouted through the opening, 'Mr Jacobs? It's DS Lewis. Are you there?'

Still nothing. Surely the man hadn't gone out? He'd asked her to call, after all, so there must have been a reason.

Now extremely annoyed, she turned and stared about her in the overgrown front garden, undecided about her next move. A sleek black and white cat rubbed against her legs and she bent to stroke it for a second. 'Where is the prick, puss?'

she said aloud, without expecting an answer, and watched the cat stalk away again into the long grass.

It was then that an elderly woman appeared in the front garden of the house next door and approached the fence. 'You after Mr Jacobs?' she called.

Kate nodded. 'Have you seen him this morning?'

The woman shook her head. 'Rarely see him anyway,' she replied, ''cept when he goes out. Must be there, though, 'cause his car is still in the garage and he never walks anywhere.'

Kate smiled. The nosy neighbour. A real boon to the police. What would they do without them? 'Thanks,' she replied, glancing at the partially closed doors of the detached garage. Even from where she was standing, she could see the gleam of a bumper bar through the gap and inwardly cursed her lapse for not checking the garage herself.

The old woman was craning her neck now, trying to peer into the front window over the fence. Kate said nothing further to her, but re-approached the front door and tried the handle. The door was not locked and opened easily.

'Mr Jacobs?' she called again. 'Can I come in?'

She did anyway, wrinkling her nose at the familiar stale smell that met her in the hallway and remembering what Hayden had said about the perils of alcohol.

She checked the sitting room first, even though she had already seen that it was empty, noting the open newspaper on the arm of the chair that was still set in front of the television. The paper carried the day's date, so either Jacobs had been out to collect it, which seemed unlikely if what the elderly neighbour had said was true, or it had been delivered by the paper boy or girl and no doubt picked up by Jacobs from the door mat.

So where the hell was Jacobs?

She next checked the heavily curtained room opposite and found it to be a bedroom with a shabby, threadbare carpet only partly covering the wooden floor and containing just an unmade bed, a double wardrobe and a dressing table – but there was no sign of Jacobs.

Beyond the two front rooms was a further bedroom and a bathroom and toilet directly opposite each other, neither of which was occupied and then, right at the back of the bungalow, the kitchen – and it was there that Kate found Austin Jacobs.

He was lying face down on the tiled floor beside the cooker and the fact that he was dead was pretty obvious. His body bore evidence of a severe stab wound to the lower back and his head was lying in a pool of blood that had apparently erupted from a severed carotid artery, spraying an adjacent cabinet with the force of a fractured hose!

* * *

The forensic pathologist looked a bit like an alien from outer space in her protective white suit and hood as she bent over Jacobs' body to carefully examine the horrendous wound to his throat. 'We'll have to stop meeting like this, Ted,' Lydia Summers said. 'People will begin to talk.'

Ted Roscoe was only too well aware of the fact that Summers had been the pathologist who had attended the majority of his crime scenes over the years, but he didn't seem to see the funny side of her remark and he simply scowled at her in characteristic fashion as he stood with Kate just outside the crime scene tapes in his blue plastic booties, chewing rhythmically. 'What've we got, Doc?' he snapped.

She glanced at him over her shoulder and sighed. 'My, Ted, you're always in so much of a hurry,' she commented, then added mischievously, 'I can tell you he didn't die of natural causes anyway and unless he's a contortionist, I doubt this is a suicide!'

Roscoe snorted. 'No time for witticisms, Doc,' he retorted. 'He's an ex-colleague.'

She straightened up, her plastic gloves, stained a nice colour of red, held out limply in front of her. 'Very "ex" now, Ted,' she went on drily. 'What can I say at this stage, apart from the obvious? Deep stab wound to the lower back, which seems to have penetrated a good six to seven inches, and a very significant incision to the trachea, which resulted in a severed jugular vein and carotid artery.'

'Weapon?'

She pursed her lips for a second, glancing back at the corpse. 'A long, narrow, double-edged blade by the look of it. PM should tell us more.' She sighed. 'And before you ask me, I would put the time of death as within the past four hours.'

Roscoe grunted and glanced at his watch. 'He rang me at around nine,' he said, 'and Kate here found him at 11.30, so probably shortly after his call to me then?'

She shrugged. 'Well, it's now just after one, so that would fit within the four-hour period I've just given you, yes, but I can't be more explicit.'

'Any other thoughts, Doctor?' Kate pressed.

Summers hesitated and frowned. 'Well, I would suggest – and don't quote me at this stage – that your assailant was possibly not very tall, hence the wounds to the back being quite low, and that he is likely to have straddled his victim after bringing him to the floor face down, then jerked his head back by the hair to slice right through the trachea and carotid artery from behind. There look to be traces of blood in the deceased's hair, some of which appears to have been torn out, and that is certainly consistent with my hypothesis. I would also suggest the wound to the trachea was made from right to left, which would indicate your man is likely to be left-handed.'

Another grunt from Roscoe as he threw a glance at Kate. 'Don't know about the left-handed bit, but Stallard is short and muscular, so that would all fit,' he said, 'and we have the motive already – revenge.'

'All nice and tidy then, Ted?' Summers added with heavy sarcasm. 'Just the way you like it.'

Kate winced, but Roscoe had the skin of a rhinoceros when it suited him and he simply ignored the dig. But he was unable to ignore the voice that suddenly spoke at his elbow, the hard-clipped accent more at home on the streets of Belfast than in rural Somerset. 'Wee bit off your patch, are you not, Ted?'

Roscoe turned to face the thin blonde woman in the smart grey suit standing just behind him, his mouth briefly frozen in mid-chew. 'Deidrie,' he finally acknowledged.

DI Deidrie Hennessey smiled thinly. 'Funny really,' she said, 'but I always thought *I* covered the Bridgwater catchment area, so I did – 'less, of course, I've missed something in standing orders to say it now comes under Highbridge?'

Roscoe coughed and pushed his chewing gum to the side of his mouth. 'Yeah, well,' he replied gruffly, 'the stiff was a former DCI and we have every reason to believe his death could be down to an escaped con, called Lenny Stallard, whom he once put away.'

She treated him to a frosty smile. 'Sure, it's awful good of you to share that info with me, Ted,' she said with heavy sarcasm. 'I'll bear the wee feller in mind as a potential suspect when I get up to speed on things, so I will.' Her smile was replaced by a cold tight-lipped glare. 'Now piss off, will you, and leave me to deal with *my* crime scene?'

Roscoe started to say something, thought better of it and headed for the front door, chewing furiously. Compressing her lips in an apologetic gesture for the benefit of DI Hennessey, Kate followed close on his heels. But halfway up the garden path, Roscoe turned quickly to face her.

'Meant to tell you something,' he said, snapping the finger and thumb of one hand together.

Kate frowned. 'Tell me what?' she queried.

He flicked a cigarette from a crumpled packet and lit up. 'Hayden's had a slight relapse,' he said bluntly. 'Hospital rang to speak to you. I took the message.'

Kate swayed slightly and grabbed hold of the gatepost to steady herself. 'And you're only telling me this now?' she whispered.

He grimaced. 'Nothing you could do anyway – and I had to get over here to see what was what before Hennessey arrived and put her oar in.'

For a moment Kate simply stared at him in disbelief. 'You bastard … *sir*,' she said slowly and distinctly, 'you absolute unfeeling bastard!' And she headed for the car at a run.

* * *

She could see Hayden through the glass partition of the ICU and his face was set in a white mask, tubes and other paraphernalia connected to him from tall canisters standing beside the bed and a VDU on a table alongside registering a green spiked line that pulsed intermittently.

'Regrettably he has lapsed into coma,' the doctor explained carefully, 'and the tests – including intensive scans – that we have carried out so far have suggested that he may have sustained a cerebral oedema and haematoma—'

'What does that mean?' Kate whispered.

He made a face. 'Put simply, a brain swell, leading to a subdural bleed, caused by the blow to the head,' he said. 'It seems the injury he received was more substantial than we thought and may ultimately require surgical intervention, though we will try other established treatments first.'

She shuddered involuntarily and gripped his white-coated arm. 'Is he going to—?' she blurted, then broke off, frightened to say the word that was on the tip of her tongue.

He made a face and carefully disengaged her hand, instead cupping her hand between both of his own.

'Early days yet, Mrs Lewis,' he said gently. 'He's getting the best attention possible. The most sensible thing you can do is to go home – there's nothing you can do for him here.'

'Go home?' she choked. 'No way. I'm staying and—'

He sighed, removing his hands and firmly pushing her own hand down to her side. 'Staying here will not help him and it will only distress you,' he said. 'You should go home and get some rest.'

She emitted a hard humourless laugh. 'Rest?' she echoed. 'You expect me to rest when my husband could be at death's door?'

The doctor winced. 'We will ring you if there is any change,' he said. 'Nothing can be gained from you staying here. He could be like this for quite some time.'

'What do you mean by "quite some time"?'

He hesitated. 'It could be several days, maybe even weeks,' he said, 'but there's every chance he will make a full recovery.'

'I don't understand. He was obviously concussed after the assault, but he was conscious at the scene and spoke to me.'

He nodded. 'It can happen like that. The condition is not always immediate. There can be a delayed reaction to the event, as there has been in this case.'

Kate ran a hand through her disordered hair and stared up at the ceiling, trying to marshal her thoughts. She knew he was right, but something inside her rebelled against the idea of what she saw as walking out on Hayden.

'What about the person who did this?' the doctor went on quietly. 'Wouldn't you be better employed trying to catch him before he does something like this again.'

'He already has,' she breathed, the agony of indecision stamped into her expression.

He shrugged again. 'There you are then,' he said and nodded at the glass partition. 'What do you think Hayden would say about it?' he said.

It was a master-stroke and Kate's jaw tightened as she thought of Lenny Stallard – still out there after what he had done, first to Hayden and then the hapless Jacobs. He was free and laughing at her. He had to be caught and put back where he belonged, otherwise Hayden's injuries would have all been for nothing.

'Ring me!' she snapped and with a last regretful glance at Hayden, she turned and headed back out of the department towards the stairs and the open street.

* * *

Roscoe was back in his office when she returned to Highbridge police station. She didn't bother to knock.

'How is he?' he asked gruffly, looking up, but avoiding her gaze.

'In a coma,' she said, her voice breaking up halfway through the reply. 'Brain bleed apparently. They may have to operate.'

'Bloody hell!' he replied. 'Do you want to go back to the hospital and wait it out? I can ask for someone else to take over from you here.'

'No point,' she replied. 'Nothing I can do and I'd rather be working.'

'You sure?' he persisted. 'Look, I know I came across as a heartless bastard earlier and I should have told you about the call immediately, but everything was coming at me and I let my concerns about the job take over. I can only apologise.'

Her eyes burned into him, but she didn't answer him directly. 'We need to find Stallard,' she said, ignoring his explanation. '*I* need to find Stallard – for Hayden's sake.'

Roscoe's looked doubtful. 'Are you in a fit state to do that?' he queried.

'Try me,' she snapped. 'I want that bastard's head on a plate!'

'Yeah,' he muttered, 'that's what worries me.'

CHAPTER 8

Kate had no idea what she expected to achieve by returning to Yardley's Cider Farm – especially as the crime scene would already have been subjected to a painstaking search by a dedicated team – but she was drawn back to it by a kind of inner compulsion that she could not explain.

The blue and white perimeter tape was still in place across the entrance when she pulled up in the lane outside the farm and a young man and woman with "Press" stamped all over them rushed towards her as she walked quickly towards the gateway. But they were too late and the uniformed constable, who had initially stepped in front of her as she was about to duck under the tape, grinned, then quickly raised it for her, effectively preventing the reporters going any further.

'Sorry, skipper,' he said, ignoring their shouted questions. 'Didn't recognise you with your clothes on.'

She treated him to a cold stare. 'Very funny,' she replied, 'but I'm fresh out of humour at the moment.'

He winced as he suddenly caught on. 'Oh sorry, skip,' he went on quickly. 'I wasn't thinking – how is he?'

'Rough!' she snapped and pushed past him without another word.

Yellow crime scene tape blocked her entry to the big warehouse where Hayden had been attacked, but she tore it free and stepped through the door. She was confronted by a uniformed sergeant she recognised from Highbridge police station.

'Kate,' he acknowledged, frowning past her at the torn tape. 'You've just missed your DC, Jamie Foster, and Mr Roscoe left ages ago.'

'I know – I've already spoken to Mr Roscoe, Tony,' she said.

He shrugged. 'We're about done here too. Scenes of Crime found sweet FA and they've long gone.'

She stared past him around the warehouse, taking in an assortment of debris including wooden pallets, broken barrels, rolls of torn plastic and bits of twisted metal scattered over the concrete floor. Her gaze then focused briefly on the rickety-looking wooden staircase which rose to an equally unstable-looking walkway running along part of one wall bordered by a safety rail, which seemed to provide access to a couple of open doors on the inner side, no doubt offices. Just below it, the forklift truck was still in situ and even from where she was standing she could see the black stain on the concrete floor beside it.

She shuddered and the sergeant compressed his lips in a tight line, squeezing her wrist sympathetically.

'How's he doing?' he queried.

She looked away from him, tears welling in her eyes. 'Not good,' she replied in a strangled voice, then got a grip on herself and cleared her throat before changing the subject. 'Any weapon?'

He grunted. 'Zilch. Lots of rubbish – pit-props, bits of steel, that sort of thing – but nothing that can be connected.'

She focused on the half-open corrugated iron doors at the far end of the warehouse through which a couple of uniformed officers had suddenly appeared.

He seemed to read her thoughts. 'Nothing outside either – except some tyre tracks.'

'Tyre tracks?'

'Yeah, I'll show you.'

He led her through the warehouse and back out into the sunlight, pointing to a patch of soft ground to one side of a concrete track that curved away from the building into some trees. She bent down and studied the deep marks.

'SOCO thought they were likely to have been made by a heavy motor, like some sort of 4x4 or u/v, going by the tyre width and the depth of the tread,' he said. 'You didn't hear a car start up after the … er … incident, did you?'

She straightened and shook her head again.

He grunted. 'Probably no connection then. The track exits on a drive which connects with the main road, so it's wide open. Maybe someone was up here looking for something worth nicking or a couple dropped by for a shag.' He coughed, adding. 'If you'll pardon my French.'

She smiled in spite of herself. 'Don't fret, Tony,' she said. 'I stopped being a shrinking violet years ago. What about footprints?'

Another shake of the head. 'Most of the track is solid concrete, so if he stuck to it, he wouldn't leave any. As for the rest,' and he waved a hand at the water-logged fields on either side, 'you'd be hard put to find a trace of anything "off piste".'

'What about a dog?'

He sighed, obviously tiring of the interrogation. 'We got one up here just after it happened, but the damned thing turned up nothing more than a bloody heron.'

She nodded. 'So we're stuffed?'

He coughed again. 'I wouldn't say that. Stallard is still out there somewhere and he can't hide from us forever. Sooner or later we'll feel his collar, you can bet on it.'

'Yes,' she agreed. 'And how many more people will he hurt before then?'

But Sergeant Tony Anderson didn't have an answer to that question.

* * *

There was no sign of the black Volvo or the MGC sports car when Kate pulled up in front of Sycamore Lodge, but the flashy red Jaguar was drawn up close to the house and Carol Slater answered the door immediately. She was still barefoot, but dressed more demurely this time in a white blouse and black skirt – work clothes, no doubt. She was still sporting her ash-blonde wig and her perfume was even stronger.

'Sergeant,' she exclaimed, her eyes widening in surprise. 'You just caught me. I was about to head back to the salon after a very late lunch – busy, busy, you know – but I'm afraid Daddy and Chas are both out.'

Kate nodded. 'I don't need to see them and I won't keep you more than a couple of minutes anyway,' she said, accepting her motioned invitation to step inside.

A pair of black stiletto-heeled shoes lay on the floor by an armchair in the sitting room and an empty wine glass and plate stood on the adjacent coffee table. Kate smiled faintly when she saw the shoes, noting the redness of the young woman's toes and heels and empathising with her desire to kick the shoes off for a while to give her feet the chance to recover from the agony of walking in them.

'Coffee?' Carol Slater queried with a smile of her own, waving her to the two-seater settee, but the quick glance she directed at her wristwatch indicated that the offer was only a courtesy and not really expected to be taken up.

'No thanks,' Kate replied, propping on the edge of the settee. 'I'm only here to update you on Stallard.'

'Stallard? Why, what's happened?'

Kate grimaced, thinking of Hayden in the ICU and involuntarily clenching her fists. 'We … we think we cornered him yesterday in a derelict farm,' she said, 'but he attacked my partner and escaped, which means he is likely to be desperate now and also very dangerous.'

'Goodness,' Carol Slater breathed, sitting down in the armchair by her shoes. 'And how is your partner now? Was he badly hurt?'

Kate swallowed hard. 'He's … he's in intensive care,' she replied. 'Nasty head injury.'

The other winced, obviously now regretting the tactlessness of her last comment. 'Heaven forbid, that's awful. What on earth did Stallard hit him with?'

'We don't know. The team are still looking for the weapon.'

'Well, let's hope they find it and that everything works out okay for your partner. You are so brave still working on with such a dreadful worry hanging over you.'

Kate's face became a taut mask. 'I have no choice,' she replied. 'Stallard has made this one personal.'

It was on the tip of her tongue to tell her about the murder of Jacobs, but then she decided against it. It would have achieved nothing and as there was as yet no evidence to positively connect Stallard with a crime that wasn't even on her patch, it would have been more than a little indiscreet for her to have mentioned it. So instead, she stood up abruptly. 'Anyway, I came to warn you to be especially careful from now on and please tell your father and brother to do the same.'

'Tell us what?' Charles Slater said, striding into the room, his car ignition keys in one hand. He was dressed in a brown suede jacket over a white, roll-necked sweater and fawn corduroy trousers. Quite the man about town, Kate thought drily, though a bit behind the times dress-wise.

Carol Slater also stood up, making a face. 'It's Stallard, Chas,' she said. 'Apparently he was flushed out of hiding yesterday at a derelict farm and attacked a police officer – the sergeant's husband – who's in intensive care.'

He frowned. 'Good lord, so Stallard is still on the loose?'

She nodded. 'We'd better warn Daddy.'

He jerked his mobile from his pocket. 'I'll ring him now.'

As he left the room, Kate stood up. 'There's no need to panic, Miss Slater,' she said. 'Stallard may have decided to quit altogether, but I felt you should be aware of the latest developments.'

Slater squeezed her arm. 'Thank you, Sergeant. It was good of you to take the trouble to let us know, especially in your own time of trouble.'

And it was her own personal "time of trouble" that Kate was thinking about as she left the house and when she rang the hospital on her private mobile from the CID car her troubles got a lot worse – they had been urgently trying to get hold of her for authority to operate on Hayden to relieve the pressure on his brain.

'*It will be a difficult operation,*' the specialist said to her in a low voice, '*and it is by no means certain it will succeed, but my advice is it is the best option.*'

Kate reached the hospital in 20 minutes, breaking every speed limit on the way, and with a hand that shook uncontrollably she signed the consent form and sat in the hospital waiting room with a cup of coffee that tasted like stale cigarettes.

* * *

Kate awoke from a dreamless sleep with a lurch, conscious of the fact that someone was shaking her gently by the shoulder. She blinked in the bright yellow fluorescent light of the hospital waiting room, for a second wondering where she was. Then she saw the doctor in his white coat standing beside her and realisation dawned. She had slumped sideways against the wall and now she jerked upright, gripping the chair arms with both hands and staring into his pale weary face.

'Hayden?' she blurted. 'Is he … okay?'

The doctor took a deep breath and she felt an icy hand clutch at her heart, but then he smiled reassuringly. 'Your husband's had his op,' he said, 'but it was a long one and very difficult. He's lost a lot of blood, but we were successful in removing a sizable clot.'

She swallowed several times before she could find her voice. 'Is … is he going to be all right?' she whispered.

He hesitated, his smile replaced by a frown. 'Well, he came through the op satisfactorily,' he said, choosing his words carefully, 'but he will have to be monitored for several days at least before we can be sure everything was a total success. I'm afraid it could be a fairly long waiting game for you.'

'Can I see him?'

He shook his head. 'It's best that you don't for the present. Why don't you go home and get a good night's sleep, then phone us in the morning.'

She nodded quickly. 'You will ring me if there is—'

'Any change?' he finished for her. 'Of course we will,' and he smiled again, 'but this time keep your personal mobile on if you are out and about at all, won't you?'

But Kate had no intention of being "out and about" anywhere that particular night and after ringing Roscoe with her news, she went straight home to a cold lonely bed and lay awake, listening to a newly risen wind off the Levels and thinking of a big untidy man with a mop of flaxen hair and a smile that could light up an entire room.

CHAPTER 9

Kate's house phone awakened her at just after eight, but it wasn't the hospital. It was DI Roscoe.

'*Any more news on hubby?*' he rasped down the phone.

Kate relaxed and fell back against the pillows. 'Nothing after what I told you last night,' she said, still angry with him for his earlier insensitivity.

'*Well, no news is good news, eh?*' he replied.

She sensed hesitation at the other end of the line and then he was blurting out the real reason for his call. '*You … er … coming in this morning, or will you be at the hospital?*'

Her eyes narrowed. 'Why?' she queried, the hostility in her tone unmistakable even down a telephone line.

He cleared his throat. '*We need to talk.*'

'About what?'

'*Just.*'

She frowned. 'I am going to the hospital this morning, yes, but I will be in around eleven, if that is ok?'

'*Do fine.*'

The line went dead.

In fact, Kate was in a lot earlier than eleven. Hayden was still uncommunicative in the ICU and she was restricted to seeing him through the glass partition.

'Risk of infection at present,' the staff nurse had explained with a smile, 'but he's doing fine. Ring us again later.'

Tearing her gaze away from the white-faced figure lying in the bed, connected to tubes and wires like some Frankenstein creation, Kate left the hospital before she broke down completely.

* * *

Roscoe was hardly visible in his small office, but wreathed in smoke after several cigarettes and chewing as usual.

'Doing all right, is he?' he asked, his manner suggesting the question was more automatic than anything else, as if his mind was on other things.

'Holding his own – just,' Kate replied. 'Now, what is all this about needing to talk?'

Roscoe scowled and looked down at his desk. 'Guv'nor is taking you off the Stallard case,' he said.

'What?'

'He thinks you are too close to this one, because of Hayden, and feels that your personal feelings might impair your judgement.'

'That's bollocks!'

There was a heavy sigh. 'Articulate as ever,' he remarked sarcastically.

'But it is bollocks and you know it.'

'Maybe, but it wasn't my decision – though I have to say I think the boss has got a point.'

'Oh, thanks – it's nice to know I can count on your support.'

'Don't give me that shit.' There was a sharpness to his tone now as his patience began to disintegrate. 'It isn't a question of my support and you know it. We can't afford to have Stallard's eventual arrest and conviction compromised.'

'Compromised?' She laughed without humour. 'Do you think I'm going to beat him over the head with my handbag?'

He ignored the remark. 'They've set up an incident room at Bridgwater to deal with the Jacobs murder, as the crime was committed on their turf, and a DCI Fairlow from headquarters has been appointed to head the thing up as SIO. I've been loaned another DS and DC with the brief to investigate the assault on Hayden and to continue inquiries into the possible whereabouts of Stallard, subject to a definite link being established with the Jacobs killing—'

'Which I would have thought was pretty obvious to start with,' she cut in drily.

'When both jobs will be made part of the main murder investigation,' he finished heavily, ignoring her interruption.

'So for the moment Hayden's assault gets just a DS and a DC?' she sneered. 'That really is an impressive team.'

'Whole force is short on resources,' he snapped defensively, 'and anyway, I've managed to hang on to Jamie Foster, as well, so I'll have two DCs, not just the one. Furthermore, I'll be reporting back to Fairlow on a regular basis, which means there'll be plenty of liaison.'

She snorted. 'Liaison? Sounds like a right pig's ear of a set-up to me. Why couldn't the incident room at Bridgwater take over the lot in one go?'

He grimaced 'Fairlow doesn't want any pre-judgements or prejudicial influences on the Jacobs investigation apparently. He sees this as a way of avoiding both and upstairs, the Super doesn't think we can justify a full incident room here in addition to the one at Bridgwater.'

'Unless Hayden actually …' and she had difficulty phrasing the word, '… *dies* and it becomes a murder case, like the stiffing of Jacobs?'

He didn't answer, but stared down at his desk, shuffling his feet.

'So, what do I do in the meantime?' she went on. 'Polish the office silver?'

He made a face. 'You will have to look after the day-to-day running of the department with our new TDC, Ann Jones,' he said.

'Who?' she ejaculated. 'Did you say TDC? A temporary detective constable? You've got to be joking?'

'She comes highly recommended,' he said. 'Mature woman and a transferee from the Met. Four years' experience in the job and has a first-class honours degree in Law. She has been a plod downstairs for over a year and although she has no CID experience, she's proved to be a very good thief-taker. Got quite a few good nicks under her belt.'

Kate shook her head in disbelief. 'I don't care how good she is, where she's come from or how long she's been in the job – she's not a fully trained DC. You really couldn't humiliate me enough, could you, reducing me to acting as a wet nurse for a bloody apprentice detective?'

He snorted. 'Now you're being totally unreasonable.'

'Am I? Am I really? So what about taking me off the case in the first place, eh? Was that reasonable? Like hell it was! And I bet you were behind the whole thing because it has happened before, hasn't it? You tried to neutralise me on the Strawfoot murders, if you remember, but it didn't work, did it? I still got our man in the end.'

'This case is different,' he retorted. 'And anyway, it's your own fault. You never do as you are told. You're a maverick, a sodding loose cannon, and you're known for it throughout the force.'

She glared at him. 'But I get results, don't I? That's the whole point – I get results!'

He slammed the flat of his hand down on the desk top in an explosion of anger. 'You're off the case, Detective Sergeant!' he yelled. 'Is that clear? You've been re-assigned. Now, have you returned Colonel Slater's shotgun, as I instructed?'

'Not yet,' she replied. 'I'll do it this afternoon.'

'No you won't!' he snapped. 'I don't want you going anywhere near the Slater's house again. I'll get a plod to do it.'

She stood up sharply. 'Fine,' she replied. 'At least I won't be held responsible if Slater blasts some innocent bystander he mistakes for Stallard.'

He snorted. 'Ever the dramatist, aren't you, Kate?' he threw back, adding, and without thinking in the midst of his anger, 'but the only thing you should be concerned with right now is your injured husband – unless that has ceased to be a priority for you.'

Kate stared at him open-mouthed. 'I can't believe you just said that,' she gasped. 'I can't believe my own guv'nor could come out with something like that.'

Immediately regretting his unforgivable retaliatory shot, which had served only to compound the "'felony" of his earlier delay in passing on the message from the hospital, Roscoe wouldn't meet her gaze, but concentrated on fumbling for another cigarette instead.

When he looked up again, she was gone, the door left wide open behind her as she stormed down the general office and out through the double doors at the far end.

Suddenly the CID man felt old and after 30 years in a job that had sucked every bit of vitality out of him, so very tired.

'Shit!' he said slowly and distinctly as he lit up with fingers that still trembled from the raw emotion that had gripped him. 'Friggin' bloody shit!'

* * *

Kate sat for a long time in the CID car in the police station yard. Not for the first time in her service, she felt like chucking everything – the department, her rank, the whole job. What was the point to it all? A former university graduate, she could have chosen virtually any career when she had graduated, yet she had plumped for the police and then CID. It had been a hard, unforgiving life with plenty of brickbats and few rewards – especially for a woman – and she had had to prove herself time and time again, but for what? In the end, who cared? Not those at the top, that was for sure; they were too focused on their own miserable careers. Hayden's current situation was a classic example of this No one had contacted her since he had been hospitalised apart from Roscoe, and he had only done so as a formality – what was expected of him as her guv'nor. He didn't really give a jot. He was too busy covering his own back. And where was the station's commander, the superintendent who was so keen on preaching the value of teamwork? Why hadn't he been to the hospital to see how Hayden was faring? She snorted to herself. He was probably at some conference or other or maybe playing golf somewhere.

Kate wasn't conscious of the woman standing beside her car until a hesitant knuckle tapped on the driver's window. Kate glanced up quickly, drying her eyes on her sleeve, then opened the door and climbed out.

'TDC Ann Jones,' the young woman said in a voice that betrayed her Welsh heritage. 'People call me Jonah – but hopefully, not because I'm unlucky. I was told by Mr Roscoe that I had to report to you.'

Kate appraised her openly. Probably in her mid-30s, she was short, stocky – bordering on the muscular – and pasty-faced, with mousey hair and large brown eyes. She was dressed in a smart grey suit with black casual shoes and carried a black handbag over one shoulder on a long strap. Not the sort of woman to stand out in a crowd or turn heads, that was for sure. Then Kate noticed something else, which gave her a jolt. When the young woman turned her head at the sound of a car horn on the road outside, she displayed a long curved scar which ran down her cheek from below her right eye to the corner of her mouth. Without intending to, Kate focused over-long on the scar and Ann Jones gave a rueful smile, feeling it tenderly with the index finger of her left hand.

'Not very pretty, is it?' she said. 'Broken bottle in a pub brawl in Aldershot when I was in the military. Some squaddie with too much jungle juice inside him.'

'Military?'

'Yes, I was a Redcap, see – nine years in the service. Came out five years ago and joined the Met a year later.' She sighed. 'Lucky to get in too.'

'Oh?'

Jones held up her right hand and Kate winced when she saw that the upper part of the second finger was missing.

'Same incident,' she said and gave another rueful smile. 'Grabbed the bottle in the struggle, see. Severed the finger and it got infected. The medics couldn't save it.'

Kate emitted a low whistle. 'You have been in the wars.'

Jones nodded. 'Met took me after a lot of argy-bargey because of my degree and the reference I got from the Army, so I've got that to be thankful for anyway.'

'But what made you apply for a transfer to this force?'

Jones shrugged. 'Met is too big – you can get lost or forgotten in it. I fancied a smaller force with a better chance of promotion. You were advertising, so I just went for it.'

Kate considered her answer for a moment, then abruptly tensed, conscious of the fact that she hadn't said a proper word of greeting. Blurting out a quick embarrassed, 'Sorry, what must you think of me,' she shook her hand. 'My mind was on other things.'

Jones met her gaze with a concerned frown. 'I can well understand that, skipper. How is he?'

Kate blinked hard to hold back more tears. 'He's had his op and we can only pray that he gets over it,' she said. 'Thank you for asking.'

'No problem. What's the agenda for this afternoon then?'

Kate stared at her blankly for a moment. 'Agenda?'

'Yes, Mr Roscoe said you would show me the ropes.'

'Ah yes, of course.' Kate looked at her watch and opened the driver's door of the CID car again. 'But first some lunch, eh? We won't bother with the canteen – food is a bit basic. I know a nice little hostelry out in the sticks where we can chat. So climb aboard.'

Jones slid into the front passenger seat, bringing with her a whiff of exotic perfume, as Kate climbed back behind the wheel. 'Trouble is, I don't drink,' she said.

'Don't . . . don't drink?' Kate stared at her in astonishment. A detective who didn't drink? That was unheard of.

'Strong chapel, see.'

'Chapel?' Inwardly Kate groaned. That was all she needed – a trainee detective who didn't drink and was one of the holy brigade.

'Oh, from the Valleys, are you then?' she said quickly in an effort to hide her surprise.

'Not originally,' Jones said, 'but I was adopted by a Welsh couple in Merthyr and brought up by them after my mother abandoned me at birth – born out of wedlock, see.'

'How awful for you. So … er … where is your real family from then?'

Jones shrugged. 'I wish I knew. My birth certificate gives a hospital in Cardiff but that's all I know. Been trying to trace my natural mother for years, but it was difficult in the mob.'

'Still no luck then?'

Jones sighed. 'Actually, yes. I finally did get lucky about a year ago – only to discover I was too late and she had died.'

Kate winced. 'Fate can be so cruel at times. So what are you going to do now?'

'What can I do? I know nothing about her and I suppose it's best left alone, don't you think?'

Kate nodded and started the engine. 'You might be right there,' was all she could think of saying in such circumstances.

Jones hesitated, then said: 'Sorry about being tee-total.'

Kate forced a smile. 'Well, there's always orange juice,' she said as she pulled away, 'or maybe a coke. You're not a vegetarian as well, by any chance, are you?'

'Funny you should say that,' said Ann Jones, 'but I do eat fish.'

* * *

There was just a white Transit van and a mud-stained Land Rover in the car park at the front of The Scarlet Dancer, but a big articulated lorry on French plates, with the name Jacques Ferron on its flank, was parked down the side of the pub, facing towards the road.

'If he's dropped into this place for a meal,' Kate commented sarcastically to Ann Jones, nodding towards the lorry as they crossed the car park, 'that should do wonders for *entente cordiale*!'

There were four customers in the bar – a couple of farming types and a man in a boiler suit (white van man?) drinking at the bar, plus a dark-skinned man in a denim jacket and jeans eating a plate of sandwiches at one of the tables – no doubt the artic driver. Otherwise the place was completely empty.

Dibble's face hardened when he saw the two detectives. 'You again?' he said.

Kate shrugged. 'Can't stay away, Mr Dibble,' she said. 'Half a pint of cider please and ...?' She turned to Ann Jones, raising an eyebrow.

'Half of lemonade, please,' the new TDC said.

'Do you do food?' Kate asked.

Dibble grunted. 'Pork pies, sandwiches and crisps, that's all,' he retorted, pouring the cider.

Kate smiled again. 'A real gourmet pub then?' she teased. 'Our continental cousin over there cannot fail but to be impressed.'

Dibble leaned across the bar in a threatening manner. 'Now you listen to me, Defective Sergeant,' he said, deliberately mispronouncing Kate's rank, 'this could be harassment, this could. I reckon I should make a complaint.'

Kate didn't like Ronnie Dibble and it showed. 'Be my guest, Mr Dibble,' she replied, thinking that Daniel Sayers had said much the same thing to her. This time, though, she cast aside the discretion she had maintained in relation to Carol Slater for the greater "good" of winding up the unpleasant publican.

'Then, you probably won't want to know about the murder.'

He spilled some of Ann Jones' lemonade.

'Murder?' he echoed. 'What murder?'

Kate took a sip of her cider. 'Chap by the name of Austin Jacobs,' she said. 'Ex-Detective Chief Inspector actually. Was responsible for putting Lenny Stallard away.'

Kate studied Dibble's face intently for a reaction and she was not disappointed. The widening of the shifty eyes was too pronounced to escape notice. She waited for the other tell-tale sign – and got it when he swallowed hard.

'We just thought you should be aware of his death,' she said, 'what with Lenny Stallard still being on the loose and you a former witness at his trial.'

Paying the now visibly shaken licensee for the drinks and ordering a round of beef and a round of cheese sandwiches, Kate steered her companion to a table in the corner of the bar.

'What was all that about?' Ann Jones queried in a hushed voice, so Kate told her about the escapee's connection with Dibble.

'So why bait him?' the other asked.

'He's hiding something,' Kate replied, watching over the top of her glass as Dibble served another newly arrived male customer and noting the frequent glances he cast in her direction.

'I thought that the first time I met him – something smells. Winding him up a little might precipitate a reaction and produce some answers.'

Ann Jones frowned. 'But why are you bothering with this at all now? Mr Roscoe said you were off the case.'

Kate studied her for a moment. 'Mr Roscoe says a lot of things, Jonah.'

'You could get yourself into a whole load of trouble.'

Kate smiled grimly. 'What's new? Anyway, the risk of upsetting our Mr Roscoe hasn't stopped me before and it certainly won't stop me now. All I know is that Hayden was nearly killed because of this job and I owe it to him to get to the bottom of it.'

'But surely, it's simply a question of finding and re-arresting Lenny Stallard and charging him with the murder of Austin Jacobs, plus assault with intent to commit GBH on Hayden?'

'That's what it would probably say in the CID training manual, but as you must have found in your own experience before, sometimes you have to think outside the box. I firmly believe there is more to this case than it appears and I intend to find out what – officially or unofficially.'

But then the conversation was interrupted by the arrival of Dibble with two plates of sandwiches, which he set in front of them, together with appropriate cutlery wrapped in paper napkins.

'Radio says a copper was done at the old Yardley's Cider Farm,' Dibble said. 'Was that the clever cove who was with you the first time you called?'

'My husband,' Kate confirmed and she leaned forward towards him. 'And now Jacobs has been stiffed, I wonder who might be next?'

Dibble scowled. 'Stallard comes here and he gets more'n he bargains for,' he boasted.

Kate nodded. 'So you said once before, Mr Dibble,' she acknowledged. 'But I would still lock my doors at night if I were you.'

Half an hour later Kate and Ann Jones left the pub and climbed into the CID car.

'What now then?' Ann asked.

Kate glanced back at the pub in her rear view mirror and gave a thin smile. 'Oh, I think we'll let things fester for a bit and see what the inimitable Mr Dibble does next,' she said. 'He might surprise us.'

CHAPTER 10

Kate was home a lot earlier than usual. After an uninspiring afternoon investigating a break-in at a laundry and the theft of a pedal cycle from a garden shed, she had dropped Ann Jones off at Highbridge police station to complete the paperwork and had headed for the hospital. But it was another wasted journey. There was no change in Hayden's condition. He was still unconscious and unaware of her presence on the other side of the glass screen and the staff nurse told her that his recovery was likely to be a lengthy process with no guarantees as to the final outcome.

Tired and dispirited, Kate could not face preparing dinner for herself in the empty cottage in Burtle so she headed out on to the Levels in her Mazda MX5 to look for somewhere else to eat, unaware of the fact that she was being followed by a man in a blue BMW.

She found a cheerful-looking inn she had used with Hayden a couple of times before, but had only just settled on a bench seat at a corner table with a large glass of red wine after ordering a meal at the bar, when the man from the BMW stopped by her table.

'Mind if I join you?' he said with a grin and pulled out a chair.

Kate glared at him. Short and plump, with a greying black beard, sharp bird-like brown eyes and a slightly hooked nose, her uninvited "dinner date" was dressed in a fawn car coat and blue jeans and wore a plastic identity card around his neck on a black strap. Kate didn't have to read the card to know it said "Press", or that the name printed on the card would be Bradley Jakes, for she had crossed swords with the local crime reporter so many times in the past that it had almost become a habit.

'No, you may not,' she snapped back. 'So piss off!'

The man chuckled and sat down anyway. 'What have you ordered?' he queried. 'I understand the lasagne is pretty good here.'

Kate took a sip of her wine and sat back against the wall. 'What do you want, Jakes?' She said wearily. 'I am off duty and have nothing to say to you anyway.'

He raised a hand and a young woman in a white blouse and black skirt came over to the table with a writing pad.

'Whisky-Mac, love,' he said, omitting the word "please", 'Bells would be good.'

'Anything to eat?'

'Not as yet.'

The girl shrugged and left them to it.

'Sorry to hear about Hayden,' Jakes said with just the right sober expression. 'Must be difficult for you at the moment. How is he?'

Kate clenched her teeth tightly for a second. She didn't like Jakes or what he represented and he knew it, but reporters tend not to have very thin skins so it made no difference to him anyway.

'You know without asking me,' she retorted. 'Now get to the point so I can eat my meal in peace when it arrives.'

His whisky was deposited on the table by his left elbow and he nodded to the waitress before taking a sip. 'Word is you've been taken off the case,' he continued. 'Seems a bit unfair when you were just getting your teeth into it, but there again that sort of thing has happened to you before, hasn't it?'

Kate leaned forward across the table and studied him fixedly. 'As I said to you just now, I have nothing to say to you,' she grated, 'so why don't you just go and play on the motorway among the articulated lorries?'

He made a face. 'That was rather a nasty thing to say to someone who has your best interests at heart, Kate.'

'DS Lewis to you. Now are you going to leave or—'

'Or what, *Kate*,' he sneered, 'you'll call the police?'

She shot to her feet, almost knocking her glass of wine over and drawing curious attention from both the bar staff and several other diners.

He held both hands up in front of him in a defensive gesture. 'Okay, okay,' he said, 'but hear me out first.'

She hesitated, then reluctantly sat down again and the bar staff and diners immediately lost interest.

'I may have something of interest for you,' he said.

'Like what?'

It was his turn to lean forwards across the table. 'I believe you've paid a couple of visits to our Ronnie Dibble at The Scarlet Dancer?'

'So?'

'What did you make of him?'

'What was I supposed to make of him?'

He took another sip of his whisky. 'What would it be worth if I were able to give you some pukka info on him that might raise a few questions in your mind?'

'Such as?'

He chuckled. 'All I ask is for a reciprocal arrangement – give me an exclusive on the progress of the case.'

'You know I would never agree to that with you – and anyway, as you rightly observed, I am no longer on the case.'

'So why did you visit him again this afternoon?'

'That's my business.'

He thought for a second. 'Let me give you a tip, Kate – no strings attached. I have it on good authority that Ronnie Dibble was a very good friend of a former DCI, named Austin Jacobs who, I gather from a source, met an unfortunate end earlier today.'

Kate's heartbeat quickened and she hardly noticed the steak and chips dinner arrive on the table in front of her, complete with cutlery and a tray of condiments.

'How much of a friend?' she queried softly, unsurprised by the fact that Jakes had already heard about the murder.

He made a face. 'Well, put it like this. Jacobs, my source tells me, had some sort of a hold over him – so much so that your ace thief-taker was a frequent visitor to The Scarlet Dancer.'

'Maybe Dibble was his snout?'

'Maybe he was, though I can't see a man like Dibble being a police informant. In any event, it seems that all your illustrious DCI's drinks and snacks were on the house.'

'You're saying Jacobs was bent?'

'Draw your own conclusions.'

'So how does that affect the present case?'

Jakes shrugged and drained his whisky glass.

'That's for you to work out,' he said, standing up sharply, 'but it might be worth your while having a quiet look around Dibble's premises.'

'Looking for what?'

Another shrug. 'Anything that might strike you as … shall we say, odd? I mean, you have to ask yourself the question how The Scarlet Dancer survives as a business on just half a dozen punters a day? Could be that Dibble has another source of income way over and above what even a very knowledgeable snout might earn – involvement perhaps in activities other than those connected with running a pub, eh?

He half-turned towards the bar counter, feeling for his wallet in his back pocket, then snapped his fingers and turned back towards her. 'Oh yes, and it might not be wise to believe everything people tell you. Hidden agendas and all that?'

'Does that include journalists?'

He just smirked and said: 'Don't forget who gave you the info if you turn up anything tasty, will you?'

Then before she could question him further, he had crossed to the counter, left some change on the towelling mat and strolled out of the bar into the car park, leaving her staring after him with her brows furrowed in thought and her steak and chips growing cold as she suffered a sudden loss of appetite.

* * *

The Scarlet Dancer closed promptly at eleven and sitting in her car in a gateway on the other side of the road, opposite the car park, Kate watched and waited as four men – presumably the only customers – trooped out of the public bar into the moonlight, got in three cars and drove off. Dibble appeared once after that to let a young woman – no doubt a bar worker – out through the same door but then, within minutes of the door closing again, the lights in the bar were extinguished and the pub was plunged into darkness. Not much clearing up to do at this particular hostelry, Kate thought, or maybe Dibble just liked to turn in early.

Kate knew full well that what she was contemplating doing was illegal and that no matter what Dibble might be guilty of, if she was caught she could end up on a serious charge herself, but there was insufficient evidence to justify applying for a search warrant. After all, what would she be searching for? So she was left with little option, but to resort to the old police "Ways and Means Act" if she wanted to follow up on her suspicions. But she had never gone into something on such flimsy grounds before. All she had was what could be very iffy information from a journalist she had never trusted, plus her own gut instinct, which had told her from the very start that Dibble was a wrong-un and was up to something. She smiled grimly as she recalled what Roscoe had said about her being a maverick and a loose cannon.

Maybe he was right, but the fact remained that without taking risks, you never achieved anything.

Forcing herself to stay where she was for a further 20 minutes, she then climbed out of the car and carefully pushed the door to behind her. Avoiding the main entrance to the car park and the direct route to the front of the premises, she followed a low boundary hedge bordering the road and turned into a rutted track, which she had noticed earlier striking across the moor between an overgrown rhyne and the side of the building.

A few yards further on she spotted a gated archway in a high brick wall, which extended from the rear corner of the building for at least 20 yards before disappearing into a patch of dense woodland. The gate was unlocked and leaning over on just the lower hinge. Through the gap this presented she could see a paved yard beyond with the back of the pub to her right and a long outhouse with a corrugated iron roof at the far end of the yard to her left. Apart from a faint glow behind what seemed to be heavy curtains drawn across an upstairs window of the pub, the whole place was in darkness.

Squeezing her slight frame through the gap between the gate and the archway, she stood for a few moments, scanning the yard in the moonlight and listening – tensing in case a dog might be on the loose. But nothing stirred, so she took a chance and crept across the yard to check on the outhouse.

Even though shadows cloaked the front of the building where the moonlight failed to reach, she could see that the door was shut and securely padlocked. Examining the padlock with her small pocket torch partially masked in one hand, she saw that it appeared to be fairly new too – and it had certainly been recently oiled, for her fingers were immediately glistening with the stuff. She spent a few moments testing its resistance, twisting it as hard as she could against the hasp, but it was apparent that the thing was heavy duty and it would take a lot more than a healthy tug to force it open. Whatever it was that Dibble had stored inside, he was obviously very keen to protect it against intruders.

Frowning, she edged along the wall to the end to check the side of the building. Immediately she saw the window. It was high up under the roof's eaves, but someone had parked what looked – and smelled – like an old fish and chip van against the wall beneath it.

Whoever owned the vehicle – whether it was Dibble himself or someone else he allowed to park the thing there – it couldn't have been more convenient for her purposes.

Throwing a fierce grin at the moon, she clambered up on to the front bumper, then the bonnet. From there it was relatively easy to reach the cab roof and then the roof of the box-shaped body. The window sill of the outhouse was now level with her waist. She examined the frame with the aid of her torch and saw that it not only opened conveniently at the bottom, but was not fastened properly. Couldn't be better!

Crouching down on her knees and inserting the fingers of one hand between the window frame and the sill she felt for the catch and managed to flick it upwards. The window had obviously not been opened in a long time, for it was very stiff, but in the end she managed it and raising it as high as she could with one hand, she thrust her head through the opening and lowered it on to her back.

The beam of her torch revealed that the outhouse was packed with large cardboard boxes, stacked four high and two deep against each of three walls, but as they all appeared to be sealed, it was not possible to see what any of them contained. A closer look was obviously required, but actually getting inside the outhouse was not going to be that easy.

Nevertheless, it had to be done and gritting her teeth as the window juddered down her backbone, she pulled herself through the opening and lowered herself, hands first, on to the stack immediately beneath her. But she hadn't allowed for the fact that some of the boxes might not be quite as robust as they appeared to be and as she leant on the stack and bent her right leg to pull it through the open window, the topmost box, which was carrying her weight, buckled under her and to her horror, pitched forward, bringing the upper boxes of the stack tumbling down and taking her with them.

The fall to the concrete floor knocked all the wind out of her and for a few moments she simply lay there among the broken boxes, her head spinning and coloured lights flashing before her eyes. She must have fallen about 20ft and it was a wonder she hadn't suffered serious injury, but moving her arms and legs experimentally she satisfied herself that while she was obviously bruised and shaken she hadn't broken anything.

Physical damage aside, however, she still had a major problem. Although the noise created by the collapse of the boxes may not have been earth-shattering, it would have been loud enough to have been heard outside the shed, which meant Dibble could now be aware that he had an intruder and already be on his way to investigate.

Gritting her teeth, she forced herself up on to her knees and using the corner of one of the poorly stacked boxes lining the back wall beside her for support, she hauled herself to her feet. But glancing up at the window through which she had made her undignified entrance and which now admitted a shaft of blazing white moonlight, she felt her stomach churn. It was apparent that the window was far too high up on the wall for her to reach, and the boxes which had been stacked so precariously under it were now lying around her, spewing their contents out all over the floor.

'Shit!' she breathed, using her favourite expletive. Now what? The boxes in the other stacks were too big and heavy for her to move into place under the window, and anyway there was now too much rubbish strewn all over the floor which would have to be cleared away first and she suspected – with good reason, as it turned out – that she was fast running out of time to do anything.

She spotted her torch, miraculously undamaged and still lit, as her glance roved around the gloom. But bending down to pick it up, she froze. The contents of one of the boxes had cascaded all over the floor in front of her through a serious rent in the cardboard and the shaft of moonlight revealed those contents to be packets of branded cigarettes, each one neatly packaged together, 20 at a time, and tightly sealed in cellophane wrappers.

'Well, I'll be damned!' she exclaimed and turning her attention to one of the cardboard boxes still stacked beside her, she pulled the clasp-knife she always carried with her from her pocket and ran the blade down the edge before wrenching the cardboard open with both hands. Bottles glittered in the light of her torch and she studied the labels with a soft cynical chuckle, despite her own personal predicament.

'Vodka!' she breathed and turned her attention to another box. This time she found the contents to be litre bottles of whisky. 'You naughty, naughty boy, Ronnie Dibble!' she breathed. 'I bet HM Revenue and Customs would be very interested in what you've been up to here.'

But her humour was short-lived for it was at this point that keys suddenly rattled in the padlock outside and even as she whirled round, the door was wrenched open and Ronnie Dibble stood there glaring at her, a sawn-off double-barrelled shotgun in his hands, which was elevated from the waist and pointing directly at her head.

CHAPTER 11

For a few moments there was a pregnant silence and then Dibble emitted a low growl. 'You yet again,' he said. 'You just couldn't leave things alone, could you, you interfering little bitch?'

Kate felt her insides churning as she stared into the twin black muzzles of the shotgun, which, at only three or four feet away, looked twice their diameter.

'Put down the gun, Mr Dibble,' she said in as calm a voice as she could manage under the circumstances, wondering how many coppers had said a similar thing to armed offenders in the past before they had pulled the trigger.

'You got a warrant, occifer?' he sneered, ignoring her instruction. Then, when she didn't reply, he emitted a harsh laugh. 'No, I thought not – which means you're just snooping around on your own account, eh?'

'Seems I was justified,' she said. 'Looks like you have almost enough contraband in here to fill a customs shed. Bring it in via the tunnel, did you – the French lorry I saw in your car park when I was last here, for instance?'

He grunted. 'Observant little cow, aren't you? But yeah, I got a nice little deal going with a couple of Frogs I'm in business with. They're each over here twice a month, delivering legit stuff to supermarkets in Bridgwater and Taunton, so they only have to make a slight detour each time to drop off the cargo they have for me.'

Kate's mind was in overdrive. She didn't need to be blessed with a top MENSA score to appreciate that she was in big trouble. The fact that Dibble was willingly giving away so much information indicated that he didn't expect her to be in a position to repeat what she had learned to anyone afterwards.

'So, what about border checks?' she blurted, desperately playing for time while she tried to think a way out of her perilous situation. 'How do your delivery men manage to get past Customs every time without being stopped?'

He snorted. 'This ain't some Mickey Mouse operation – been going for a lot longer than you could imagine, with a lot of people and big money involved on both sides of the Channel, including in the Customs sheds and bonded warehouses.'

'It's not just a one-man band then?' she commented, encouraging him to part with more information. 'DCI Jacobs part of it too, was he?'

But he wasn't biting. Instead, he just grinned. 'Migrants at Calais have done us proud too without even knowing it. See, everyone is too busy trying to deal with the hundreds of illegals from the refugee camps trying to sneak into the country to check the loads or paperwork of every lorry that goes through.'

'Worth the risk then?' she went on, wondering if she could somehow get hold of the barrel of the shotgun and wrench it from his grasp. It would be the last move he expected her to make, but it could also precipitate the very thing she was trying to prevent and she dismissed the reckless plan as potential suicide in such a confined space.

'You can say that again. Plenty of call for duty-free ciggies, baccy and booze on the network we run. But we don't do nothin' else – no drugs or nothin' – just this. I wouldn't be involved otherwise – I got me principles.'

'Ah, the good old-fashioned smuggler,' she said drily, 'Do you think the Revenue would see the difference?'

‘It don’t really matter how they would see it,’ he retorted, ‘’cause they’ll never know nothin’ about it. And you won’t be tellin’ ’em either – not where you’re goin’.’

‘Don’t be fool!’ she snapped as she sensed his finger tightening on the trigger. ‘So far you’ve only defrauded the Revenue, which means you’re looking at just a heavy fine or a suspended sentence, but murder is something else – kill a copper and they’ll throw the key away.’

He snorted. ‘They won’t know where to look,’ he countered. ‘Ain’t no one knows you’re here.’

She swallowed hard. ‘You sure about that? How do you think I found out about your illicit stash? I just needed to confirm the fact before I alerted the Revenue.’

He hesitated. ‘That’s bollocks.’

‘Is it? Can you afford to take the chance?’

Another shrug. ‘I’ve taken chances all me life, so one more won’t make no difference. Now toss your mobile phone over to me.’

She made a grimace and jerking her phone from her pocket, she dropped it on the floor in front of him.

Without taking his eyes off her, he felt for the phone with his foot and stamped down several times until he was able to crush it under his heel. Then, nodding his head towards the open door behind him, he said, ‘Outside. I don’t want your brains all over me merchandise.’

She didn’t argue, but walked slowly around him and out into the moonlight.

‘Any tricks and I’ll let you have both barrels,’ he warned, following closely behind her. ‘Now go straight through the archway over there.’

She felt the barrel of the shotgun nudge her roughly in the back and obeyed with a sense of resignation, her throat drying up and her legs beginning to shake at the thought of what was in store for her. He was no doubt taking her out on to the moor where he could do the deed and dump her body afterwards without anyone being the wiser.

Whether a low-level criminal like Dibble was ruthless enough to actually be capable of going through with her cold-blooded execution when it came to it was not a hundred percent certain, but as it turned out, he was not put to the test anyway, for they never got as far as the archway.

The crunch of tyres on loose gravel coming from the direction of the front car park had an immediate effect on her would-be assassin and the barrel of the shotgun found her spine again in a savage dig as he snarled: 'Stand still!'

She could practically hear his brain working as they stood there in the moonlight, effectively frozen to the spot. Should she make a run of it, she thought quickly? If there was a possible witness just yards away, would he dare use the shotgun? It seemed unlikely. But what if he panicked or the driver of the newly arrived vehicle was only using the car park to turn around in and head back the way they had come? There were too many ifs and buts to be sure. But there again, what other option did she have?

The muscles in her legs tensed and she took a deep breath. It was now or never – after all she was going to die anyway – but Dibble seemed to sense her intentions and the shotgun was pressed into the back of her neck.

'Don't try it,' he hissed. 'Back to the shed.'

The engine of the vehicle in the car park was cut just as they reached the outbuilding and seconds later there was the sound of a car door opening, then closing with a bang.

'I'll deal with you later,' Dibble grated, pushing Kate into the shed and closing the door. 'But make a sound and I'll kill you and the visitor. Got it?'

She heard the padlock being applied and as Dibble's heavy footsteps receded, there was the sound of loud hammering, presumably on the front door of the pub.

In the gloom of the shed, Kate's heart sank lower than she had ever thought possible.

* * *

Kate thought a lot about Hayden as she prowled around the tight confines of the shed, wondering if he might have regained consciousness by now and be asking for her – refusing even to contemplate the other awful possibility – and also wondering whether she would ever see him again.

She had spent some time clearing away the packets of cigarettes which had littered the floor before trying to move some of the other boxes into position under the window through which she had entered the shed. But the boxes were stacked at too greater height to be reached and handled individually, while moving the stacks themselves by sheer brute strength proved to be impossible. Maybe Dibble's powerful frame could have managed it, but at just over eight and a half stone, Kate was not even in with a chance and in the end she had to admit defeat.

Facing the inevitability of a final – potentially fatal – confrontation with Dibble, she took the only action left open to her. Jerking a bottle of whisky from the box she had cut open earlier, she tapped it sharply on the concrete floor several times until it shattered at her feet, the contents forming a sickly-smelling puddle which gleamed with a brief rich golden lustre in the moonlight before it spread out across the floor as a formless black stain.

Then, holding the top half of the broken glass shell up in front of her, she touched the jagged edges with the fingers of her other hand. As she did so, she thought of the damage she had seen a broken bottle do to a human face in the numerous bar-room brawls she had attended as a uniformed copper – a classic example of which was what had happened to poor Ann Jones – and wondered if she would be able to get close enough to Dibble to do the same thing to him before he blew her away with his shotgun. The more she thought about it, though, the more the futility of what she was contemplating dawned on her, but she was fresh out of options – the clasp-knife in her pocket had such a short blade that it would have been useless as a weapon, except at very close quarters and she had left her CS gas spray at home – so she had no choice but to go with the bottle.

It was at this point that she heard the muffled sound of a car starting up and seconds later, the roar of an engine as it sped away. The visitor had gone, which meant Dibble would soon be back. She took a deep breath and positioned herself to the right of the door – the opposite side to the hinges – which she felt would give her a slight advantage as she would see him a fraction of a second before he saw her.

Outside the shed she heard the distant sound of a siren and smiled grimly. It sounded like the distinctive warble of a Traffic unit on its way to a "shout". No chance they would be heading her way, though – she was on her own.

She waited … and waited, but there was no sound of approaching footsteps or the turning of a key in the shed padlock. She frowned and flexed her leg from the knee downwards to relieve the cramp that was beginning to knot the muscles in her calf.

More precious minutes followed and she glanced at her watch with the aid of her torch. She had been standing there for at least 15 minutes. Where was Dibble?

There was a scrabbling sound above her head and then the mournful hoot of an owl as it lifted off the shed roof. Straight afterwards, a vehicle – an HGV, she thought – growled past the pub, its engine soon fading into the immensity of the moor. She glanced at her watch again … 20 minutes now. Was Dibble deliberately hanging things out to torture her? But no, she couldn't see him doing that; he wanted her out of the way as quickly as possible. So where the hell was he?

She waited a few minutes longer, then bent down on one knee to press an eye against a gap between the door and the frame. The moonlight revealed that the yard was completely deserted. There was a light on at the back of the pub opposite, but otherwise no sign of life at all. She was mystified. Surely Dibble wasn't just going to leave her locked inside the shed? It didn't make sense.

Straightening up, she took hold of the door handle and turned it. The door gave a lot more than she had expected, but she felt and heard the padlock bite. She stood there for a moment, biting her lip. She remembered how new the padlock had seemed when she had first examined it, but the door itself was quite old and split in places. Maybe a good kick would force it open? But what about the noise? That would be sure to bring Dibble running to investigate. She pressed her eye against the gap again and confirmed that the yard was still deserted.

'In for a penny …,' she breathed and stepping back, lifted her foot and slammed it into the door. There was a loud rattle, but it stayed shut. Gritting her teeth, she did the same thing again and this time had the satisfaction of feeling the door give a little more. Two more assaults on it produced the desired result and it flew open, admitting a more intense gush of moonlight.

She studied the yard narrowly. Still not a sign of anyone. Surely Dibble must have heard the noise? Yet the pub appeared totally dead, although lights now glowed dimly through heavy curtains drawn across one downstairs window and a couple more upstairs. What was the matter with the man? Had he suddenly gone deaf?

She took a deep breath. There was only one way to find out.

Still clutching her broken bottle, she stepped out into the open and half-turned towards the archway. Then she hesitated. The most sensible thing for her to do in the circumstances was to get well away from the pub and back to her car while she still had the chance. She could then find a phone and call for armed back-up to deal with Dibble. But taking the easy option had never been her forte and in any event, her natural curiosity had got the better of her.

So instead of quitting the scene at the fastest rate of knots possible, she headed for the back of the pub and flattened herself against the stone wall in a patch of shadow thrown up by a dilapidated-looking water-butt.

Then, resorting to a trick she had learned from the "old-timer" who had tutored her in practical beat-craft during her first year as a rookie constable, she closed her eyes tightly for a few moments to maximise her sense of hearing by temporarily disabling that of sight. But the night was now dead – not even the murmur of distant traffic or the call of a night bird to disturb the stillness. It was strangely disturbing.

Edging past the water-butt and along the wall, she paused by the lighted downstairs window and peered around the edge of the frame. Curtains had been drawn across the square pane, but through a chink she could see into the room beyond, which turned out to be an ultra-modern fitted kitchen, equipped with an island in the centre and a Range cooker and expensive-looking built-in cupboards and worktops occupying the opposite wall. There were more built-in cupboards and worktops along the wall to her right and a Welsh dresser flanked by an internal door to her left while a smart stainless steel sink and double drainer had been fitted just below the window beside the external door to the yard. It was clear that the room was empty, but Dibble had obviously been there recently as his sawn-off shotgun had been left on the island, alongside a bottle of single-malt Scotch whisky and a glass containing a tell-tale amber residue.

She gnawed at her lip, once more considering her options. Venturing into the house would be the height of stupidity. Dibble could re-enter the room at any time and his shotgun was all too handy for him on the table. But she was nonplussed as to why he had left it on the table in the first place – and more important, why he hadn't responded immediately to the noise of her break-out. She had no desire to confront the powerfully built thug, but at the same time, she found the silence confronting her strangely disquieting. Where on earth had Dibble gone? Surely he wouldn't simply have driven off somewhere with his visitor and left her alive and kicking inside the shed? It didn't make sense and she didn't like unsolved mysteries.

Leaving the window, she reached down and tried the handle of the kitchen door. The door opened without resistance and her nostrils were assailed by the smell of recent cooking. Crossing the room inside, she paused for a few seconds by the table to stare down at the sawn-off and ran a finger along the cold metal barrels with a shudder. Then, making up her mind, she put her bottle down on the table, picked up the weapon, broke it and ejected the cartridges before slipping them into her pocket and returning the gun to the table.

Feeling safer now that the weapon was empty, she left her broken bottle where it was and turned her attention to the internal door, peering through the gap into a short windowless hallway lit by a brass table lamp on a half-moon table.

There was still no sign of anyone, so she pulled the door wider and stepped through on to a thick pile carpet and stood there for a moment, looking around her. To her left, at the far end of the hallway, a narrow staircase flanked on one side by another door, ascended into darkness, while at the other end, a further door, which had been left wide open, revealed what was obviously the public bar, with its row of counter-top pump handles silhouetted in a blaze of moonlight, like motionless Lilliput sentries.

For some reason she gave the public bar a miss and approached the closed door flanking the staircase instead. Holding her breath, she turned the handle and eased the door open. It creaked a little but swung back with relative ease and she found herself staring into what appeared to be a small sparsely furnished sitting room, illuminated solely by moonlight penetrating the gloom through a small window. It contained a couple of green leather armchairs, a matching settee and a big, wide-screen television, but little else and the room was otherwise empty.

Moving quietly out into the hallway again, she turned her attention to the upper floor, starting up the thickly carpeted staircase only to stop abruptly, her heart thumping wildly, when one of the treads gave a despairing groan. But the silence remained profound and she moved on.

A door opened off the landing immediately on her left and even without seeing the edge of a wash-hand basin through the gap, she could smell that it was the bathroom and toilet. A step up just beyond it and to her right accessed a corridor, running from the front to the back of the building, obviously in line with the hallway downstairs, with several doors visible on each side. She stepped up into the corridor and tried the first left-hand door, which was also ajar. The moonlit bedroom inside was empty.

She moved on, wondering, with a stab of apprehension, what she would do if she was suddenly confronted by the muscular Ronnie Dibble, conscious once again of her own stupidity in pushing on, yet unable to stop herself.

The next doorway was brightly illuminated and she tensed as she approached the wide open door, taking a deep breath before peering round it into a huge room – no doubt two former bedrooms knocked into one – which boasted the sort of opulence that was in stark contrast to the grim, rundown appearance of the building itself .

With walls painted a delicate shade of pink and a white ceiling resembling the top of an extravagant wedding cake, it boasted two glittering chandeliers, heavy brocade curtains drawn across the two windows and a thick Persian style carpet. Each corner was occupied by a chaise-longue with gold-coloured upholstery and part of one wall was taken up by a long cocktail bar constructed of stainless steel and patterned glass, above which was an enormous wall-hung television.

Even more striking were the finishing touches to the décor – several risqué statues of naked men and women in erotic poses placed strategically around the room and similar themed gilt-framed pictures adorning the walls. It didn't take much imagination to work out what the room was probably used for and Kate pursed her lips in a silent whistle as she returned to the corridor. It seemed that Ronnie Dibble was involved in a lot more unsavoury practices than smuggling, despite his so-called principles.

Tearing herself away from the vulgar extravagance of Dibble's pink "bordello" and now at the far end of the corridor, Kate set about checking the three rooms on the other side, anticipating a sudden confrontation with the man himself at any second. But the thuggish licensee never appeared and she only got as far as the first room anyway.

This one was furnished as a study or office, but in a smoky glass and stainless steel modernistic style, with a stand-alone computer on a pedestal, a deep swivel armchair, and a row of three-drawer filing cabinets, which were all closed. A bunch of keys had been left on the top of the pedestal beside the computer, several of which looked like filing cabinet keys.

Ordinarily her curiosity would not have allowed her to leave the room without checking on the cabinets first. The fact that she didn't was due entirely to a significant and rather gruesome distraction – the body of Ronnie Dibble lying face down on the thick pile carpet just in front of them, blood drenching his shirt and the carpet under him, and a familiar red pattern spattered across the drawers of the cabinets like some chilling entry for the Turner Prize.

CHAPTER 12

'Deep stab wound to the lower back,' Lydia Summers declared, straightening up from Dibble's body, 'plus a nicely severed trachea and carotid artery. I would suggest your man was attacked from behind as he was walking into the room from the corridor, hence the trail of blood from the door to where he was lying. He was then finished off with the deep incision to the throat.'

Roscoe nodded gloomily from the hallway. 'Just like Austin Jacobs.' he summarised.

The forensic pathologist shrugged. 'Very similar,' she agreed, 'but I am not able to say positively that there is a connection – that is down to the eventual conclusions of your own investigation.'

'Bit of a coincidence, though, isn't it, Doc? MO seems to be the same.'

Summers smiled. 'Ah, the all-important modus operandi or method of operations, Detective Inspector. Well, that remains to be seen. You see, an MO, as you sleuths love to call it, can also be applied to forensic pathology. We also look for a common denominator in a case involving more than one similar death, but this requires a little bit more than prima facie assumptions; we need to establish definite facts and these can only be gleaned from a full post mortem.'

Roscoe scowled, acutely conscious that Summers was being deliberately obtuse in an effort to rile him.

'Okay, Doc,' he growled. 'You can cut the crap. In your expert opinion, could we be looking for the same killer?'

Summers' smile broadened. 'Very possibly, Ted,' she replied, moving away from the body and peeling off her surgical gloves as she stepped back out into the hallway. 'But I wouldn't want to tramp on the toes of your esteemed SOCOs. I am doing the late DCI Jacobs' PM tomorrow at two and if I have time, Mr Dibble's will follow. I will let you know what my findings are in my report.'

Kate, standing very much in the background, winced. Winding Roscoe up was not a good idea – especially as she knew she would be next in his line of fire. So far since arriving on the scene he had hardly spoken to her, merely turning up with her junior colleague, DC Jamie Foster, and a couple of uniformed officers and stomping past her into the pub, leaving her to wander in after him. But she knew he wouldn't ignore her for long and she wasn't looking forward to the eventual confrontation.

Fortunately for her, however, she was spared this for a while by the arrival of the SOCO team and she left Roscoe talking to their supervisor while she seized the opportunity to step out of the pub into the cool night air.

As she stared at the jewel-spangled heavens, she thought of Hayden and wondered if no news was good news where he was concerned. The trouble was, the hospital had promised to ring her if there was any change, but Dibble had smashed her mobile, so if they had rung her on it after being unable to contact her at home, she would be none the wiser. Somehow she had to get hold of a phone and check.

The uniformed constable guarding the entrance to the car park was only too pleased to oblige her with the loan of his own private mobile, but the hospital took ages to answer the call and when they did, she was unable to glean much information from them other than the fact that Hayden was stable, but still not conscious.

She had only just returned the phone to the policeman when she sensed a presence behind her and swung round quickly to face Roscoe.

'My car!' the DI snapped, indicating his old Honda Civic. Kate nodded and walked ahead of him to the car, climbing into the front passenger seat. The interior smelled of cigarettes and beer, but fortunately her window was open so she leaned as close to it as possible.

Roscoe settled into the driving seat and switching on the interior light, flicked a filter-tip out of a battered packet of cigarettes and slipped it in his mouth. Then, glancing sideways at Kate as if suddenly sensing her disapproval, he emitted an irritable grunt and stuck the cigarette behind his ear instead, tossing the packet on to the dashboard in front of him and sucking some gum from the side of his mouth to begin rhythmically chewing.

'So,' he said, a brittle edge to his voice, 'do you mind explaining what you think you were doing prowling about a dodgy boozer in the middle of the night without a warrant – especially after being told to keep your nose out of the Stallard inquiry?'

So she told him, omitting only the fact that she had been acting on information received from Bradley Jakes. As she did so, she tried hard to read a reaction from the side of his slab-like face, but he kept his gaze focused on the far end of the moonlit car park through the windscreen without giving anything away. Surprisingly, he made no attempt to interrupt her either and even when she had finished with a resigned shrug of her shoulders, he just sat there, staring in front of him and chewing his gum. In fact, he was remarkably controlled and she didn't like it. An enraged snarling Ted Roscoe she could handle but this silent, brooding man sitting beside her in absolute silence was something else.

'The motor that turned up, then drove away …' he said finally, '… any ideas what kind it was? Car, van, lorry? Anything?'

She took a deep breath, still waiting for him to explode.

'Something heavy, by the sound of it,' she replied. 'Maybe a large van or a 4x4.'

He stiffened in his seat and cast her a brief glance. 'SOCO found what they thought might be 4x4 tracks at the back of the cider farm,' he said slowly. 'Could be a connection—' He broke off, adding: 'But that would mean Stallard has access to a motor of his own.' He shook his head. 'Can't see that.'

He stared at her fixedly. 'If there ever was a car at the pub, of course?'

She frowned. 'If? But I told you there was.'

'I know what you said.'

'I don't understand. What are you getting at?'

His lips compressed into a tight line. 'You claimed Dibble shut you in the shed,' he said. 'Is that all he did? Didn't come on to you, did he? Maybe you followed him afterwards and skewered him when his back was turned?'

She shot upright in her seat, her eyes wide and angry. 'You what?'

'Well, think about it. You were on the property unlawfully – without authority and without a warrant. All we have to go on is your own explanation as to what happened, plus a corpse with nasty knife wounds. Someone might decide to question your account of things in these circumstances.'

She gaped at him. 'And you think—'

'It isn't about what I think!' he snarled, now obviously rattled and regretting the blurted off-the-wall accusation that had been made out of bad temper. 'This is now a murder inquiry and all angles will have to be considered.'

'What angles? If you seriously suspect me of "skewering" Dibble, as you put it, where's the bloody knife?'

He turned his head away from her to concentrate on looking through the windscreen again, seemingly reluctant to meet her angry stare.

'I'm not suspecting you of anything,' he muttered almost as a retraction. 'I was just pointing out how bad it looks.

At the very least, you are likely to be under investigation, not only for disobedience to orders, but also for illegally trespassing on private property, but it could get a lot more serious than that—'

'Illegally trespassing? Dibble was a bloody smuggler. He's got a shed load of contraband – not to mention a room upstairs he's obviously using as a sodding knocking-shop!'

He grimaced and threw her a quick glance. 'Which, if he had lived, would have made the job of prosecuting him almost impossible since the evidence which we would have had to rely on would have been obtained illegally and therefore treated as inadmissible.'

'But … but all this is total rubbish and you know it.'

He held up his hand sharply to silence her. 'Enough!' he barked, regaining his former bullishness. 'I know nothing of the sort and you'd be well advised not to say anything that might incriminate you. Just remember, you got yourself into this mess so you will have to face the consequences.'

Then, to her surprise, instead of continuing the conversation, he abruptly threw open his door and climbed out.

'Go home, Sergeant,' he threw back over his shoulder. 'You've done enough damage for one night.'

Then he was a short dumpy figure striding back across the car park towards The Scarlet Dancer, leaving her staring after him in stunned disbelief.

* * *

The little thatched cottage on the outskirts of Burtle village seemed cold and hostile when Kate turned her key in the front door and she hesitated for a moment before stepping inside.

She tossed her car keys on to the coffee table and interrogated the 1571 facility on the main phone, but there was no message waiting for her. No news had to be good news, though, didn't it, she asked herself? After all, if there had been any change in Hayden's condition and the hospital had been unable to reach her on her mobile after Dibble had smashed it, they would have left a message on the cottage's answer phone, wouldn't they?

Suddenly realising how tired she was, she pulled off her coat and tossed it on to the settee before kicking off her shoes and slouching into the kitchen to flick on the light and plug in the kettle for a coffee.

She stared at her reflection in the window while she waited for the kettle to boil, her mind still numb after what Roscoe had said to her. First poor Hayden and now this. Her whole world was on the verge of collapse and it would only need one more push to bring it crashing down completely. Okay, so maybe she was too headstrong and she had certainly had enough gipsy's warnings in the past about going off at what Roscoe liked to call "half-cock", but as she had pointed out at her previous rollicking, it wasn't as though she hadn't got results – and wasn't that what being a detective was all about?

She poured herself a black coffee and settled on to one of the stools at the breakfast bar with it cupped in her cold shivering hands.

But what about Hayden? He was in hospital because of her. She should have listened to him from the start. Going into the derelict cider farm in search of a violent criminal without proper back-up had gone against all the rules that had been dinned into her since her early days as a rookie constable. Arrogance and impetuous stupidity had taken over, as always, and because of that she had put the life of the man she loved right on the line. If Hayden failed to make it …

She choked as she forced some of the scalding coffee down her throat and it was because of this that she failed to hear the creak of the floorboards in the living room behind her. 'Any chance of a coffee for me then?' a voice said quietly.

She whirled round, remembering too late that she had not closed the front door after her.

Bradley Jakes gave a thin smirk. 'How'd it go?' he queried.

Kate hauled herself off the stool and glared at him. 'Who said you could waltz in here without being invited?' she rapped. 'Get out – now!'

He held up both hands in a defensive gesture. 'Keep your hair on, Kate,' he said. 'I just thought I'd pop by to see how my info turned out.' He leaned a shoulder against the door frame and pulled out a packet of cigarettes, proffering her the packet.

'You've got a bloody sauce,' she breathed, but with her nerves stretched to breaking point, a cigarette was just what she needed even though she professed to be a non-smoker, and snatching one from the packet, she let him light it up for her.

'Why are you up so late?' she demanded. 'Shit the bed or something?'

He shrugged. 'I just told you, I wondered how things went at The Scarlet Dancer tonight.'

She sank back on to the stool. 'What makes you think I was at The Scarlet Dancer?'

He chuckled and coming off the door frame, stepped into the kitchen to prop himself against the edge of the work surface, blowing rings with his cigarette.

'Let's not play games, Kate,' he replied. 'You and I both know you couldn't resist checking poor old Ronnie Dibble out. Find his stash, did you? Is that why half of Highbridge nick is camped on his doorstep?'

'You were there?' she exclaimed.

'Close to the action,' he admitted, 'where every good journalist should be.' He frowned. 'Bobby on the car park entrance said it was a crime scene, though. What sort of crime scene would that be then? I saw Roscoe and the SOCO van there – "Scientific Investigations" on the side. Can't see them turning out over a few hundred smuggled cigarettes and bottles of booze.'

She took a pull on her cigarette and exhaled through a wheezing cough, avoiding his stare. 'You'll have to ask the nick,' she blurted before she could stop herself. 'As you seemed to know when we last spoke, I'm no longer on the case.'

He raised both eyebrows and chuckled again. 'Yeah, but maybe you're in much deeper shit than you were before, eh? Old Roscoe read you the riot act in his car before he sent you packing, did he?'

She felt sick as she realised that the canny journalist must have actually been watching her from somewhere close to the scene, but she didn't satisfy him with the indignant retort he obviously expected and instead, calmly dropped her cigarette in the sink and watched it fizz to extinction among the unwashed dishes piled up in the cold soapy water.

'Nothing of the sort,' she lied. 'It's just that I have been assigned other cases.'

But Jakes was no fool and he studied her with a crafty glint in his eyes. 'Old Dibble come on to you, did he?' he queried. 'Tried it on and got a slap?'

She stood up sharply from the stool. 'I want you to leave now, Mr Jakes,' she countered, 'or I will have to eject you.'

He didn't budge an inch. 'Or maybe it's something more serious?' he went on. 'Maybe your slap was a bit too heavy? On the critical list is he, love?'

'Don't talk bollocks, Jakes,' she shouted. 'Now, for the last time, get out – and if you print any of that crap, I'll sue your arse off!'

He eased himself away from the work surface, once again holding up a hand in a defensive gesture. 'Okay, okay, sweetheart, I'm going, but if you won't tell me, it means I'm going to have to go back to the scene and ask that nice Mr Roscoe.' He shook his head in mock regret. 'I'd have to tell him, of course, that my partner won't keep her side of the bargain to share our info—'

She started towards him, her fists clenched and her eyes blazing. 'You wouldn't dare! We had no such bargain.'

He sighed. 'You followed up on the information I gave you, didn't you? How do you think that would look to a press-hating DI like Roscoe? I don't think he would be too happy about one of his detective sergeants working hand-in-glove with a newspaper reporter, do you?'

Kate swallowed hard. Ordinarily she would have dismissed his threat with the contempt it deserved, but in her present precarious position and after all that Roscoe had said to her at the murder scene, she knew that a word from Jakes on top of it all was likely to finish her completely.

'Dibble is dead,' she said flatly, reasoning that he would find that out soon enough anyway.

'How do you mean "dead",' he replied. 'Dead like a heart attack, or dead like stiffed by someone?'

'It's a murder investigation,' she confirmed. 'But that's all I'm telling you.'

He nodded slowly. 'Murder, like ex-DCI Austin Jacobs?' he queried.

She stiffened. 'What makes you think Jacobs was murdered?'

He snorted. 'Oh come on, love. I wouldn't be much of a hack if I didn't know about that by now, would I? Are the two crimes being linked?'

'I don't know.'

'Same MO, was it?'

'I'm not prepared to go into that.'

'Lenny Stallard the key suspect, is he?'

'What makes you say that?'

'Well, it's common knowledge he's on the loose in the area – you've got half the force looking for him – and he certainly had an axe to grind with both Jacobs and Dibble, so it's pretty elementary, my dear Watson, isn't it?'

'No comment.'

He tossed his cigarette into the sink to join hers. 'Thing is,' he went on, the crafty glint back in his eyes, 'you could be on the wrong track.'

Her inbuilt antenna quivered. 'What do you mean?'

He tapped the side of his nose with the index finger of his free hand. 'Well, maybe – just maybe – Lenny Stallard didn't do old Mrs Slater in the first place.'

'What? But Stallard admitted at his trial that he broke into the house.'

'Yeah, but he always denied the murder.'

'Well, he would, wouldn't he? And there was enough witness evidence against him to prove the case beyond reasonable doubt.'

'Exactly, which brings us to two of those witnesses – Jacobs and Dibble. See, the word is that Jacobs was not only on the take, but as I told you when we chatted before, he also had a hold over Dibble.'

'But you never told me what sort of a hold?'

He stretched and yawned. 'Jacobs was a shrewd old bastard. Made it his business to know a lot about a lot of people, so he could use that info to his own advantage when the opportunity arose. In Dibble's case there was plenty to know too, as you've just found out, so your former colleague would have been able to play poor old Ronnie like a harp – make him do anything and more important, *say* anything he wanted.'

Kate caught on quickly. 'Are you alleging Jacobs got Dibble to give false evidence in the Stallard case?'

'I'm not alleging anything. I'm just suggesting things may not be as cut-and-dried as your lot seem to think.'

'So why would Jacobs want Dibble to lie?'

He raised an eyebrow. 'We still partners?'

Her mouth tightened. 'We're not partners, Jakes, and never will be.'

He shrugged and turned towards the door. 'In which case, I think we'll just leave it there. If you decide to change your mind later on, we'll talk again. You know where to find me.'

Kate's hands clenched into tight fists. 'If you know something that could help the investigation, you have a duty—'

'Duty?' he echoed with a derisory laugh. 'Don't give me that load of balls, love. I'm a press reporter. I only have a duty to my newspaper and the reading public.'

Then he gave her a mock salute and left.

CHAPTER 13

Kate sat for a long time on the kitchen stool after she'd heard Jake's car drive away, her thoughts in a hopeless tangle. How the hell did Jakes know so much about everything? Where had he got all his information? What exactly was he implying with regard to the Stallard case? Dibble's integrity was obviously blown away now, especially after what she had discovered at The Scarlet Dancer, so maybe he had lied to the court, as Jakes had implied, but why? And what about Jacobs himself? Had he been a corrupt copper and if so, why would he have decided to lean on Dibble to give false evidence? What would he have got out of it? And most important of all, why were both Jacobs and Dibble murdered? Revenge by Stallard or was it something – and someone – else? Which raised another question: if Daphne Slater had been murdered by someone else and Stallard had been framed, who on earth could that someone else have been? There were so many imponderables and to make matters worse, she felt that Jakes was leading her by the nose; dropping an interesting morsel in front of her – like his information on Dibble in the first place – then leaving her to chew on it.

One thing was clear however; there was no point in tying her brain up in knots, trying to work things out. Consulting her watch, she saw it was past three in the morning. She was exhausted after the night's events and needed to get some sleep, if only for a few hours, before facing whatever ordeal was in store for her when she returned to work later in the morning.

But as it transpired, Fate had other ideas and she had only just climbed the stairs to the bedroom with a large glass of red wine in one hand when the telephone rang. Red wine from her glass slopping over her wrist and acid surging up into her throat from her stomach, she stood for a second, staring at the extension phone as if it were about to explode. A call at after three in the morning was never likely to bring good news and with Hayden in the hospital ICU, she felt sure it could mean only one thing.

Feeling her legs starting to buckle under her, she stumbled to the bed – the glass finally slipping from her hand to spread a large red stain over the coverlet – and picked up the receiver with a shaking hand.

'Mrs Lewis?' a deep voice queried. 'Hospital security here. No panic, but I've been instructed to let you know that an intruder has been disturbed in our ICU. Police have been informed and are on their way as we speak.'

'An intruder?' Kate whispered. 'My husband—'

'He's fine,' the voice said, 'but it seems someone tried to tamper with the equipment at his bedside.'

* * *

There were police cars everywhere when Kate got to the hospital. It seemed that the "shout" had attracted units from all over the place, drawn to the hospital as if by a giant magnet. Two Traffic cars were parked at an angle over three ambulance bays at the front of the A & E building, one with a door left open, and a dog van and two area patrol cars had been "abandoned" in the service road. Torches were flashing in the shrubberies adjoining the car park and it seemed that every light the hospital possessed had been turned on, its high buildings looking like electrical circuit boards framed against the night sky.

Kate jumped out of her car without setting the handbrake – unaware that it had rolled forwards into the back of one of the Traffic cars – and charged through the double glass doors of A & E, heading straight for the ICU. A security guard with a torch stepped in front of her, but he didn't stand a chance and slight as she was, she bowled him over before he could open his mouth to say "you can't go through".

She could hear the shouts on the floor above her as she mounted the stairs and came face to face with a uniformed sergeant in the doorway of the ICU.

'Hayden's fine,' he growled, 'but the bastard's gone to ground somewhere in the hospital.'

Kate pushed past him and stared through the glass screen at the motionless figure in the bed. There was a nurse and a man in a white coat – obviously a doctor – by his bedside and the nurse, glimpsing Kate standing there, came out to see her.

'Your husband is okay, Mrs Lewis,' she said, recognising her from a previous visit. 'Our staff nurse saw the intruder crouched over the bed in time. She challenged him and he pushed her out of the way and took off.'

Kate took a deep trembling breath, staring at Hayden again. 'What did he do to my husband?' she queried.

The nurse grimaced. 'We don't really know, but it's possible he was trying to disconnect some of the apparatus,' she said, 'although he obviously didn't know what he was doing and didn't manage to do it. Doctor Singh is just making sure everything is as it should be.'

Kate took another deep breath, this time of relief. 'So who are we looking for?' she demanded, turning on the policeman.

The sergeant gave a quick shrug. 'Shortish, stocky guy in a dark hoodie and jeans.'

'Nothing else?'

He shook his head. 'He moved too quickly apparently and the staff nurse didn't get much of a look at him, but she said he seemed quite athletic.'

'Stallard!' Kate breathed, then glanced at the still-open door to the corridor, then back at the nurse. 'So how did he get in here in the first place when there's a keypad controlling entry? I've always had to ring to gain access.'

The nurse made an apologetic grimace. 'One of our cleaners wedged the door open to bring a trolley through,' she replied. 'She said she was only gone a minute.'

Kate shook her head in disbelief. 'Wonderful!' she commented grimly. 'Why bother with a keypad at all?'

'He may not have got far, though,' the sergeant put in. 'Hospital security were pretty much on the ball and had the building sealed within minutes.'

Kate stared through the open door again, following the long corridor's strip-lights with her eyes. 'Then let's see if we can find the arsehole!' she grated, turning back towards the door – only to be stopped in her tracks by a sharp 'Sorry, but I can't permit that'.

Kate swung round to face the young Asian doctor who had left Hayden's bedside to come up behind her.

'What do you mean, you can't permit it?' she snapped back. '

'This is a hospital,' the doctor said quietly. 'We have patients to consider and it is now …' he glanced at the clock on the wall '… a quarter to four in the morning. I cannot permit an intrusive search of the premises which is likely to disturb chronically ill people.'

The uniformed sergeant stared at Kate and made a face, which said it all. Kate closed her eyes for a second in resignation, then nodded.

'Just make sure this security door stays shut from now on,' she said tartly. 'There had better not be a repeat performance!'

Outside in the cool fresh air, she stood by her car for a few moments, sipping a mediocre coffee she had bought from the machine in the foyer, her gaze roving around the car park as she nursed the paper cup in both hands. The intruder was obviously long gone, no matter what the sergeant had said, and deep down she knew that a search of the hospital would have proved fruitless anyway, but that did little to alleviate her frustration. First the murder of Jacobs, then Dibble and now an audacious attempt on the life of her own husband – yet not a single sighting of Stallard save for that first intrusion at the home of the Slaters. Where the hell was the man hiding and was it possible that he did have wheels of his own, as had been suggested? If so, he could be anywhere – even on his way out of the county by now.

She was so lost in her thoughts that the sudden movement she caught out of the corner of her eye at one end of the building didn't register at first and then, when it finally did, the figure in the hooded coat had melted into the shadows.

Dropping her cup, she raced in pursuit. She found an open fire-escape door, then turned the corner and glimpsed her quarry sprinting along the service road towards the rear of the hospital. She was just in time to see him lurch sideways and disappear among some out-buildings.

Stunted grass tugged at her shoes as she stumbled between two long sheds, crunching discarded cardboard and plastic detritus underfoot. Then she came to an intersection. There was no sign of the figure, but even as she hesitated, trying to decide which way to go, she heard the sound of an engine starting up. Instinctively, she jerked round and raced back to the service road, but she was too late and caught just a brief glimpse of a large black shape, displaying no lights, disappearing at breakneck speed round a curve in the road towards the exit. A flash of brake-lights and then the vehicle became a fading growl on the road outside the hospital.

'Shit! Shit! Shit!' she snarled at the moon. 'What are *you* laughing at?'

Then, kicking a buckled Coco-Cola can across the road into the bushes, she turned on her heel and walked back, head-down, to her car – and straight into Ted Roscoe.

'Talking to yourself now, are you?' the DI said gruffly. 'Bad sign, that is.'

Even in just the moonlight, he looked dishevelled and bleary-eyed and as usual, smelled strongly of beer. The pork-pie hat he often liked to wear was almost as buckled as the coke can Kate had kicked across the road, suggesting he had rammed it on to his head in a fit of temper, and the collar of his overcoat was twisted under itself.

'Did you see the car?' Kate snapped. 'It … it was him and he just drove out.'

Roscoe shook his head and followed the direction of her gaze towards the hospital exit.

'Just been to the ICU,' he said. 'Got called out half an hour ago.' Then he added, 'You sure it was our man?'

She gave an irritable snort. 'Short, stocky, hooded coat and running away? Pretty obvious to anyone, I would have thought!' she snapped, her anger overruling her inbuilt deference to rank.

Roscoe's eyes narrowed, but he didn't pull her up on her blatant insolence, no doubt because of the attempt on her husband's life.

'What sort of car?' he queried. 'Did you get the reg?'

She shook her head, suddenly deflated. 'Just saw a big black wagon – like a 4x4 of some sort. It wasn't showing any lights.'

Roscoe nodded. 'Maybe Security will have something on their cameras?' he said.

But they didn't, for, sod's law being what it was, the CCTV system covering the hospital and its grounds was temporarily out of action. The senior security man on duty could not have been more apologetic about the situation, but that didn't wash with Kate in her present mood.

'What a dipstick,' she muttered as they left his office. 'Seems everything is conspiring against us on this case.'

'We'll get a break eventually,' the DI replied. 'I'm sure of it – we always do.'

She hardly heard him. 'So why would Stallard want to stiff poor old Hayden anyway?' she blurted. 'He had nothing to do with the Slater murder investigation.'

Roscoe shrugged. 'Maybe the arsehole was worried that he might be able to identify him after the assault at the cider farm.'

She shook her head firmly. 'That doesn't make sense. He's already sus for two murders. Why would he care about a less serious assault charge?'

She leaned back against her car with a heavy grimace. 'If only I had got the number of that bloody car. At least we could have circulated it. At the moment, Stallard could go anywhere and we wouldn't be any the wiser.'

Roscoe grunted. 'I'll get Ann Jones to troll through the PNC, see if we've got any 4x4 motors recently nicked. That's if he didn't just hire one from one of our dodgy dealers.'

Kate shook her head again. 'After the press circulation, he wouldn't risk doing that.'

'Then we're just down to old friends who might have helped him out.'

She snorted. 'As far as we know, he's only got Daniel Sayers and I can't see that toe-rag loaning a motor to the man who got him a double helping of porridge for the GBH on that postmistress.'

Roscoe studied her intently for a moment. 'Go home, Kate,' he said quietly. 'Nothing more you can do here and you've got enough shit to worry about already after the Dibble job. I'll arrange for a plod guard to be put on your husband from now on.'

She met his gaze and held it. 'Just make sure Stallard doesn't get to Hayden again, *sir*,' she said. 'Or the shit that I'm in won't smell half as bad as the shit that drops on you!'

He stiffened at her second insubordinate remark, but once more chose not to bite. 'I'm not your enemy, Kate,' he said in the same quiet tone. 'Far from it.'

She threw open the door of her car and climbed into the seat. 'You could have fooled me, Guv'nor,' she replied, then slammed the door and reversed back from the Traffic car before driving off.

CHAPTER 14

Sleep did not come easily to Kate when she got home following the shenanigans at the hospital, and even after she had finally drifted off, trapped in a web of dark tangled dreams, her refuge from reality didn't last long and she surfaced at just after eight in the morning to the sound of her telephone ringing.

The receiver slipped out of her hand the first time, but then she managed to haul it up on to the pillow by the cord and acknowledge the call with an unintelligible grunt.

'You can forget the lie-in,' Roscoe barked. 'Get your arse down to the nick pronto; there's a DCI from the big house wants to see you.'

All vestiges of sleep left Kate in an instant and her heart sank, knowing that the "big house" meant headquarters.

'What about?' she queried.

He snorted. 'You'll find out. Just get down here now!'

Then, before she could ask anything else, he cut off.

There was a slim young man with carrot-red hair and pale blue eyes sitting on the edge of the window sill in Roscoe's office when Kate walked in, and he stood up with a disarming smile and held out a warm, dry hand which she took after a moment's hesitation.

'DCI Peter Fairlow …' he said, while Roscoe watched him covertly from behind his desk, his eyes hooded in disapproval. '… SIO in the current murder investigation.'

Kate gave Fairlow the once-over, catching a whiff of delicate aftershave as she took in the expensive-looking blue suit, which she guessed would be bespoke Italian silk, the police special course tie and the highly polished Italian-style brown shoes. One of the new breed of senior officers, she mused: young – this one probably about 28 – well-educated, personable and totally ruthless; a complete antithesis to the rough, aggressive, hard-drinking, chain-smoking senior CID officers she had been familiar with in her early years of police service. An improvement? Looking at Roscoe, she gave a brief cynical smile. In one way, maybe; in another, she was not so sure – the jury was still out on that.

'So, you're the officer who found both Jacobs and Dibble?' Fairlow went on, adding quickly: 'Look, do sit down.'

Surprised at the warm reception when she had been expecting something a lot different, Kate settled into the chair he had pulled out from against the wall for her.

'Yes, Guv,' she replied.

The grin disappeared and he frowned. 'Peter, if you don't mind,' he corrected smoothly as he dropped into another chair. 'I hate all this "Guv" and "Sir" stuff. Modern police service now, eh? Time we got in line with 21st century thinking, don't you think?'

Inwardly, Kate cringed. Like most experienced street-hardened police officers, she felt uncomfortable with the fashionable push away from a disciplined rank-structured organisation towards a new liberal, corporate-style regime where everyone was a Tom or a Sheila and gobbledegook and bullshit ruled the day. Fairlow seemed pleasant enough, but she couldn't help thinking that maybe she preferred Roscoe, warts and all – at least his heart was in the right place, even if he could be an arse at times.

'Sorry, sir,' she said, 'but I don't feel comfortable being on first-name terms with a senior officer.'

There was a flash of something – irritation – in Fairlow's eyes but then he raised both hands, palms upwards in a deprecating gesture, and said: 'As you wish, Sergeant. We must beg to differ, though.'

Out of the corner of her eye she saw Roscoe was grinning. The shit-bag was enjoying all this, wasn't he, she mused?

'Anyway,' Fairlow went on, 'I must congratulate you on your contribution to this inquiry so far. Of course, entering The Scarlet Dancer without a warrant was rather out of order, but as Mr Dibble is no more, he will not be in a position to complain and there can, of course, be no prosecution now that he is deceased. Furthermore, both your superintendent and myself feel that the end result makes up for the … er … technical illegal entry and I understand that our Revenue colleagues are cock-a-hoop over what you have turned up.'

He beamed. 'Therefore, instead of pursuing a full discipline inquiry, which will do no one any good, it has been decided, with the approval of HQ Professional Standards, of course, to give you a formal caution instead, so consider that done here and now.'

She breathed a sigh of relief. 'Thank you, sir.'

Another flash of even white teeth in gracious acknowledgment. 'I don't know whether you know it,' he went on, 'but the stash of liquor and cigarettes you found was just the tip of the iceberg where Master Dibble was concerned. In addition to the rather … er … unusual room upstairs, it turns out that he was a very naughty boy indeed. SOCO found around 1500 photographs of child porn in the filing cabinets in his study and we suspect he was part of an internet paedophile ring. The hard drive on his computer is currently being interrogated.'

Kate drew in her breath sharply. 'Child porn?' she echoed, thinking of the pink room and what Jakes had said about other activities Dibble was involved in. Maybe this, rather than the publican's smuggling racket, was the hold Jacobs had had over him. She was, however, careful not to blurt anything out which would have indicated her prior suspicions, though she could feel Roscoe's eyes burning into her – almost as if he had sensed something in her reaction.

Fortunately Fairlow didn't seem to notice and abruptly stood up. 'Right then, well I'll be off. Incident room to manage, you know, and since it seems I'll be taking over the Dibble murder investigation now as well as that of the unfortunate Mr Jacobs, I'm likely to be up to my ears in it. Glad to have you and Mr Roscoe here on board. Keep up the good work, eh?'

Kate also stood up and shook the extended hand again, but Roscoe simply stayed put, nodding in a perfunctory way as the still-smiling DCI made his exit, after which he sat back in his chair and eyed Kate almost balefully.

'Off the hook again then, eh, Lewis?' he growled. 'You really are a lucky cow.'

She flushed. 'Not sure I like the analogy with a cow, Guv,' she replied. 'But you know what they say – the sun always shines on the righteous.'

He gave a grim smile. 'Do they?' he retorted, lighting up a cigarette. 'Well, seeing as you're back in the fold *Miss*, and we seem to be part of the main investigation now, you might as well earn your keep. I know how much you like post mortems and you're in luck this afternoon – we have two you can attend. I shall be there, standing in for the DCI. Two o'clock sharp then, eh? Starting with Austin Jacobs, I believe. Enjoy!'

* * *

Kate wasn't really surprised to see Bradley Jakes waiting outside the mortuary when she drove into the car park with Ann Jones. The man seemed to have an uncanny knack of knowing the best place to be at any given time. He grinned as he pushed off the wall he was leaning against and strolled over to her with his hands in his pockets.

'Hi, Sarge,' he said as she climbed out of the CID car. 'Big day today, isn't it? Two PMs for the price of one.'

'Very funny,' she replied, slamming the car door shut and turning to face him. 'Maybe you should write comic scripts instead of crummy newspaper stories?'

He manufactured a hurt expression, then abruptly changed the subject. 'So, how's your old man after his near miss last night?'

She stiffened. 'What near miss?'

He rolled his eyes contemptuously. 'Oh come on, Kate,' he said. 'Do you really think half a dozen cop cars screeching into a hospital in the middle of the night with blue lights flashing wouldn't arouse a little local curiosity? I gather someone tried to finish poor old Hayden off for good.'

There was no point in denying the incident because Jakes obviously had most of the details already – maybe supplied by a member of the hospital's security staff for a nice little bung – but Kate had no intention of confirming it either.

'You'll trip over that nose of yours one day,' she said, pushing past him.

'Guy got away, I hear. Do you think it was Lenny Stallard?'

'Haven't a clue,' she threw back over her shoulder as she headed for the double doors of the mortuary building.

'Bit like the rest of Highbridge CID then,' he chortled after her. 'They don't seem to have a clue either!'

Ann Jones chuckled as she followed Kate into the building. 'Bit of a wit, your man, isn't he?' she said.

'Yeah,' Kate agreed, 'with a big "T" in front of the word "wit".'

Lydia Summers smiled as they entered the mortuary. 'Just in time, ladies,' she said, the scalpel in her gloved hand glinting under the overhead strip-lights and the green-robed assistant standing on the other side of the table awaiting her instructions.

Roscoe was there too, dressed in his short coat and pork-pie hat, standing beside a photographer with a video camera who would be recording the entire proceedings for the coroner. The DI was chewing, as usual, making disgusting sucking noises while his boot-button eyes flicked first one way and then another, as if he had an itch.

Kate winced as her gaze took in the stainless steel dissecting table and the naked white corpse of Austin Jacobs lying there on his back. Despite numerous post mortems in her career, she had never got used to the grisly experience: the revolting smell that was released when the abdomen and stomach were cut open; and the horrible sound as the top of the skull was sliced open with a special saw, like the top of a tin, before the brain and other organs were removed, weighed and dissected. It was a skillful exercise, but conducted with such cold clinical precision that it seemed somehow so callous and inhuman. What had once been a living, breathing person, with the individual characteristics and personality that made up the unique identity of a member of the human race, had now become just an empty shell – an inanimate object, exposed in an obscene, degrading and semi-public way to horrific dismemberment. Even the features were subjected to the ritual of disfigurement – peeled back over the face, as if just a Guy Fawkes-type mask, to allow the skull to be opened, then pulled back in place once the "lid" had been replaced, to hide the awful incision that had been made. The horror was unimaginable to anyone spared the experience and Kate had never got used to it.

Glancing sideways at Ann Jones, she saw the first tell-tale beads of perspiration appear on the TDC's forehead even before the pathologist had started, noticed the colour slowly draining from her face and the cobweb of tiny blue veins surfacing on one cheek. As unobtrusively as possible, Kate reached out and took her wrist in one hand, squeezing once before releasing it. Jones smiled briefly – and then collapsed in a dead faint.

It was quite chilly outside in the car park, but it suited Kate fine and she sat Ann Jones on a wooden seat that had been placed to one side of the double doors, though for what purpose outside a mortuary was a matter of conjecture. Jones had recovered as quickly as she had passed out, but she was trembling and her eyes were wet with tears.

'Sorry,' she whispered. 'I made a right fool of myself.'

Kate gave a harsh laugh. 'Actually you helped me out,' she replied. 'I also hate those bloody things and you gave me the excuse to leave.' She frowned. 'I am surprised, though – with four years in the job already and ex-military as well. I would have thought you'd seen plenty of this sort of thing before.'

Jones nodded. 'I've had my fair share of it in the force, yes, but I've never got used to it. As for the military, most people assume that because you were a squaddie, you've been in the thick of it all, you know, Iraq, Afghanistan – blood, bullets and wall-to-wall corpses. Truth is, I never served in any of the action zones – just Gib, Germany and army camps at Aldershot and others on Salisbury Plain. Pretty tame really.'

Kate smiled. 'Nothing wrong with that. Better than an early grave—'

Then she broke off as a voice drawled at her elbow. 'Rough in there, was it?' Bradley Jakes queried, a malicious grin on his face as he studied Ann Jones' white face.

'Why don't you just piss off?' Kate snarled, turning and pushing past him.

Jakes was undeterred and emitted a humourless chuckle. 'I will once I've got all the SP I need,' he called after her. 'But I suppose they're still doing the cutting are they?'

The journalist didn't expect Kate's next reaction and he was caught completely unawares as the chunky heel of her knee-length boot slammed into his shin, then scraped down the tibia to his instep in one agonising movement.

His shout of "Bitch!" was wasted, for Kate was already walking ahead of Ann Jones to the car and she blew him a kiss as he crouched on the ground rocking backwards and forwards and clutching his badly bruised leg.

'That could have been a mistake, skipper,' Ann Jones said, dabbing perfume behind her ears from a small bottle as if to get rid of the clinging smell of the mortuary before climbing back into the CID car.

Inwardly, Kate was inclined to agree with her – especially if Jakes chose to approach Roscoe, as he had threatened to do, to claim he and she were in cahoots – but she wasn't about to acknowledge the fact.

'Then it can join all the other mistakes I've made,' she replied. 'Now, seeing as I appear to be back on the inquiry, let's go hunting.'

'Shouldn't we go back inside?' the TDC queried with a worried frown. 'Mr Roscoe won't be very happy if we just push off now.'

Kate started the engine and threw her a grim smile. 'Mr Roscoe is never happy, Jonah,' she replied. 'And I'm sure anyone as ugly as him can cope with being miserable for another day.'

* * *

Daniel Sayers was getting into his old red Land Rover Defender parked outside his house when Kate turned the corner into the street and she pulled over to the kerbside in the CID car to let him drive off. Even from over 40 yards away she could see he was on his own.

'So the prick is off out, is he?' she commented to Ann Jones sitting in the front seat beside her, 'and I wonder where he's going – without his dear old mum too?'

The TDC popped a Polo mint in her mouth and offered her the packet. 'Only one way to find out, skipper,' she said, pocketing the mints again when Kate refused her offer.

Kate nodded and pulled out slowly to follow Sayers as he drove away. Okay, so maybe the toe-rag had been telling the truth about having no contact with Lenny Stallard, but there was nothing to lose by tailing him to wherever he was going anyway – just in case he was lying through his teeth, as toe-rags like him usually did.

But it was a wasted effort. Sayers simply went to the nearest Tesco supermarket and spent 40 minutes shopping before returning home. And to make matters worse, he had obviously been aware of Kate on his tail, for after unloading the Volvo and locking up, he waved at the two detectives parked up 20–30 yards away before disappearing indoors.

Ann Jones went into a fit of laughter at Sayers' gesture, but Kate couldn't see the funny side of things and she used every expletive she could think of to reinforce that fact as they finally drove off.

'What a bloody waste of time,' she grated, swearing again when a speed camera flashed as they drove through a small village at speed.

'Now what? We've reached a total brick wall on this case. Two bloody murders, Hayden still in a coma and not even one positive sighting of Stallard, apart from his appearance at the Slater's place and the likelihood that he was the intruder who was disturbed at the hospital. Where the hell can the bastard be hiding?'

She glanced quickly at her colleague. 'Roscoe said he was going to get you to check the PNC database to see if we'd had any 4x4's nicked in the area recently.'

Ann Jones crunched her second Polo mint. 'Did it this morning. Didn't take long. Very few vehicles stolen in the area in the last week and no 4x4's or large utility wagons. Most modern cars are too difficult to steal nowadays anyway, what with electronic alarms, immobilisers and all the other security gizmos they have on them. I checked the whole of the South-West and right up to Manchester too, but again, nothing relevant since Stallard escaped.'

Kate shook her head. 'So, another dead-end then?'

'Something'll turn up.'

Kate remembered that Roscoe had said much the same thing a short time before, though in a much less optimistic tone, and it was on the tip of her tongue to deliver a suitable cynical response when the police radio barked out an "*any units vicinity of Mark?*" call.

Ann Jones grabbed the handset and responded immediately.

'Intruder, Sycamore Lodge, Mark Moor,' the operator advised.

Kate threw her colleague a swift glance. 'That's the Slater's place,' she exclaimed and sent the car into a fish-tail as she stamped on the accelerator.

'What did I tell you?' Ann Jones shouted, hanging on to her seat. 'I said something would turn up.'

CHAPTER 15

There were two marked police cars on the forecourt of Sycamore Lodge – a powerful Traffic car and one of the local patrol cars – when Kate and Ann Jones pulled up behind the red Jaguar they had seen parked there before. Carol Slater met them on the doorstep, looking worried. She was dressed in a neat black skirt and white blouse and was wearing shoes this time.

'It was Stallard again,' she exclaimed. 'I caught sight of this man in a hoodie at the front of the house when I was in my bedroom and I recognised him when he glanced up at me. He'd obviously come through the side-gate from the back of the house.' She waved an arm in the direction of the gate. 'I dialled 999 straight away, but when I looked again he had disappeared and there was no further sign of him by the time the first police officer arrived.'

Kate looked puzzled. 'But how were you able to identify him? When I first came to see you, I thought you said that you were out when the murder was committed and that illness prevented you attending his trial?'

She nodded. 'That's true, Sergeant, but I saw his picture enough times on television and in the newspapers and it is one that is indelibly etched on my memory, I assure you.'

'Anyone else see him?' Kate queried as Ann Jones strode off quickly in the direction she had indicated, disappearing through the open gate.

She shook her head. 'Chas went off early this morning on a business trip and I only came home for lunch and to change out of my trouser suit – I spilled some hair lotion down it at the salon.' She bit her lip. 'I'm very worried about Daddy though.'

'Why? Where is the Colonel now?'

She shrugged helplessly. 'That's it; I don't know. When I got home he was not in the house. He must have gone out for a walk.' She waved a hand towards the black Volvo, parked as usual in the far corner of the forecourt. 'As you can see, his car is still over there and the Jag is my own car, so he couldn't have driven off anywhere. He … he often takes a stroll around the grounds after his lunch to get some exercise and I am terrified that he might have run into Stallard.'

Kate's glanced at the black Volvo XC90 and her lips tightened. 'Could he have taken his shotgun with him this time?'

Carol Slater shook her head. 'No, I checked the gun cabinet immediately after ringing the police – I know where he keeps the key, you see – and the shotgun is still there.'

'Is there a particular route he follows?'

'Not really. He … he just wanders. We have several acres here, some of it woodland and scrub, but most of it marsh.'

Kate turned on her heel and crossed the forecourt to the local patrol car. A uniformed woman constable was speaking into her radio and she glanced up quickly as Kate's slim figure darkened her window. Kate recognised her as one of the local Highbridge officers.

'Where's the officer from the Traffic unit?' she queried when the woman wound down the window.

There was a shrug. 'Only just got here, skipper. Must be out in the grounds somewhere.'

'Call up Control and see if they can get some more back-up,' she said. 'We may have a vulnerable missing person as well as this bloody intruder.'

'ARV?' the other queried, reaching for her handset.

Kate hesitated. 'Not at this stage. There's no suggestion our man is armed, so an armed response vehicle would be a bit OTT.'

Then, leaving the patrol officer to do the necessary, she marched back to the front door of the house. Carol Slater was still standing there, her gaze roving nervously around the forecourt towards the shrubbery that partly obscured the high perimeter wall and lined the long driveway to the front entrance.

'Did you hear a car drive away on the main road after you lost sight of the man in the hoodie, Miss Slater?' she asked.

Carol Slater shook her head. 'No, I can't say I did.'

Kate frowned, thinking of the 4x4 she had glimpsed at the hospital and the distinctive tyre tracks at the cider farm.

'It's just that I wonder how he got here in the first place. I saw no parked vehicles in the vicinity when we arrived and you're a bit out in the wilds here – I can't see an escaped con risking a hike along somewhere like Mark Causeway in full view of all the traffic.'

'Perhaps he's … what do you say … "holed up" somewhere close by?'

Kate grunted, thinking now of the square miles of open country that made up the Somerset Levels.

'It's possible, but it would take an army to find out exactly where.'

Ann Jones returned at this point, followed by another uniformed policewoman. 'Waste of time trying to search a place this size with just the three of us, skip,' she said.

A moment later the policewoman from the local car rushed over to them. 'All available units tied up, Sergeant,' she said breathlessly. 'Apparently we're it.'

Kate took a deep breath and turned to Carol Slater again. 'Have you absolutely no idea where your father could have gone? Is there a favourite place he might have headed for – somewhere he enjoys visiting, which he can manage to get to with his injured leg?'

The young woman thought for a few seconds, then snapped her fingers. 'The lake – there's a small lake at the southern extremity of the grounds. It … it has a bird-hide on the edge and there's a jetty. Dad's a keen twitcher and—'

'Can you take us there?' Kate cut in, adding impatiently. 'Like now!'

Carol Slater jumped. 'Oh yes; yes, of course. I'll get my gumboots on. It will be quite wet by the hide.'

* * *

Five minutes later she was leading the four police officers across the back lawn into the woodland which fringed it, magpies squawking angrily at them accompanied by the distant rapid tap of an elusive woodpecker as they followed a muddy track through the trees.

They got to the lake within ten minutes, the trees falling back to reveal a wide expanse of marshy field traversed by a boardwalk, leading to a ragged line of trees some 30–40ft away. They didn't see the hide until they were almost on top of the thing. It was a wooden shed-like structure, raised on stout piles and cleverly concealed among the trees, with bushes hemming it in on both sides.

Three wooden steps led up to the door and they creaked in protest as Kate mounted them to reach for the wooden latch – alarming what looked like a moorhen, which shot out from under the hide with panic-stricken squawks and hit the lake with a series of loud splashes. The door seemed to have jammed and resisted her at first, but then, after a determined tug, it opened outwards with the crack of rusty hinges and her nostrils were immediately assailed by the dank odour of stagnant water and decaying wood.

The room inside was only about 10ft wide, with three small shuttered windows facing the lake, which had not been closed and now admitted strands of weak sunlight. There was a shelf running the length of the hide under the windows and a long wooden bench set a couple of feet back from it – obviously provided for the comfort of would-be twitchers. There were no twitchers using it at the present moment, though – but the hide was nevertheless occupied.

The man was lying motionless on the floor and Kate almost tripped over him. Despite the fact that he was lying face downwards, she knew she was looking at Colonel Stephen Slater. Furthermore, it was apparent, even before she checked one out-flung wrist and found no pulse, that he was dead – the savage wound in his back, the dark pool, which had spread out from under his body and the spattered wall and frames of the open windows telling their own story.

* * *

Roscoe snatched off his pork-pie hat and ran his stubby fingers across his balding scalp. His frustration was evident in the way the fingers of his other hand continually drummed on the guard rail of the wooden jetty, which advanced from the bank beside the hide a short distance out on to the lake.

A man who liked to be close to the action at all times, Roscoe was furious with Lydia Summers for ordering everyone out of the hide while the forensic pathologist conducted her examination of the corpse.

'Not enough room in here for all of us, Ted,' she had said firmly – before adding with a mischievous glint in her eye, 'especially someone of your girth.'

Roscoe was not noted for his sense of humour and that remark, made as it was in front of several other officers, had certainly not been favourably received. But he'd had no option but to comply with her instructions and remain outside, like a little boy waiting to be called back into the headmaster's study, and standing a few feet behind him Kate could tell from his body language that he was close to exploding. She could only hope that Summers would complete her preliminary examination soon to relieve the tension building in the air around her boss, for it was also beginning to infect her as well. To calm her taut nerves, she turned her attention to what was happening around her.

The sunlight reflected in the lake was gradually fading as dusk began to spread her wings and undaunted by the activity in and around the hide as the police forensic team moved back and forth between the exterior of the wooden building and their large van, flocks of ducks continued to home in on the still waters like squadrons of World War II bombers returning from a mission, leaving frothy trails in their wake before congregating in the centre in noisy, animated camaraderie. It was a haunting, stabilising scene far removed from the macabre work going on in and around the hide, and for just a few moments Kate was able to immerse herself in its normality and forget what had brought her to the spot.

'Getting ready to bed down for the night, Guv,' she found herself murmuring, as she noted the direction of his gaze.

'Eh?' The DI swung around and glared at her.

'The ducks,' she explained, throwing an uneasy glance into the gaps in the wooden jetty on which they were both standing as it stirred under their feet with the gentle movement of the water. 'It will soon be their bedtime.'

'Bollocks to the ducks,' he snarled. 'You'd be better employed saving your observation skills for this bloody crime scene!'

'I already have,' she bit back.

He failed to pick up on the irritation in her tone. 'And?' he said.

'Did you see Colonel Slater's shoes?'

'What about them?'

'The soles were clean.'

'So?'

'The track here from the house was muddy and you'd have expected his shoes to have picked up some of it on the way, but the leather was smooth and shiny.'

He grunted. 'Meaning what?'

'Meaning, he couldn't have walked here. Someone must have brought him in a motor. Yet his Volvo is still parked in the driveway, Carol Slater was using her Jag when he would have gone missing and Charles Slater has apparently been out in his own car since early morning.'

She turned to stare along the edge of the lake to the gateway at the back of the property through which the SOCO team had driven a short time before. The dying sunlight glinted on the tin cap badge and buttons of the policewoman who had been positioned there to keep out unwanted visitors, and beyond she could just see the drove curving away across the moor.

'The killer could only have come in through that gate,' she said, pointing. 'You can't get to the lake from the house by vehicle – there's only the track I just mentioned.'

Roscoe stared in the same direction. 'Then, as we thought, Stallard must have access to a wagon of some sort,' he said. 'Which suggests he would have left tracks, just like he did at the cider farm?'

Kate shook her head and waved an arm around the field behind them, where the SOCO van and several other police vehicles were parked. 'I hardly think so. Ground's wet and will be pretty badly churned up after this lot drove in.'

Roscoe swore savagely. 'So nothing for us yet again,' he grated. 'DCI won't be very happy about that when he turns up.'

He eyed her with open hostility, obviously looking for an opportunity to vent his spleen on someone. 'Any more than I was when you just buggered off from the morgue this afternoon without my say-so.'

Kate cleared her throat. 'Sorry about that, Guv,' she replied, 'but you could see how ill Ann Jones was.'

There was the suggestion of a sneer on his face. 'Yeah, and Bradley Jakes is not too well either,' he added. 'Someone stepped on his leg, I hear.'

Kate tensed, wondering if the reporter had made good his threat to tell the DI that they were sharing information and anxious to avoid trying to explain *that* away after everything else.

'What was the result of the PM anyway?' she queried quickly, in an effort to distract him.

He made a grimace. 'Nothing we don't already know. Weapon with a long, narrow blade, wound to the lower back and a slit throat in both cases. Hardly worth attending the event in the first place.'

He glared at her again. 'But you should have been there anyway – not skiving off to attack bloody reporters. What we don't need right now is an official complaint from Bradley Jakes – and what I want to know is why you did a stupid thing like that? What's your beef with that low-life prat?'

Kate felt sick. So it had actually happened; despite her distraction tactics, he had come right back to her with the very question she had most dreaded having to answer.

But even as her befuddled, panic-stricken brain tried to cobble together some sort of credible but non-incriminatory response, she was saved by the bell – the door of the hide was suddenly thrown open and Lydia Summers appeared, dressed in her hooded nylon overalls and carrying her medical bag in one gloved hand. Roscoe immediately lost interest in Kate and wheeling round, strode towards the pathologist, his chin thrust out aggressively and his fists clenched by his sides.

'Well?' Kate heard him bark as the pathologist carefully negotiated the short flight of steps and turned to meet him, nodding to the waiting Scenes of Crime supervisor on the way to indicate that his team could now carry out their examination.

'Well what, Ted?' she said, feigning puzzlement.

'You know bloody well what, Doc,' Roscoe snarled back. 'Your verdict?'

'Well, he's dead,' she replied. 'I can tell you that for nothing.'

Kate closed her eyes tightly for a second as she joined them, waiting for Roscoe to blow completely. That he didn't was a miracle under the circumstances. Instead, he took a deep breath and said harshly: 'Just tell me what you've got, will you?'

Summers shrugged. 'More or less the same MO as in the other two cases,' she replied. 'Long, narrow blade used. Deep penetrating wound to the back and a deep incision to the throat, severing the trachea and a carotid artery – inflicted, I would suggest by a left-handed killer, as with the other two cases. Death comparatively recent – three to four hours ago, I would say.'

Roscoe might have been angry, but he was still on the ball. 'What do you mean more or less the same MO?' he queried.

She frowned. 'In the previous two cases, it was apparent from the wounds the deceased received that they were stabbed from a horizontal position in the lower back. In this case, the incision was made in the upper back just below the neck. This would indicate that, while the assailant and his earlier victims were all standing at the moment of the attack, this one was sitting and his assailant standing over him – hence the fact that the blade was driven in at an obtuse angle.'

'So the Colonel was sitting on the bench in the hide, bird-watching when he was stiffed?' Roscoe surmised. 'And his attacker crept up behind him to do the business?'

'Very good, Ted,' Summers patronised, and with heavy sarcasm added: 'What a razor-sharp mind you have!'

'Except for one thing,' Kate put in before Roscoe could hit back. 'It would have been impossible for the assailant to have climbed the steps up to the door of the hide without making a noise. The timber is badly warped and creaks underfoot. Coupled with which, the hinges on the door are badly rusted and make a loud crack when you pull the door open.'

Roscoe shrugged. 'So our killer was waiting inside when Slater arrived,' he said.

Kate shook her head. 'Not possible. There was nowhere for him to hide, if you'll pardon the pun, and the Colonel would have seen him the moment he opened the door which, incidentally, swings outwards.'

Roscoe's bad temper was returning now. 'So what are you suggesting, Miss Marple?' he snapped. 'That he was fast asleep when the killer entered the hide?'

She shrugged. 'He was an old man and it was quite warm in there, so that's a possible – though not very likely – explanation or maybe he knew his attacker and trusted him. Maybe he was driven to the hide by this man in the first place – that would explain why the soles of his shoes were so clean.'

'Ah, his shoes,' Summers said. 'You noticed them too, Sergeant. And there's another thing worth bearing in mind – if your victim was bird-watching at the time, he must have had extremely good eye-sight because there are no binoculars in the hide.'

'What if he wasn't murdered in the hide at all?' Kate queried. 'What if he was murdered somewhere else and then dumped in there afterwards?'

Summers shook her head. 'Not according to the quantity of blood on the floor and the splatter pattern across the wall and window frames. That is entirely consistent with the hide being the scene of his demise.'

'What then?' Roscoe blurted angrily. 'He was brought here from the house at the point of a gun, sat down on the bench and then stabbed to death in the hide? What would be the sense in that? Why not just top him where he was?'

Summers sighed and turned away from them. 'That's for you to work out, Ted,' she said. 'Me? I'm off home for a spot of supper and a nice glass of white wine.'

Roscoe snorted. 'All right for some,' he muttered, then scowled again as the DCI's car pulled up just inside the gate. 'Looks like my pint of beer has gone for a Burton now anyway.'

CHAPTER 16

Carol Slater looked unnaturally pale as she sat on the armchair in her sitting room. The newly returned Charles Slater sat beside her, holding both her hands in his in a comforting gesture. The policewoman who had escorted her from the grisly murder scene was standing in the background, her radio turned right down as a mark of respect.

Bent forward in the armchair opposite the shocked woman, Kate waited quietly for her to find her voice after a protracted period of sobbing, but it was a long time coming.

'How many more victims have there got to be before you catch this swine, Sergeant?' Charles Slater snapped, his anger barely concealed.

'We're doing our best, sir,' Kate replied lamely, thinking privately of Hayden and what had happened to him. 'But there's an awful lot of moor and marsh out there and our man could be anywhere.'

Slater bit his lip. 'Sorry, Sergeant, I am being very tactless after Stallard targeted your husband at the hospital?'

'Someone did, but we don't know for certain that it was him,' Kate said, her voice betraying a lack of conviction.

He nodded. 'But it's pretty obvious, isn't it?' he went on. 'As it is in relation to the murders of that retired DCI of yours and the unfortunate publican?'

Kate shook her head. 'We can't even be certain in that regard either,' she said, conscious of the fact, much too late, that it must have seemed to the Slaters that she was seeking to defend Stallard.

'But it's a bit of a coincidence that all the people who have died so far were witnesses in my mother's murder case, isn't it?'

Kate nodded. 'Of course Stallard is our chief suspect,' she agreed hastily, picking up on the sudden hostility in Carol Slater's eyes. 'But we have to keep an open mind until the culprit is actually arrested.'

'So how do you explain the fact that both Sis and I have been able to identify him as our intruder and that this time he was spotted in the grounds less than two hours before our father was found brutally murdered?'

Kate was on a hiding to nothing and she knew it. 'Look,' she said, 'I am not saying that Stallard was *not* responsible; I am merely saying this will have to be proved when we apprehend him.'

'And when will that be, Sergeant Lewis?' Carol Slater said suddenly. 'Tomorrow? Next week? Next month? Never?'

Kate was taken aback by her aggressive attitude, which seemed completely out of character, but she had to admit to herself that it was nevertheless understandable under the circumstances.

'I can't give you a time-scale, Miss Slater,' she said in a sharper tone than she had intended, 'but we'll do all we can to put him back where he belongs.'

The distraught woman stiffened and seemed about to snap back at her, but before she could get the words out, her brother bent closer to her with a heavy sigh. 'I'm sure the police are doing their best, Sis,' he said quickly, no doubt anxious to avoid a scene, and Kate saw his hands tighten on those of his sister in what seemed to be a censuring gesture.

His tactic worked too and she swallowed the comment that had obviously been on the tip of her tongue and nodded. 'I … I'm sorry, Sergeant, that remark was uncalled for, but I was … was very close to my—'

Her voice trailed off and Kate stood up abruptly, seeing this as an opportune moment to bring the conversation to a close.

'I think I should leave you and your brother to grieve, Miss Slater,' she said. 'This dreadful business must have come as a terrible shock to you and I can't even begin to imagine how you must feel.' She waved a hand towards the policewoman standing in the background. 'I will leave this officer here for a little while to ensure the press don't become a nuisance and in the meantime, I will arrange for a police presence outside for the rest of the night as a security measure. I will see myself out.'

The night air that greeted Kate was cool and sweet and she stood for a few moments staring around the forecourt, which, she was pleased to see, was well lit by a number of low-level floodlights.

She thought about what the pathologist had said after her examination of Slater's body and the other issues attached to the murder, which both Roscoe and herself had briefly touched on, and tried to make some sense of it all.

It had been established that Slater had been murdered in the hide, but it was by no means certain how he had got there. He obviously hadn't driven himself to the scene as no parked vehicles had been present in the vicinity and all three cars available to himself and the family had been accounted for. Yet his clean shoes had indicated that he couldn't have walked to the spot. The only possible answer to the puzzle was that his killer – almost certainly Stallard – had driven him there in the vehicle he was using, either under duress or in an unconscious state. But why would Stallard go to all that trouble when Slater could have been killed in his own house while his two children were out? And in any event, Carol Slater was certain she had seen Stallard leaving the property on foot from the front of the house. Why would he do that if he had access to a vehicle and had used it to convey the Colonel to the hide via the back entrance? Also, what had happened to his vehicle afterwards? And last, but by no means least, how was it that, despite a mammoth police manhunt and massive media attention, a wanted criminal like Stallard was able to drive around the area with impunity, murder three people and disappear each time in a car that could only have been stolen, hired from an agency or borrowed from a friend, without it being brought to the notice of the police by someone?

She needed to talk things over with Roscoe – do a brainstorm – to see if they could arrive at some sort of conclusion, but the DI had been carted off to the Bridgwater incident room for a debrief by a very unhappy DCI Fairlow shortly after the young SIO had visited the scene and Kate had not been invited. In normal circumstances, being excluded from things would have hurt like hell, but with Hayden still unconscious in the hospital's ICU, she felt she had enough to worry about already without getting worked up over anything else.

And as if her thoughts about Hayden had acted as a communication trigger, the new mobile she had purchased to replace the one Dibble had smashed rang for the first time.

'It's the hospital, Sergeant Lewis,' the female voice at the other end announced. *'Would you like to call in to see us? Your husband has regained consciousness.'*

* * *

Kate's journey to the hospital was a blur to her and the only recollection she had of it afterwards was the flash of another speed camera as she raced through a 30mph speed limit at a little over 60mph. Damn! Her second ticket in a few hours!

She left the CID car in an ambulance bay directly outside the hospital's main entrance and took the stairs two at a time, her whole body on fire at the news she had received.

Hayden was not going to die; he was conscious. She could hardly believe it and the tears were streaming down her face even before she got to the security door of the ICU and was admitted by a smiling staff nurse.

'He's very weak,' she said as Kate brushed past her, 'but he's demanding some food, which is a good sign. Just ten minutes, though.'

This time Kate was not relegated to a place behind the glass partition and no one tried to stop her entering the little softly lit room. Hayden was sitting up in bed, propped up by several pillows and most of the equipment to which he had been connected had now been removed, but there was a thick bandage wound around his head and Kate gave a little shiver as she tried not to think what it concealed.

He gave her a tired smile as she bent over his bed to kiss him on the cheek. 'Hello, old girl,' he murmured. 'They tell me I've overslept again.'

Kate wiped the tears away with the back of one hand and switched off her police radio. 'Yes,' she joked, 'you've been a lazy sod.'

He sighed. 'Apparently they're bringing me some buttered toast,' he went on. 'Rather have a medium rare steak and a glass of red wine, though.'

Kate chuckled and squeezed his hand, propping herself on a chair by the bed. 'When you come home, I'm going to cook you the biggest steak you've ever seen,' she replied, 'and pour you a glass of the most expensive bottle of wine I can find.'

He frowned. 'Hey, steady on, old girl. 'No need to take out a mortgage.'

She laughed again, wiping more tears away. 'I thought … I thought—' she blurted, but he held up one hand to cut her off.

'Always had a pretty thick skull,' he said, 'so you needn't have worried.' He frowned. 'Darned feller certainly clocked me one, though. Some sort of pole, I think.'

Her smile faded and her expression was suddenly serious. 'You didn't see who it was that hit you, I suppose?' she queried.

He shook his head, then winced. 'Just a dark figure in a hoodie,' he said. 'But the bounder stank of deodorant, I can tell you that.'

'Deodorant?'

He grunted. 'Or aftershave. Last thing I remember. Reckon he must have bathed in it. Potent stuff too by the smell of it.'

Kate looked dubious. 'Are you sure about that? You didn't dream it? I can't see Stallard wearing aftershave.'

He kept his head still and shrugged with his eyebrows. 'Maybe it wasn't him – someone else hiding in there?'

'What, a vagrant, you mean? Certainly can't see one of them smelling of aftershave either – maybe vomit, but not aftershave.'

He tutted. 'That's a bit unkind, old girl. The PC Brigade would hang, draw and quarter you if they heard you say that.'

But Kate wasn't listening. Her thoughts had jumped to something else – the memory of a man they had met not too long ago who had worn a lot of deodorant. 'And he owns a 4x4 and knew we were going there,' she said to herself.

Hayden sighed. 'Who knew we were going where?' he asked.

Kate patted his arm. 'Nothing for you to worry about,' she said and turned quickly as a nurse stepped into the room, carrying something on a tray hidden under a white linen serviette.

'Ah, your buttered toast, I believe,' Kate said as the young woman removed the serviette, 'and what looks suspiciously like a cup of tea.'

Hayden's eyes lit up as she swung a small table attached to a steel column on a pedestal across the bed in front of him and placed the tray on it.

'Just think of it as a medium rare steak,' Kate laughed as he tucked in with gusto. 'Now, I must be off.'

He frowned, wiping butter off the tip of his nose. 'Off where – can't you stay for a bit?'

She shook her head and climbed to her feet. 'I'll see you again tomorrow,' she said. 'You look very tired and once you've eaten that, you should get some rest.'

'So where are you going then?'

She smiled again, but there was a grimness to it this time. 'To see a man about some deodorant,' she replied.

He looked worried. 'No Lone Ranger stuff,' he warned. 'I know what you're like.'

She shook her head. 'Promise,' she lied, then added with a grin, 'Oh by the way, Roscoe sends his love.'

* * *

Ann Jones was not happy when Kate returned to Highbridge police station and apologised for leaving her stranded at the Slater house. 'You just drove off,' she said. 'I had to come back to the nick with Roscoe – have you any idea what that was like?'

Kate gave a thin smile. 'An experience?' she suggested.

Jones snorted. 'Experience? The man is a menace. He shouldn't be on the road at all.'

Kate nodded, thinking of the times she had been a passenger in the DI's ancient Honda Civic. 'I can only say sorry,' she replied. 'But I wasn't thinking. Got a message from the hospital – Hayden's regained consciousness. I just shot off to see him. Wasn't thinking of anything else.'

There was a stunned silence for a moment. 'Now it's my turn to say sorry,' the TDC replied. 'I … I didn't realise.'

Kate shook her head. 'You weren't to know. But it's a weight off my mind anyway. Where's Roscoe?'

Jones made a face. 'Still with the DCI at Bridgwater,' she replied, 'and I don't envy him after what's just happened.'

Kate grunted. 'At least that keeps him out of our hair for an hour or so. Fancy staying on a while.'

'Why?'

'There's a man I want to see again.'

'What, tonight?'

'Might as well strike while the iron is hot.'

Jones shrugged. 'Nothing to do tonight anyway. Only go to the gym and cook dinner for myself.'

'The gym?'

'Yes, I work out at least three times a week – keeps me fit.'

Kate nodded, thinking that she was not really surprised. Her colleague looked to be quite a tough cookie and it was good to have her by her side.

'And what about the cooking?' Kate went on. 'Have you no one to do it for you?'

Jones ran a hand down the scar on her face. 'I don't think I'm very marketable with this, plus a missing finger,' she replied. 'Last proper boyfriend – another Redcap – dumped me straight after it happened. Since then I've had nothing more than casual relationships, so I make do with a cat for company.'

Kate chuckled. 'More fool your ex,' she said, then winked. 'So our next job when this case is over is to find you a man, eh?'

'Maybe I don't want one anymore – more trouble than they're worth.'

'Don't you believe it,' Kate responded, thinking of Hayden. 'They can be indispensable.'

* * *

Daniel Sayers said nothing at first, just glared at Kate with undisguised hostility, still reeking of deodorant, which caught Kate right at the back of the throat. 'What do *you* want yet again – and at this time of night?' he said. 'Me ma's in bed.'

Kate glanced at her watch. 'What, at nine-thirty in the evening?' she exclaimed.

'She's old.'

'I don't want her anyway. It's you I've come to see.'

Sayers made no effort to move aside to let them into the house, but Kate pushed past him anyway, making her way into a small bedroom opening off the hallway.

Sayers stumbled through after her, with Ann Jones close behind him. 'About what?' he demanded. 'You got no right—'

Kate turned to face him. 'About several things – like you're a friend of Lenny Stallard, you own a 4x4, and you knew my colleague and I were going to check out Yardley's Cider Farm before we went there.'

'Dunno what you're on about.'

'I'm on about murder, wasting police time and conspiracy to pervert the course of justice – crimes which could get you sent down for 14 years to life.'

Sayers visibly paled. 'I ain't stiffed no one and I ain't done none of them o'ver fings noi'ver.'

Kate glanced past him at Ann Jones. 'Okay, but first off, my colleague and I would like to check out your Land Rover.'

'Don't have it no more – sold it couple of hours ago.'

'That was pretty sudden, wasn't it? Who'd you sell it to?'

'Bloke I met in a pub.'

'What bloke?'

'Dunno. Pikey I reckon. Paid me cash and I didn't get his name. Only met him by chance when I called in for a pint'

Kate snorted. 'A gipsy, eh? How convenient. If I had a pound for every time someone spun that load of crap, I'd be able to retire on the proceeds.'

He shrugged. 'No crime selling a motor to someone.'

'So what car have you got now then?'

'I ain't.'

'Seems a bit stupid losing one set of wheels without having something to replace them with?'

'Gonna buy an old Volvo V70 from ano'ver bloke I know.'

'But why sell the Land Rover in the first place?'

Another shrug. 'Fing was full of rust and I got a good deal.'

'How much?'

'That's my business.'

'What was the name of the pub where you met this man?' Ann Jones put in.

He half-turned towards her. 'Can't remember, but it were out Cheddar way.'

'Did anyone see you there?'

'Probably lots, but we done the deal in the car park anyway.'

'How did you get home?'

'The guy drove me.'

Kate changed to another tack. 'Get rid of the motor to stop us finding any trace of Colonel Slater's DNA inside, did you?'

Sayers stared at her. 'Who? Dunno what you're talkin' about?'

'The old man whose wife your mate, Stallard, stiffed around two years ago – he got stiffed himself this afternoon. But you'd know that anyway, wouldn't you?'

If Sayers was putting on a show, he was a superb actor, for his jaw almost hit his chest. 'Slater? Lenny done old man Slater?' he gasped, then stared wide-eyed at Kate before throwing a quick glance behind him at Ann Jones.

'Why would you immediately jump to the conclusion that Stallard was responsible?' Ann Jones put in again. 'With him when he did it, were you?'

His Adam's apple jerked spasmodically. 'I already told you, I ain't seen Lenny since he got put away, so don't try that one on me. I just said him, 'cause you've already put him in the frame for the o'ver jobs.'

Kate gave a non-committal grunt. 'Knew Colonel Slater well, though, did you?'

'No,' he retorted, 'but I've heard all about the bleedin' Slaters.'

'How so?'

He snorted, naked envy rearing its ugly head. 'Everyone knows about 'em. Arseholes, all of 'em. Fink they're better than everyone else. Big house, flash motors, noses in the air. I were sorry about the old girl what got stiffed by Lenny –

she didn't deserve that and as the old boy's new "trouble and strife", she weren't like the rest of 'em anyhow.'

Kate raised an eyebrow. 'New? Are you saying she was the Colonel's second wife?'

He nodded. 'I heard the first one croaked a few years ago.'

'So the Colonel's children were from the previous marriage?'

'That's what they say.'

'What do you say?'

'How would I know?'

Kate grimaced. He was playing with them, introducing useless information to try and throw them off course.

'So what about the police officer?' she said. 'My other half incidentally, who was attacked at Yardley's Cider Farm? What do you know about that? After all, you were the only one who knew he and I were going to Yardley's before it happened.'

His grin vanished as he cottoned on to what Kate was implying and she was pleased to see the alarm back in his eyes.

'Yeah, but I had noffink to do with him bein' done over and I can prove it. I was wiv' me mum here all afternoon when you left – I'll even wake her up so she can tell you herself if you want?'

Kate ignored the offer. 'Maybe Lenny Stallard has got himself a mobile now. You could've called his number to warn him the police were on their way to his bolt-hole?' she suggested.

'Bollocks!' Sayers snarled. 'I ain't never seen nor heard from Lenny since he were banged up and I wouldn't want him to know I'd talked to you lot anyway – he's a violent bastard and he don't like grasses.'

Kate pursed her lips in thought for a moment before giving a quick nod to indicate that the interview was over.

'Fine, Mr Sayers, we'll leave it there for now and we'll be in touch if we need anything further from you.'

'That's it?' he exclaimed as she pushed past him again, virtually shepherding Ann Jones towards the still open front door. 'You barge in here, freaten me and accuse me of stiffin' old man Slater, then you just piss off as if noffink has happened?'

Kate gave him her sweetest smile. 'You've got it in a nutshell,' she replied. 'Goodnight, Mr Sayers. Give our regards to your mother, won't you?'

Ann Jones looked thoughtful as they climbed back into the CID car. 'Something smells there,' she said.

Kate nodded. 'Not as sweet as you, though,' she replied with a grin. 'Maybe you should offer to lend Sayers some of *your* perfume?'

Jones snorted. 'I don't think Chanel No. 5 would suit him somehow,' she commented, then added, 'but I wasn't referring to his BO. He was obviously lying about the sale of that car.'

Kate paused in the act of turning the key in the ignition. 'Maybe he was,' she agreed, 'but we'll never prove it and as he said, there's no crime in selling a car.'

'Is he a suspect, do you think?'

'A prime one, I would say.'

'So what do we do about it?'

Kate started the car and glanced in her offside wing mirror as she pulled away. 'Nothing we can do at the moment,' she replied. 'And anyway, my immediate plan is to go home, open a nice bottle of red wine and go to bed.'

Jones grinned. 'Sounds good to me,' she agreed, 'except the bit about the red wine, of course.'

CHAPTER 17

Kate lay awake in the big double bed for a long time after she had dropped Ann Jones off at the police station and had returned to her cottage in Burtle. She couldn't help dwelling on Sayers and the sudden sale of his Land Rover directly after the murder of Colonel Slater, and the more she thought about him, the more the frustration welled up inside her.

He was obviously up to his neck in something, but it was a moot point as to whether that had anything to do with the murder of Colonel Slater and the others or the assault on Hayden. So the man was an out-and-out villain, with the form to prove it, but whether he was capable of murder was another matter, and in the absence of proper evidence to support the commission of an actual crime, there was nothing she could do.

So why torture herself thinking about his possible culpability then? She kicked the duvet off the bed and lay there naked and perspiring in the moonlight that now blazed white and cold through the window where the drawn curtains only stirred slightly in the breeze stealing through the open fanlight. That was the trouble with knowing things; if you couldn't do anything with the information you had acquired, what was the point in possessing it in the first place? It was best to be left in the dark.

She was still ruefully considering this pearl of wisdom when she heard a series of crunching sounds coming from the direction of the back garden.

For a few seconds she lay there, not moving, wondering if she had imagined it, but then she heard the sounds again – definitely heavy feet biting into the loose ornamental gravel path Hayden had only laid a few days before.

Climbing quickly out of the bed and silent in her bare feet, she approached the window and stood to one side of it to peer down into the garden, now shivering a little in the unheated room.

A patchwork of flat, empty fields met her gaze, stretching away to infinity, and scanning the small back garden with its patch of lawn and strip of gravel immediately below the window she saw that it was deserted. Imagination? Somehow she didn't think so.

Leaving the window and snatching her robe from the end of the bed, she grabbed the CS gas spray she had left on the dressing table with her notebook and mobile and carefully opened the bedroom door, making her way along the short passageway to the stairs, but stopping to peer down into the moonlit living room before going any further. Nothing.

Frowning, she started down the stairs, pausing only when she felt the woodblock floor beneath her feet. Then, bending down to pull on a pair of wedge-heeled shoes she had left beside the little half-moon table pushed up against the wall, she crossed the living room to the patio doors.

The moonlight flooding the garden showed it to be still deserted, shadows from the tall hedges reaching towards the house across the patch of lawn like knobbly alien fingers.

She carefully turned the key in the lock of the left-hand door, gritting her teeth in anticipation of a loud "crack", but Hayden must have oiled it recently, for the key turned easily and without a sound. Cool air stole into the room, a faint breeze ruffling her robe.

She stepped out on to the gravel path and turned left towards the driveway where the cars were parked, stopping briefly at the end of the cottage to peer round the corner.

Hayden's Jaguar was parked nose in to the front of the wooden garage, which was locked up and never used, her Mazda MX5 close behind it. The cars were shadowed by the end wall of the cottage and the adjoining hedge and she inwardly cursed her stupidity for not bringing a torch with her.

She stood there for several seconds, watching and listening, but nothing moved. It was only when she was about to leave the cover of the wall and check the cars that the dark hooded figure suddenly straightened up behind her Mazda and stood there for a moment, staring in her direction.

Whether the intruder sensed her presence before she stepped out into the blaze of moonlight or only became aware of her when she emerged from behind the wall, it is impossible to say, but he was a lot quicker to react than Kate. Even as the toes of her shoes dug into the soft gravel of the path as she launched herself across the driveway, he was away like a startled deer, racing off down the road towards the local school. She was in no position to go after him, particularly in just a robe and wedge-heeled shoes, and watched from the end of the drive as he lurched sideways through a gateway or gap in the hedge lining the long straight road and disappeared from view.

'Damn!' she breathed as she turned back towards the parked cars behind which he had been hiding. 'Now what the hell were you after?'

Checking the cars over for any damage, she saw no obvious sign of scratches or dents on the bodywork of either of the vehicles and the tyres did not seem to have been slashed. Going over Hayden's car again, just to make sure, she breathed a sigh of relief. She wouldn't have had the nerve to face him if he had come home to find that his beloved Jaguar had been vandalised, for she had long been resigned to the fact that she was a definite second in his affections to that classic 3.4-litre monster.

Returning to the living room, she shut and locked the patio doors and kicking off her shoes, went back to the half-moon table where she stood for a moment with one hand on the telephone. The most obvious thing to do was to ring the control room to report what had happened – that's what she would have told any member of the public to do in such circumstances – but what was the point? The intruder was gone now and even if Control could rustle up a unit to attend, it would probably be a good half-hour at least before they turned up; all too late. She compressed her lips in a grimace as she remembered the last time she had called the station to report an intruder during the Strawfoot murder inquiry. The uniformed sergeant who had attended the scene then had treated the whole thing as a joke and she had no intention of suffering the same embarrassment again.

Removing her hand from the telephone, she went into the kitchen and opened a fresh bottle of red wine, then returned to the living room with a half-full glass and sat in a corner of the settee.

She had to have time to think. The intruder had been wearing a hoodie and the possible significance of this in relation to the current murder inquiry was glaringly obvious. Lenny Stallard was said to have stolen a similar garment from a house he had burgled following his escape, Hayden had said his attacker had been wearing a hooded coat, and the intruder spooked at the hospital and clocked twice in the grounds of Sycamore Lodge had been described as being similarly attired.

Yet at the same time, many youngsters today wore hoodies – they were a sort of fashion statement – and they were also the ideal cover-all for professional criminals. Her intruder could have been nothing more than a potential burglar or car thief – or even a vandal, keen to damage one of the cars in the drive because she and Hayden were Old Bill.

She took a sip of her wine and leaned her head against the back of the settee with her eyes closed.

But why now? Why would a burglar, car thief or vandal choose to target the cottage on this particular night? She and Hayden had lived there for several years – even before they were married – and nothing like it had happened before.

No, the intrusion had to be connected to the Stallard murder inquiry and if that was the case, the man who had fled from her driveway could only have been Stallard himself which, in turn, raised another question: why had he decided to pay her a visit in the first place? Not to give himself up or to plead his innocence, that was for sure, otherwise he wouldn't have run off. To do her harm then? Most unlikely. There was no reason for him to want to single her out any more than any of the other officers on the inquiry? So why, why, why?

Abruptly she stood up, draining her wine glass. Maybe she would never know. And right at that moment, she was too worn out to care anyway. Bed beckoned again and she headed for the stairs with a heavy yawn, wondering, as she threw off her robe and climbed on to the rumpled sheet covering the mattress, what sort of a night Hayden might be having. She was still thinking of Hayden as she finally drifted off with her arms clutching what would have been his pillow and a wistful smile on her face.

* * *

Kate had overslept. The realisation hit her when she awoke suddenly from a deep dreamless sleep and her blurred gaze focused on the alarm clock beside her bed. It was already half-past eight and she had forgotten to set the damned thing, which was hardly surprising after the shock incident of the previous night – something that would nevertheless elicit little sympathy from her crusty intolerant boss.

'Roscoe will crucify me,' she breathed as she scrambled from the bed.

There was no time for breakfast or a shower, so she pulled on her clothes, washed her face – more to wake herself up than anything else – then cleaned her teeth and ran a comb briefly through her hair before running to her car parked in the drive.

The Mazda roared into life first time at just a flick of the ignition key and briefly checking over her shoulder to make sure there was no passing traffic, she reversed out into the road at speed and slammed the car into first gear even before it had jolted to a stop, her tyres scrabbling frantically on smooth tarmac as she took off like a rocket towards Mark.

Fortunately the road out of Burtle was straight and brazenly ignoring the 30mph limit, she was able to clock up a good 50mph within seconds, the powerful engine responding instantly to her touch, as if it sensed it was being given its head and was determined to meet expectations.

Kate could have taken a left to Highbridge just beyond the village, but conscious of the fact that the road she was following was a lot faster, she stayed with it, accelerating even more along the straight until she reached a sharp left-hand bend at the end and applied the brake prior to changing down through the box. But instead of encountering the anticipated resistance from the brake pedal as the discs were applied, she found there was nothing there and the pedal went all the way to the floor.

For an instant, blind panic froze her brain, but almost at the same moment her police driver training kicked in and she reacted. As the bend hurtled towards her, she crashed through the gearbox, heedless of any damage she may have caused, reducing the speed of the car by using the gears as a brake. She made the bend in a cloud of smoke from the tyres and with a tortured screeching from the gearbox.

But she was still going too fast and even as she fought to keep control and prevent the little sports car careering off the road into the adjacent rhyne, she caught the glint of sunlight on polished metal. Then, just yards in front of her, the massive front of an articulated lorry suddenly filled her windscreen, horn blaring, coupling clanking as it cut its corner and lurched towards her on the wrong side of the road. In that split second she saw the narrow mouth of the drove to her right and wrenching the steering wheel in that direction, away from the curve of the bend, she sent the car streaking across the road directly in front of the lorry.

It was touch and go, but he missed her by a hair's breadth. Then her wheels tore into the gravel of the drove and the car slewed round in a rear-wheel skid. As she came to a juddering stop right on the edge of the rhyne which curled round the bend on the opposite side of the road, she heard the asthmatic hiss of airbrakes behind her and in her rear view mirror saw the big trailer swing towards the rear of the Mazda like a battering ram, also in the midst of a heavy skid, stopping just a couple of feet from her bumper bar with a thudding lurch.

For a moment there was absolute silence and then a door slammed and a heavy- set man in a sweater and jeans hauled her door open. His face was white and his eyes were almost starting from his head.

'You stupid bloody cow!' he snarled, grabbing her by the arm. 'You almost killed both of us.'

'Sorry,' she croaked, allowing him to lever her out of the car. 'My … my brakes failed.'

'Yeah?' he snarled. 'That's what they all say.'

She tore his hand away and leaned back against the Mazda, her legs shaking and her chest heaving in long trembling gasps.

At once he stepped back a couple of paces and shook his head, his initial fury abruptly subsiding.

'You okay?' he said, peering into her face with obvious concern.

She nodded weakly. 'Just shocked, that's all,' she replied. 'Don't know what happened. No pressure on the brake pedal.'

He grunted. 'Let me take a look.'

She moved to one side while he ducked into the car and tested the pedal with one hand.

'Looks like you're out of fluid,' he said and briefly straightening up, dropped down on all fours to first peer and then half-crawl under the car. Kate heard his low whistle almost immediately and when he emerged and climbed to his feet, he stared at her intently for a moment.

'Someone obviously doesn't like you very much, love,' he said. 'Your brake pipes've been partially cut through.'

Kate returned his stare with a look of disbelief.

'Cut?' she said.

He nodded. 'Someone must've used a hacksaw or something like that,' he said. 'But they didn't finish the job, so the fluid must've only dripped out until you put pressure on the pedal. Where've you just driven from?'

'Burtle.'

He grunted. 'Well, you're flippin' lucky to be alive, I'll tell you that. Maybe whoever cut your brake pipes didn't want you to be, eh?'

CHAPTER 18

Someone wanted her dead! Kate stood for a long time in the now gathering mist, leaning against the wing of her car and trying to come to terms with the cold reality of what the artic driver had exposed. He was gone, of course. After an exchange of names and addresses and a muttered word of sympathy, he had driven off to meet his delivery targets, but his words lingered in her head: "You're lucky to be alive – maybe someone didn't want you to be." And could that someone be Lenny Stallard, she mused? But if so, why? She had got nowhere in relation to the inquiry or where he had gone to ground. Furthermore, killing her would not have put a stop to the manhunt or improve his chances of avoiding a return to prison on a multiple murder charge. But what if Stallard was not responsible? The thought was even more chilling.

It was a good half-hour before she was picked up by the patrol car sent to the scene, following her mobile call to the police control room. She had been given no option but to leave her beloved Mazda where it was to await the arrival of the recovery vehicle which would transport it to the police pound for a SOCO team examination and although she was not entirely happy about this, she had to recognise that the car was no longer drivable – the gearbox was finished, seized up and a total write-off.

As for herself, although having escaped serious injury, she was still very shaky after the incident, with painful bruising to her chest and shoulder from the wrench of the seatbelt and to the side of her head where it had come in contact with the driver's window. She was tempted to ask the patrol car driver to take her home where she could lie down for a couple of hours, but she decided against it and allowed him to drop her off at Highbridge police station where she found the general CID office deserted save for Detective Constable Jamie Foster.

'On your tod then, Jamie?' she queried as she pushed through the double doors.

He got up from his desk and came towards her. ''Fraid so,' he replied. 'Ann Jones has called in to say she is going to be late – problem with that rough old Discovery she drives – and the two bods loaned to us from Bridgwater are out on inquires.'

Kate glanced towards the DI's office, where the door stood open. 'And the guv'nor?' she queried.

He grinned. 'In the shit, skip,' he said.

She threw him a puzzled frown. 'How's that?'

He chuckled. 'Super walked in ten minutes ago and caught him lighting up in his office. Went potty and ordered him upstairs.'

Kate grimaced. 'I warned him about his bloody fags. He just refuses to move with the times.'

'Well, he's gone and done it now. He's not only in breach of police regs, but the law as well.'

Foster's grin faded as he seemed to suddenly become aware of Kate's white face. 'You all right, Sarge? I hear you had a prang on the way here?'

She nodded and sank on to the chair behind her desk. 'Bit more than a prang,' she corrected. 'Someone cut my brake pipes. SOCO will be giving the car the once-over shortly.'

He whistled. 'Bloody hell. I've been out on a job. Didn't know about all this. You sure you're all right?'

She nodded again. 'Bit bruised, that's all, but the car's gearbox is smashed to buggery.'

Another whistle. 'That's going to cost. Want a coffee?'

She forced a weak smile. 'Be nice. I'll have to wait to see the DI anyway.'

Foster glanced over her shoulder and cleared his throat. 'You won't have to wait long,' he murmured.

Kate glanced quickly to one side and saw Roscoe standing there staring at her with a familiar scowl on his slab-like face. 'Five minutes, my office,' he snapped and walked past her in the direction of his "inner sanctum".

Kate waited a few minutes for Foster to make her the promised coffee – in no hurry to join Roscoe, having sensed from the look on his face that it would be far from a pleasurable experience. Then, taking a couple of sips from the plastic cup the DC set on the desk in front of her, she finally hoisted herself wearily out of her chair and headed for the DI's office.

She found him slumped in the swivel behind his desk, staring at the scarred top and idly playing with a crumpled packet of cigarettes, as if unsure what to do with them.

He didn't respond to her knock and only looked up when she dropped into the chair in front of him, his eyes cold and hard. 'Why did you call out scenes of crime?' he queried.

'My car—' she began, but he cut her off.

'You had a prang,' he finished for her. 'I know all about that, but why SOCO?'

So she told him about the brake pipes and her nocturnal visitor. 'I think he must have been responsible for it,' she finished.

His scowl returned with a vengeance. 'Why didn't you call in at the time to report that you had an intruder?'

She shrugged. 'No point. He would've been long gone by the time back-up arrived.'

He looked unimpressed. 'Do you reckon it was Lenny Stallard?'

'I can't think who else it could have been – he had the right build and was wearing the same sort of dark hooded coat.'

He grunted. 'So why would he target you?'

'Perhaps he thought I was getting too close.'

'How?'

'I don't know.'

'Don't know a lot, do you?' he retorted, adding with the suggestion of a sneer in his tone, 'except maybe who the cowardly shit was who whispered sweet nothings in the Super's ear about me smoking in my office.'

Her eyes narrowed. 'What do you mean by that?'

He treated her to a mirthless smile. 'What do you think I mean? After all, you for one have never made any secret of your objections to my fags, have you?'

She stared at him. 'Are you suggesting I verballed you to the boss?'

His own hard gaze never left her face. 'I don't know. Did you?'

She took a deep trembling breath. 'You should know better than that. I'm really shocked that you would even think such a thing.'

For a moment he continued to study her, as if trying to read what was in her head. Then abruptly he relaxed and sat back in his chair. 'Maybe not then,' he growled, 'but someone did and when I find out who it was, they'll be in a lot deeper shit than I am right now.'

'Well, thanks for the apology,' she said with heavy sarcasm.

'I didn't realise I had given one,' he replied, 'but if I decide to, you'll be the first to know.' He pushed a half-full mug of cold coffee across the desk towards her. 'Now, if you want to be really useful, you can get me a fresh coffee – then you and me have a short trip to make to the mortuary for the PM on Colonel Slater before we head for the incident room at Bridgwater for a briefing with the DCI – and this time you can bloody well drive. Oh, by the way, good news about Hayden, isn't it?'

'As if you cared,' she thought and picking up the mug, she walked out, toying with the idea of slipping something particularly nasty in his coffee.

* * *

In life, Colonel Slater had been a hard uncompromising man with a forceful, overbearing personality that would have intimidated most would-be opponents, but death had stolen all that from him and on the mortuary slab he seemed to have shrunk in statue, his thin emaciated looking frame, with its horrendous wounds now even more clearly apparent, somehow pathetic and almost childlike in its vulnerability under the mortuary lights. Once an important man in the military, no doubt well respected and highly decorated, he was now just another insignificant, characterless cadaver to be dismembered and probed, essential organs weighed and dissected with a dispassionate clinical precision, before being stitched up and returned to the -40 degree embrace of one of the big refrigerators. There to await the eventual findings of a coroner's inquest and in the event of a trial, the final decision of the designated crown court jury. Sliced up and preserved like a joint of meat, with no "Best Before" or "Use By" date label on his corpse. That very unfunny thought, which came unbidden into Kate's mind, made her want to vomit and when the post mortem was finally over, she left Roscoe talking to the pathologist and stood for several minutes in the misery of the now wet afternoon, savouring the clean fresh air as if she had never tasted it before.

Once again, Roscoe was unimpressed by her departure and when he joined her shortly afterwards, fouling the air with a cigarette, he grunted: 'Losing your touch, are you, Lewis?'

She threw him a quick glance. 'What the hell are we doing in this shitty job, Guv?' she queried, without answering him.

'If you start thinking like that,' he replied, 'you'll go round the bend.' He jerked his head back towards the mortuary. 'That was a waste of time anyway. Nothing new. Like the other PMs, just a confirmation of what we'd been told already.'

He headed for the car. 'You coming? Maybe the DCI will come up with some brilliant new ideas.'

But he didn't. In fact, DCI Fairlow was in a pretty downbeat mood and there was a tautness in his facial muscles, a noticeable tenseness in his demeanour which provided a clear indication of the stress he was now under. Three murders, a policeman hospitalised and the only suspect an escaped criminal who seemed to have disappeared into the mist of the Somerset Levels. No leads, forensic or otherwise, the press clamouring at the door of Bridgwater police station – Roscoe and Kate had had to wade through them on the way in – and a twitchy hierarchy at headquarters anxious for a breakthrough. It was the usual scenario during the early days of a major crime investigation, but that didn't make it any easier to endure and Kate mused unkindly that youthful sophistication, a suave personality and a flashy Italian suit would be of no help to Peter Fairlow in these circumstances. He needed hard results and so far there weren't any. But at least from Kate and Roscoe's perspective, being made part of the inquiry at last, rather than left stuck out on the edge, was to be welcomed. Not that Roscoe's old rival, DI Deidrie Hennessey, was particularly happy to have them on board, especially after their brief run-in with her at the scene of Austin Jacobs' murder, and the cold atmosphere which had greeted them on their arrival for the briefing could be felt all the way out into the street afterwards.

Roscoe had little to say on the journey back to Highbridge police station, but seemed to be in a particularly truculent, uncommunicative mood despite the fact that they were now officially part of the inquiry team. She was glad to see the back of him and barely let him out of the CID car before driving off, muttering that she was going to sort out her own car.

That proved to be quite difficult. SOCO had finished with the vehicle and it was in the police pound, but it was apparent from the damage to the gearbox that it would not be drivable until major repair work had been carried out. She got in touch with the insurance company, who began the long process of issuing an insurance claim form in the next post and arranging for an assessor to attend the pound in due course to carry out the necessary vehicle examination.

In the meantime, arrangements were made for Kate to be issued with a temporary replacement car, which was delivered to Highbridge police station and turned out to be an embarrassing bright yellow Fiat 500.

Disgusted with the thing, weary from lack of sleep the previous night, and feeling the bruises from her accident really starting to come out now, Kate checked with the hospital on her mobile to make sure Hayden was still okay. Then, absenting herself from the station by means of a call to Jamie Foster, she headed back home for a bite to eat and more important, a glass of red wine. One became two and she was asleep on the settee when Foster turned up on the doorstep, knocking loudly.

Bleary eyed, Kate threw the door wide and stared at her colleague with a quizzical look on her face.

'Love your little car, skipper,' Foster said.

'Piss off,' Kate replied, sweeping her dishevelled hair back off her face. 'What are you doing here?'

He grimaced. 'Been trying to ring you,' he said, 'but your mobile's off and your mainline phone seems to be out of order. You said you were going home, so I thought I'd drop by to pick you up.'

Kate frowned and glanced behind her. Even from where she was standing, she could see that the receiver was not sitting properly on its cradle. She turned back into the room and adjusted it. 'Satisfied now?' she said as Foster followed her into the living room. 'So what's up?'

He shrugged. 'Not much,' he said drily. 'Just another body.'

The fug evaporated from Kate's brain in a rush. 'A what?'

'A plod patrol found it when they responded to a three nines about half an hour ago,' he said.

'Where?'

'Yardley's Cider Farm.'

'Yardley's?'

He nodded, studying her face. ''Fraid so – and from the circulated description, they think the stiff might be Lenny Stallard.'

* * *

It *was* Lenny Stallard! For a frozen few seconds Kate simply stared down at the bloodied corpse lying on the concrete floor of the warehouse, just feet from the forklift truck where Hayden had been attacked what seemed like an eternity ago.

'Passing motorist found him,' the middle-aged uniformed sergeant explained. 'He slipped into the yard for a slash apparently, became curious about the remains of the crime scene tapes at the entrance, poked his nose in here and Bob's your uncle.'

Kate nodded absently, remembering the torn tapes fluttering from the gateposts when she and Jamie Foster had arrived. 'Funny he should happen to choose this particular place for a wee,' she commented. 'Who was he?'

The sergeant shrugged. 'Dunno. Control said he refused to give his name.'

Kate frowned. 'That doesn't sound right.'

'He probably didn't want to get involved. A lot of people reporting incidents like to remain anonymous.'

'Maybe, but surely they could trace his mobile?'

He nodded.' I gather that's already in hand, but it's not a speedy process, and it could prove inconclusive anyway – there are ways someone can avoid a trace.'

The uniformed man turned and pointed towards a wooden staircase climbing the wall behind the forklift to a narrow walkway. 'Looks like the dead man was up there, leaned against the rail, which gave way. Classic accident—'

He didn't finish the sentence, but he didn't need to. Even from where she stood, Kate could see the broken wooden rail which now lay on the floor near the corpse.

'We'll still need to treat the thing as sus until we know different,' she said, squinting back at the walkway. 'What's up there?'

'Offices, I believe,' he replied. 'Managers would obviously have been able to keep their eyes on what their staff were doing more easily from up there than down on the shop floor.' He hesitated, then added, 'Seems like what happened to him, after what he did to Hayden in here, was sort of … er … poetic justice.'

Kate compressed her lips in a tight grimace as she thought about Hayden, but before she could reply, Foster stomped into the building from the CID car. 'I've called for SOCO and the pathologist as you instructed,' he said. 'Guv'nors are on their way too.'

'Gov'nors plural?' Kate queried over her shoulder.

The DC gave a dry chuckle. 'Big chief and Little Chief,' he quipped.

Kate threw him a critical glance. 'Don't be so disrespectful,' she snapped. 'And let's get this scene secured. Any tape in your car?'

Foster nodded and turned back towards the door only to stop again when Kate called out after him: 'Any idea what's happened to Ann Jones? I thought she'd be here.'

Foster shrugged. 'Haven't the faintest. Her car apparently—'

'So you told me earlier, but that was ages ago. If she wants to learn about detective work as a TDC, she should be with us now. Call up Control and get her here pronto.'

'No need,' said a quiet voice and Ann Jones materialised in the doorway behind Foster.

Kate studied her pale face narrowly as Foster eased past her in the doorway and disappeared. 'You'll have to get used to grisly things like this, you know,' she said, remembering her reaction at the last post mortem. 'It's part and parcel of the job.'

Jones nodded, peering past her at the body lying on the floor. 'Is it Lenny Stallard?' she asked.

Kate glanced back at the corpse. 'None other,' she said.

The TDC came closer and peered at the body with a shudder. 'What an awful way to go,' she commented.

Kate snorted. 'Don't tell me you feel sorry for him?' she queried.

Jones shook her head. 'Of course not,' she retorted quickly, 'but he was a human being after all.'

Kate made a grimace. 'The Slaters and my husband might dispute that,' she said, then nodded towards the corpse. 'Any observations?'

Jones belched in reply and abruptly turned away from Kate, bending over at the waist and retching violently.

'Outside!' Kate snapped and grabbing her elbow, led her back out into the fresh air. 'The last thing we need is for you to vomit over everything.'

Almost as soon as she had spoken, Kate regretted it and quickly put her arm around the TDC's shoulders, leading her across the concrete hard-standing to where two CID cars were now parked. 'Keep taking deep breaths,' she instructed, opening the driver's door of one of the cars, 'and just sit in here for a few moments.'

Jones nodded and climbed behind the steering wheel. 'Skipper, I'm … I'm so sorry,' she said. 'It's just that—'

'Forget it,' Kate replied gently, though inwardly she was annoyed at her colleague's embarrassing reaction and critical of her squeamishness, despite what she'd said before about her sheltered army service. 'This sort of thing affects different people in different ways. You'll get used to it in time. Just take it easy for a few minutes.'

Then she closed the car door gently on her and turned back towards the derelict building just as DCI Fairlow's powerful black Audi swept in through the gateway behind her, closely followed by a familiar red BMW X5 with forensic pathologist, Lydia Summers at the wheel.

Death certainly seemed to pay dividends for some people, she mused cynically?

CHAPTER 19

Roscoe seemed to be in a more upbeat mood than he had been for a long time and Kate could see that Lydia Summers had picked up on it.

'Pleased with this one then, are you, Ted?' the pathologist asked from behind the crime scene tapes as she glanced up from her crouched position over the corpse.

Roscoe grunted. 'Relieved would be more accurate, Doc,' he growled back. 'We've been looking for this bastard for days. It's likely that he was responsible for three murders and a serious assault on a police officer.'

'Well, he won't be serving time for any of it now, that's for sure,' she said.

'Pity,' Fairlow commented. 'It would have tidied things up nicely.'

Roscoe grunted. 'At least he won't be stiffing anyone else either,' he said, 'and we can wrap this bloody case up at last.'

Fairlow threw him a critical glance, but ignored the remark. 'What can you tell us, Doctor Summers?'

The pathologist shrugged and straightened up. 'Not much to tell from my perspective,' she said. 'Multiple injuries which, to put in layman's terms, include a broken neck, crushed skull and severe fractures to both legs, resulting in a massive haemorrhage and internal trauma – all consistent with a fall from a significant height. Death instantaneous I would have thought, and probably within the last few hours. Does that answer all the questions you might be thinking of asking?'

'So it could have only just happened?'

'More likely an hour or so ago.'

'Straightforward accident, do you think?'

Summers shrugged again. 'That's up to your SOCO team to determine from any evidence they find at the scene,' she replied. 'I can only tell you what I see here on initial examination of the body.' She gave a waspish smile, then added with heavy sarcasm, 'There are no bullet holes or knife wounds, so I think it's fair to assume he wasn't shot or stabbed.'

Kate actually heard Fairlow's sigh of relief. 'So an accident then?' he persisted, ignoring her last facetious comment.

Summers gave a thin smile. 'I suggest you await the result of the PM and the report of your forensic team,' she said firmly, picking up her surgical bag and turning towards the door. 'And if I'm not mistaken, they've just arrived.'

As she marched out of the warehouse, with a brief passing wink at Kate, the three alien figures dressed in the familiar overalls who had filed through the open doorway ahead of her approached the small knot of police officers.

Kate left Fairlow and Roscoe to brief them and followed Summers out of the building to get some fresh air and check on Ann Jones. She found the TDC out of the CID car, talking to the pathologist by the boot of her BMW.

'Feeling better?' Kate asked her.

Jones gave a weak smile. 'A lot better, thanks,' she said. 'Thought I'd get the low-down from Doctor Summers on Lenny Stallard's death, seeing as I chickened out on things.'

'Don't be so hard on yourself,' Kate replied. 'It was a bit grisly in there.'

'I sensed you thought it was more than that,' Summers commented as she pulled off her overalls.

Kate sighed. 'That obvious was it, Doctor?' she said. 'It's just that I can't buy into the accident thing just yet. I'd need to be convinced – it's all a bit too convenient.'

'Convenient for who?'

'Well, the DCI and DI for a start. It would mean a nice tidy conclusion to the case for them and I can see how attractive that might be. Thing is, though, while Stallard was a nasty thug who may well have committed the three murders we're currently investigating and no doubt deserved all he got, I can't see him being so careless as to lose his footing and fall off a walkway in the way he's supposed to have done. And what the hell was he doing up there in the first place? There are plenty of other places on site he could have chosen for a doss. In fact, why did he come back here at all?'

Summers shrugged and tossing her overalls into the boot of the car, bent down to remove the protective booties from her shoes before dumping them in after the overalls. 'Not my province,' she said, 'but the PM should reveal anything I might have missed here.' She hesitated, then said: 'Do you think you might be getting a bit paranoid, though? Accidents like this do happen from time to time.'

Kate nodded. 'Maybe I am paranoid, but my gut feeling tells me something is not quite right.'

Summers laughed. 'Ah, the old police gut thing,' she said. 'Well, maybe you should keep it to yourself for now. Poor old Roscoe thinks he's on to a winner at the moment with the possibility of a "case closed" within reach. Might be a bit unkind to disillusion him until, and if, you have something concrete to go on.'

Then, giving another chuckle, she threw open her car door, climbed in and very soon afterwards pulled away with a cheerful wave.

'Do you think Lenny Stallard's death is suspicious?' Ann Jones asked Kate as they watched the BMW drive off.

Kate frowned. 'I wish I knew,' she replied. 'But I intend finding out one way or the other, you can bet on it.'

'But if it was an accident, what would there be to find out?'

'Probably very little, but if it wasn't, we still have a killer walking about out there somewhere and he can't be allowed to get away with it.'

'If that is the case, though, shouldn't you be a bit careful?' Jones went on. 'I heard about your narrow escape after your brake pipes were cut. Someone obviously saw you as a threat and if it wasn't Stallard, they could well try again.'

Kate shrugged. 'There's not much I can do about that, is there?' she replied. 'And I'm certainly not going to let it stop me doing my job.'

Jones nodded slowly. 'That's all well and good,' she agreed, seemingly choosing her words with care, 'but if you don't mind my saying so, this isn't your personal fight, is it? It's a major crime investigation.'

'Whoever attacked Hayden and then tried to kill me made it personal,' Kate snapped back.

Jones made a face. 'Mr Roscoe won't like it,' she warned.

'Then I won't tell him.'

'That could land you in even more trouble.'

Kate smiled grimly. 'I think you and I have had this conversation before,' she reminded her, 'and I'll repeat what I said then: what's new?' At which point, she frowned again. 'Anyway, why are you so keen for me to drop the whole thing? Touch of cold feet, is it?'

Jones flushed. 'That's not fair,' she said defensively. 'I will back you up regardless of what you decide to do, and you know it. It's just that pursuing this thing seems so pointless. After all, we have absolutely nothing to go on.'

Kate gave another shrug. 'Maybe SOCO will come up with something before we finish here,' she replied, turning back towards the warehouse. 'Miracles have been known to happen!'

* * *

But to her intense frustration, SOCO didn't and shortly after Jamie Foster had dropped her off at home from the crime scene in the CID car, she had something a lot more pressing to worry about than the cause of Stallard's death when she heard the scrape of gravel from the side of the cottage as she was walking up the path to the front door. It was after seven in the evening and pitch black and with the experience of the nocturnal intruder still fresh in her mind, she wheeled round defensively – picking out the glow of a cigarette at the side of the cottage. Then abruptly fear turned to anger when a dark figure stepped into the long tongue of porch light.

'You're skittish tonight,' Bradley Jakes remarked, flicking his cigarette back into the gloom.

Kate glared at him, fists tightly clenched by her sides. 'You've got a bloody nerve coming back here,' she grated. 'Now get off my property.'

'But I've only just arrived,' he said in mock protest. 'Surely you're not going to send me away, like last time, without even a cup of coffee?'

'Just cut the crap and leave, will you,' she retorted savagely, 'unless you want another sore shin?'

He tutted. 'Threats of more violence? That's not a very friendly attitude towards a fellow investigator, is it?'

'You're not a fellow investigator, Jakes, just a pain in the arse. Now exactly why are you here?'

'Isn't it the duty of every citizen to help the police with any information they might have?'

'So, pass on the information and piss off, will you? I've had a long day and I'm very tired.'

Jakes sighed. 'So impatient and so ungrateful,' he murmured and lit another cigarette. 'Have a meaningful chat with Daniel Sayers, did you?'

Kate's anger flared again. 'Have you been following me?'

'Just keeping an eye on my investment.'

'Your what?'

He ignored her indignant retort. 'Tell you everything, did he? For instance, why he sold his Land Rover so suddenly?

Was it because he had carried his old mate, Lenny, in it when Stallard turned up here again and he thought you might do a DNA check and establish an incriminating match?'

She felt a stab of excitement at his suggestion, but did not mention her own suspicions that those DNA traces could just as easily have been those of Colonel Slater.

'You *saw* Lenny Stallard in Sayers' Land Rover?' she said cautiously.

'Not exactly,' he replied, abruptly dashing her hopes, 'but it's a pretty logical conclusion to draw from the speed with which Master Daniel got rid of the vehicle, don't you think?'

'Assumptions aren't evidence of anything,' she retorted, both surprised and relieved that his interest seemed to be focused entirely on Daniel Sayers and not the death of Lenny Stallard. It suggested that he had not yet heard about Stallard's untimely end – which, given his track record, struck Kate as little short of incredible – but she was certainly not about to enlighten him.

'Maybe not,' he went on, 'but they can often be right and I bet Sayers came out with the usual bullshit about "selling his motor to a man in a pub", eh? That must have grated a bit, as you've probably heard similar sort of crap a million times before in your service?'

She exhaled with an irritable hiss. 'What I've heard or haven't heard, Jakes, is none of your damned business,' she said and turning her back on him, continued walking up the path to her front door.

He was undeterred. 'Thing is, Sayers isn't as innocent as he makes out,' he called after her.

She stabbed her key in the lock of the front door. 'Tell me something I don't know already,' she retorted sarcastically.

'Okay,' he replied. 'What about the fact that he was working at The Scarlet Dancer just before Dibble died?'

'What?'

The journalist grinned as she turned back towards him, leaving the door to swing open in front of her.

'Part-time barman,' he went on. 'Had been working there Fridays and Saturdays for about six months apparently – cash in hand. Bet he never told you that?'

She walked slowly towards him. 'How do you know this?'

'Let's just say I have my sources.'

Now Kate couldn't conceal her interest. 'Go on?' she encouraged.

He chuckled. 'Thought you weren't interested?'

'Don't piss me about, Jakes,' she snapped. 'Just get on with it.'

'And our agreement – does that still stand?'

She swore. 'We don't have an agreement. Never have and never will.'

He dropped his half-finished cigarette on to the gravel and stepped on it. 'Now that's a pity,' he went on. 'Because there's so much more I *could* tell you.'

'Like what, for instance?'

He chuckled. 'Well, here's a taster for you. Word is, Ronnie Dibble was not the main man in his illegal enterprises – there was someone else who called the shots.'

'Like who? Jacobs? Stallard?'

'Oh, I couldn't possibly go into all the detail unless you and I were partners.'

'You mean I do your dirty work for you – dig up the facts so that you can then run a good story? Forget it.'

'Life is full of injustices, Sergeant, but at least in your official capacity you will be better placed to follow things up than me. Thing is, though, now that I have provided you with the information, can you afford not to follow it up?'

'All right,' she said heavily after a long pause, 'I hear what you say, but what possible relevance does all this have to the current multiple murder inquiry?'

'I have every faith in your ability to find the connection,' he said. 'Oh by the way, I hope your squeamish friend with the scar has got over her aversion to PMs?'

Then, before she could respond, he stepped back into the darkness and shortly afterwards, Kate saw the tail lights of what was obviously his car disappearing in the direction of Mark village, leaving her standing there wondering who would ultimately prove to be the better detective – Kate Lewis or Bradley Jakes?

* * *

Hayden was much improved when Kate dropped into the hospital to see him and to her relief, he was no longer in the ICU but in a private side ward – though still with a police guard on the door – showered, shaved and with his hair neatly combed.

Dropping clean pyjamas on to the bed, she pulled up a chair and sat beside him, gripping his hand so tightly that he winced.

'Hey, steady on, old girl,' he complained, 'I'm a sick man.'

She smiled. 'Maybe you are, Hayd,' she replied, 'but you're a damned sight tidier than I've ever seen you, so hospital care is obviously good for you.'

He looked pained. 'The food!' he exclaimed. 'It's awful – you have no idea. Even your meals are better than those I've had to endure here.'

She raised an eyebrow. 'Just for that, fat man,' she breathed, 'you can bloody well stay where you are – permanently!'

He grinned. 'How's the old inquiry going?'

So she told him everything, including details of Lenny Stallard's shock death and her doubts that he was their killer, before finishing up with Bradley Jakes' revelations, but was very careful not to mention the incident involving her car.

'I just can't work out what possible relevance Jakes' information has to this inquiry,' she said. 'Though Sayers seems to be a pretty dodgy character, I can't see why he would want to kill Dibble, Jacobs or the Colonel. Any sort of link in that respect just eludes me.'

'At least Stallard is now dead, so he is one worry less,' he pointed out.

She shook her head irritably. 'That doesn't help at all, Hayd. With him on a slab, we lose any opportunity we might have had of interviewing him and either eliminating him from the inquiry or confirming his culpability.'

'So maybe you should leave well alone,' he advised. 'Keep clear of that snake Jakes, and let the DCI and old Roscoe stew in their own juices.'

She grimaced. 'I can't, Hayd. I have to get to the bottom of it all.'

He sighed and gingerly adjusted one of the pillows behind his head. 'Then for goodness' sake be careful,' he said. 'There could be a lot more at stake than your job in this case. Think about the lengths someone went to in an effort to finish me off in here.'

Kate nodded. 'Yes, I've been wondering about that. They must have thought you knew or had seen something that could put them at risk – but what?'

He grunted. 'No idea, but it suggests to me that the intruder at the hospital is unlikely to have been our man, Stallard,' he said. 'After all, why would he bother to try to silence me if he was hell-bent on committing multiple murder anyway? A crack on the head is nothing compared to a knife in the back, is it? He wouldn't have cared whether an injured copper recognised him or not – he'd still have been going down like forever when he was caught.'

She nodded again. 'I've already raised that point with Roscoe, but I got nowhere.'

'What did you expect? The man's a cretin.' He shook his head, this time without wincing. 'No, I reckon whoever tried to do me was someone who was afraid I might be able to identify them – someone either working with Stallard, or who was keen for him to take the rap for murders they had committed.'

'Which brings us to the question of why? And if not Stallard, who?'

He smiled brightly. 'Can't help you there, old girl, though despite what you say this feller Sayers seems to be a good bet. He had it in for Stallard after being given a longer prison sentence because of what Stallard did to the postmistress, and the fact that he quickly got rid of his Land Rover might have had nothing to do with the risk of forensics finding traces of Stallard's DNA in the vehicle, but the DNA of Colonel Slater, who you yourself suspected of having been conveyed to the bird hide by someone before he was killed.'

He hesitated, now frowning heavily. 'Oh, and another thing. You know I said to you before that I couldn't remember much about the character who slugged me? Well, talking to you now, seems to have jump-started the old memory and I do recall one thing. When my assailant came at me from behind the forklift, he didn't simply lash out from the side, but stepped in front of me before wheeling and belting me with whatever he held in his hand.'

'Why would he step out from cover? He could just as easily have clobbered you from behind the truck.'

'No idea, I can only think that he was hiding rather than lying in wait for me and he didn't hear me approaching. I think I heard a sharp intake of breath – like surprise – before it all went black.'

'Go on.'

'Well, the forklift was on my right and although he was facing me, he managed to land his blow to the right side of my head.'

Kate stared at him. 'Which means he must have been—'

'Left-handed,' he finished for her, 'unless he was a contortionist. Ironically, if I had been a murder victim, the pathologist would probably have sussed the fact, but as I was almost certainly on my way to hospital before SOCO arrived it was missed at the scene and for some reason was not picked up afterwards.'

Kate gave a low whistle. 'The pathologist has already sussed the fact that the killer was left-handed,' she said.

'There you are then. I'm only sorry I didn't remember it before. So now maybe you should see if there is any way you can check whether Stallard was left-handed – it should give an indication in his old file. If he was, it could add weight to the presumption that he was my assailant and probably the murderer of Biddle, Jacobs and Slater as well. If he wasn't, then that would open up a whole new bag of worms and justify a further call on the inimitable Mr Sayers.'

Kate climbed to her feet and planted a kiss on his cheek. 'Hayd, you're a genius!' she exclaimed, 'a bloody genius.'

He nodded. 'That's true, of course,' he said soberly, 'but so few tend to recognise this glaringly obvious fact.'

Kate hardly heard him, however, for she was already out the door and heading for the car park.

CHAPTER 20

Roscoe was wearing his pork-pie hat and on his way out of his office when Kate button-holed him.

'Can I have a word, Guv?' she asked.

He closed his eyes briefly in resignation and turned back into his office, switching the light back on.

'This better be good,' he growled. 'I've only just got time for a couple of pints down the road as it is.'

Dumping his short coat on the desk, he sat on one corner, arms folded, boot-button eyes fixed on her warily.

'Shoot,' he said.

Careful not to mention anything Bradley Jakes had told her to avoid awkward questions about her involvement with him, she said instead: 'Have we discovered whether Stallard was left- or right-handed?'

His scowl was back. 'What has that got to do with anything?'

She took a deep breath, reminding him of the pathologist's observations before telling him what Hayden had said. She then waited for it to register and for the volcanic magma to start building up inside his dumpy frame. To her surprise, however, it didn't happen.

'So,' he said after a pause, 'Sherlock has experienced a memory retrieval, has he? Well, bully for him. But in answer to your question, no, I have no idea whether Stallard was right- or left-handed and it doesn't make any difference anyway.'

He eased off the desk, went round to the other side and unlocked a drawer. Then, pulling out what Kate recognised as a folio of scenes of crime photographs, he tossed it across to her. 'Feast your eyes on those,' he invited.

Kate picked up the file and flicked open the cover. There had to be a dozen photographs at least, all obviously taken at the scene of Stallard's death.

'SOCO were bloody quick with this,' she commented admiringly.

'I leaned on them for a rush job,' he growled. 'Wonderful thing, digital kit, though. You get instant results. Last pic is the one you should see.'

She flicked through to the final photograph and tensed when she saw the picture of a knife with a long narrow, sharply pointed blade and a foil grip – which had dark lumpy deposits attached.

'Discovered in one of the upstairs offices of Yardley's warehouse, above where Stallard's body was found, together with piles of sacks and other evidence of someone sleeping rough,' Roscoe continued. 'It's an old army commando knife, still bearing the regimental insignia. We believe it to be the weapon that was used on Colonel Slater and probably the other two victims. It is already on route to the lab and when we get a DNA sample from Slater's corpse, I'm quite sure we'll find there's a match.'

Kate appeared unconvinced. 'I just can't see a professional criminal like Stallard hanging on to incriminating evidence of this sort instead of just chucking it in the nearest rhyne?'

'Maybe he kept it for protection after his last hit or he had another target in mind?'

Surprised that Roscoe was being so communicative, Kate said: ‘I still think it’s a bit too clear-cut to be true. Too convenient.’

Roscoe sighed, returned the photographs to his desk and locked it. ‘Suit yourself, Sergeant,’ he said. ‘But I don’t happen to share your off-the-wall misgivings. And a word to the wise – this inquiry is now over, got it? Over! So we waste no more time on it, just wait for the lab report and the result of the PM, both of which I am quite sure will confirm what we already know to be fact. In short, Lenny Stallard broke out of prison to exact revenge on those who put him there and went on to stiff each one in turn. Then the nasty bastard lost his footing on a narrow walkway and fell to his death. End of!’

‘And Hayden?’

‘Simple. He got in the way and got clobbered.’

`‘So why try to finish him at the hospital?’

‘Who knows? Maybe Stallard feared your hubby might be able to identify him and tie him to the area where he was planning to go on his killing spree.’

Kate shook her head. ‘Sorry, Guv, that doesn’t compute with me.’

Now the molten magma was at last starting to stir and Roscoe’s face noticeably darkened. ‘I don’t give a toss what computes or doesn’t compute with you, Sergeant,’ he grated. ‘And I’m through explaining any more. All we have to do is to make sure none of this gets to the ears of the press until after the PM result and we are ready to make our well-rehearsed public announcement. Now clutter off home before I lose my rag again and destroy our imperfect relationship!’

Then he snatched up his coat and pushed past her out of the office. ‘I’ll be in the pub,’ he threw back over his shoulder. ‘Drowning thoughts of you in a nice cold Guinness.’

‘Arsehole,’ Kate muttered to herself. ‘I hope you choke on it!’

* * *

It was a long time since Kate had broken into a senior officer's desk – not since she had raided the superintendent's steel cabinet four years before, in fact, to check her personal file and see what was being said about the nervous breakdown she had suffered after a particularly traumatic case. The stakes had been high enough then – if the boss had caught her in the act, it could have got her into serious trouble – but at least she could have fallen back on her illness as an excuse. This time, with her worsening relationship with Roscoe and the fact that she was already on a gipsy's warning after previous perceived transgressions, discovery was likely to cost her a whole lot more – maybe even her stripes.

But she had to do it; she had to find out what was in the hard copy prosecution file on Stallard's old GBH conviction. She knew Roscoe had sent for it a few days before, seeking information on the thug's likely contacts, but after checking it, had then dumped it in his bottom drawer as irrelevant to their inquiry. Somewhere in that file would be the critical information detailing the use of the knife by Stallard on the postmistress, hopefully including evidence from the unfortunate victim as to whether their assailant had held the knife in his left or right hand during the attack. Kate was conscious of the fact that she could have interrogated the original crime report on the force's digitised system, which would have been a lot easier and less risky, but there was no guarantee it would contain the detail she sought, and anyway she didn't want to advertise her interest at this stage.

Aware that Roscoe kept his spare key under the battered wooden clock on his desk, it took her seconds to retrieve it and unlock the drawer. The file was still there, but she had the good sense not to try leafing through it in the DI's office, but instead, withdrew to the Ladies' toilet for the purpose, propping herself on the closed toilet seat with the door securely locked.

She found what she was seeking within ten minutes – it was in the court committal summary – and she was so excited that she almost dropped the file on the wet, recently mopped floor.

There didn't appear to be anyone in the general office when she returned to it, but appearances can often be deceptive and she was caught red-handed – though fortunately not by Roscoe. She had replaced the file in the drawer and was in the process of relocking it, when the soft voice spoke from the doorway.

'Hi, skipper, you're working late.'

Kate stiffened and her gaze flicked upwards. Ann Jones was standing in the doorway, a mug in each hand. The TDC smiled and held out one of the mugs.

'Saw you in here and thought you might like a coffee,' she said.

Kate finished locking the drawer and straightened up, pushing the key back under the clock. 'Just off home actually,' she said and frowned. 'What are you doing back here anyway? Thought you'd gone home already.'

Jones put the two mugs on a table behind her and turned back into the office. 'Left my mobile on my desk. Had to come back for it. Has Mr Roscoe already gone then?'

Kate sighed. 'Pub,' she said, coming out from behind the desk. 'I was just—'

'Checking to make sure his desk was locked?' Jones said innocently.

Kate grinned. 'Okay, you've got me bang to rights. I needed to check an old prosecution file on Stallard.'

Jones' eyes twinkled. 'You certainly live dangerously, skip. Did you find what you were after?'

'You bet and it will blow a nice big hole through Roscoe's tidy "case closed" aspirations.'

Jones seemed surprised. 'You mean Stallard wasn't our killer?'

Kate shook her head grimly. 'Unlikely to have been. You see, Hayden has now remembered that his assailant was left-handed and in Stallard's old prosecution file, re a nasty GBH on a postmistress, it clearly indicates that he was right-handed.'

Jones looked doubtful. 'But surely that's not enough to eliminate him as our murderer? Even if he didn't assault Hayden, he could still have been responsible for the three current murders.'

Kate nodded. 'Of course he could, but it throws a great big doubt on things doesn't it, and it gives me a perfectly valid reason for pursuing more inquiries.'

'Except that you'd have to admit to Mr Roscoe that you screwed his desk for the information.'

'I don't intend telling him until I am sure where all this is going.'

'And where is it going?'

Kate slumped on to a corner of the desk and released her breath in a heavy frustrated sigh as Jones leaned sideways against the door frame.

'I wish I knew. My first inclination is to tackle Daniel Sayers again. There's just so much that is wrong about that arsehole – think about it.'

She began tapping the thumb and fingers of her left hand with the index finger of her right. 'First, he was an old friend of Lenny Stallard and was able to tell us exactly where Stallard was likely to be hiding. Second, I've since found out that he worked as a part-time barman at The Scarlet Dancer pub, which establishes a connection between him and Ronnie Dibble – something he has obviously been keeping very quiet about. Third, immediately after Colonel Slater is murdered he decides to get rid of his Land Rover by selling it to "a man in a pub" – why? Fourth, he is a tough character and is of the sort of short stocky build that fits both Hayden's assailant and the intruder spotted in the hospital and at the Slaters' home. And fifth, apart from what Hayden told me about his attacker being left-handed, which may or may not fit Sayers, he also remembers the man was wearing strong aftershave or deodorant—'

'And Sayers stank of the stuff when we called on him?'

'Precisely.'

'So why don't we just bring him in for a little chat? If he turns out to be left-handed, that should clinch things.'

'Where our own suspicions are concerned, maybe, but if he denies everything, that's all we're left with – suspicions – and then he walks.'

'So what *do* we do then?'

Kate frowned. 'Not rush in anyway. See what else we can find out first. The trouble is, there are all sorts of other angles to this business. There's a suggestion that Austin Jacobs was bent, with some sort of a hold over Dibble, and we know from the search of The Scarlet Dancer that our dodgy publican was into the provision of some sort of sexual service and had around 1500 images of child porn on his computer – which may be the lever Jacobs was using.'

Jones pushed herself away from the wall. 'A right devil's brew, it seems.'

'You can say that again. And the question is, if Stallard wasn't responsible for stiffing Jacobs, Dibble and the Colonel, Sayers seems our most likely culprit. But if he hated Stallard, what possible reason could he have for killing the three witnesses who put Stallard away and why would he then kill Stallard afterwards? It just doesn't make sense.'

'Does that really matter? We should be concentrating more on securing enough evidence to justify an arrest rather than worrying about why the crime was committed?'

'Yes, it does matter. Motive is always the most important element in a murder investigation. Establish the motive and nine times out of ten, you'll discover the perpetrator.'

'So what is the motive here, do you think?'

'I'm buggered if I know. But maybe Daniel Sayers will be able to tell us when we pop and see him tomorrow. Now, where's that bloody coffee?'

CHAPTER 21

Sayers was not at home when Kate and Ann Jones called by in the CID car early the following morning and Sayers' mother was the embodiment of hostility when she opened up, still wearing her grubby house coat.

'What do *you* want?' she snapped. 'You told me you was the Social, but you're Old Bill, ain't yer?'

'We need to speak to Daniel,' Kate said, peering into the crack where only a nose and hairy chin were visible.

'Well he ain't here.'

'Do you know where he's gone?'

'In the shit again, is he?'

'No, we just want to talk to him.'

'Yeah, that's what they said last time and he didn't come back for three bleedin' years.'

Kate took a deep breath. 'Mrs Sayers, we need to talk to Danny, so where is he?'

'Why should I tell you?'

'Can we come in for a moment.'

'Why? You got a warrant?'

'We don't need a warrant just to talk.'

'Well, you can talk from where you are then.'

The door opened a fraction more, revealing the old lady's pale, haggard face and an ugly-looking black eye.

Kate drew in her breath sharply. 'Heavens, Mrs Sayers, what happened to your eye?'

There was a snort. 'Bastard clobbered me, didn't he? Ain't the first time neither.'

'That's awful. You need to see a doctor or go to the hospital.'

'No way. I ain't seein' no doctor and that's that.'

'Do you want to make a complaint of assault? Your son needs to be taught a lesson.'

'Complaint? You got to be joking. Me complain to Old Bill? Not bloody likely. Anyway, shouldn't have done what I done.'

'So what *did* you do?'

There was a rasping, humourless chuckle. 'Listened to him talkin' to some mate on that fancy mobile of his, didn't I? Said I was a nosy old bag and it were private. Then he belted me.'

Kate's in-built antenna quivered. 'You mean he thumped his own mother just over a phone call?' she encouraged. 'That's sick – especially as you couldn't have heard much of the conversation anyway.'

'Oh, I heard enough,' came the cackling reply. 'I'm not as daft as I'm cabbage-lookin'. Told me he was going down the bookies, but that's not what he said on the phone and it were a load of old crap anyway.'

She frowned as she apparently tried to recall the conversation. 'Something to do with a woman, I know that.'

Kate raised an eyebrow. 'A woman? Sounds a bit naughty.'

Another cackle. 'Yeah, probably some tom he's dug up from somewhere.' The wrinkled face was screwed up in another frown, then abruptly a new light burned in the open eye. 'A dancer, that's what he said – going to see some dancer. Got a funny name, she had, too. Can't remember what it was.'

But Kate was already ahead of her. 'Wouldn't be Scarlet, would it?' she said.

The old lady started. 'That's it!' she exclaimed. 'How did you know that? Some whore called Scarlet, that's where he's gone – dirty bastard.'

Kate tried to contain her excitement. 'Well, when he comes back, tell him we called, will you, Mrs Sayers,' she said and nudged Ann Jones back down the short path to the gate.

'Yeah,' the old lady shouted after her, 'And if you find him, tell him he can get his own bleedin' dinner!'

And the front door slammed with a resounding bang.

'That's a turn up for the books,' Jones said as she climbed into the CID car beside Kate. 'But I can't believe that the old girl didn't know what The Scarlet Dancer was. Dibble's murder has been in the papers, on radio and on TV. Surely she must have picked up on it?'

Kate nodded. 'Maybe she did and this was her way of dropping her son in it for thumping her, without making it too obvious. But it's more likely that she knows nothing about Dibble or the pub. She must be at least 80, probably doesn't see a newspaper and watches nothing but soaps on the box. I reckon she's regularly three sheets to the wind – didn't you smell the booze off her when she answered the door? And apart from a little primitive cunning when she's sober, she probably doesn't know what day it is half the time.'

Jones grunted, only partially convinced. 'But why on earth would Sayers want to go back to The Scarlet Dancer? The place is still taped off as a crime scene. There's nothing for him there.'

Kate pulled away from the kerb and headed off down the road at speed. 'That, my dear Watson, is what we are now going to find out,' she said. 'Hold on to your knickers.'

* * *

The Scarlet Dancer seemed to have shrunk into the moor since Kate was last there, as if it had given up the ghost and had lost the will to stand up to the marsh mist and constant creeping damp. It was distinctly spooky and Kate repressed a shudder as she and Jones cautiously approached the pub on foot after parking the car further down the road to avoid announcing their arrival.

The main car park at the front of the old building was deserted. No lights showed in the windows on what was a cheerless, murky day as they picked their way along the same muddy track running down the side of the building, which Kate had used before. A pair of mallards rose with a noisy flapping of wings and cackling cries from the rhyne beside the track when they reached the gated archway at the end and they both froze instinctively, waiting until the birds had disappeared into the thin, eddying mist before squeezing through the gap between the archway and the half-open gate.

An old red Volvo V70 estate was parked at the back of the building, close to the kitchen door Kate had used on her previous nocturnal visit, and she smiled grimly. So Sayers had managed to get his Volvo, had he? Red too – obviously his colour, going by the colour of the Land Rover he'd owned before. Even from a distance, the car looked to be a wreck and she wondered briefly how much he had paid for it.

Nodding at the car for Jones' benefit, Kate headed across the paved yard towards it, pausing by the front wing. Keys dangled from the lock of the kitchen door. Obviously after the murder had been reported, Sayers had hung on to the set originally issued to him as barman. At least they wouldn't have to climb through the window.

Hearing a faint sound behind her, Kate swung round and saw Jones crouched beside the front wheel of the car. The hiss of air escaping from the tyre sounded very loud in the still air, but she grinned and gave her colleague the thumbs up as the other moved on to the back wheel. Two deflated tyres should prevent their quarry from making a quick exit if he managed to get past them. Good thinking, Jonah, she mused.

Carefully turning the handle of the kitchen door, she stepped into the room and crossed to the internal door leading to the hallway, pausing for a few seconds with the door a quarter open to listen. She could feel Jones' breathing close behind her, but there was no other sound.

She stepped into the hallway and glanced quickly at the still-open door to the bar, but nothing moved inside and no light showed to relieve the day's gloom. Turning left towards the staircase, she saw that the door to the small sitting room was wide open and she could see immediately that it was empty. So where had Sayers gone? Upstairs? Had to be.

She glanced behind her at Jones, made a face and as on her previous visit, started very slowly up the staircase, holding her breath in case, like before, the treads groaned under her weight. They didn't this time, but something else brought her to an abrupt halt and she felt Jones bump into her from behind. It was a series of squeaking, scraping sounds. As she stood there, listening, she heard them again, from directly above her head, followed by a clattering thud, like something being dropped.

She moved on, reached the landing and paused again to peer round the landing wall to study the corridor.

All the doors appeared to be closed this time, except the one on the opposite side, next to the study where she had found Dibble's body. It was wide open, allowing a faint wandering light to creep out into the corridor from the room inside.

Kate frowned again. The interior of the pub was gloomy, but not dark enough to justify the use of what seemed to be some sort of torch from the way the light constantly roved around. Sayers appeared to be searching for something, but what?

Keeping as close to the wall as possible to reduce the risk of falling foul of another protesting floorboard hidden under the thick carpet, Kate advanced slowly along the corridor towards the light, motioning to Jones behind her to stay put as she did so. Despite her caution, however, the floor let her down and the creak she had feared was actually a loud "crack".

At once the light in the room was extinguished and gritting her teeth, Kate stopped dead, sensing that Sayers was listening intently. She forced herself to remain motionless, determined to wait him out, even though she had stopped with her feet in an awkward, uncomfortable position and could feel the muscles in one leg beginning to tremble.

For what seemed like minutes, but which in reality was probably just a few seconds, nothing happened and then, just as Kate feared the cramp in her calf was going to give her away, the torch flicked on and she heard the squeaking, scraping sounds resume. She started forward again, this time throwing caution to the winds, but the floorboards didn't react and she reached the doorway and peered into the room.

She saw immediately that the curtains had been drawn across the double window of what was obviously a bedroom. The bed and a section of the carpet had been pulled back from the corner of the room, exposing bare floor from which the floorboards had been removed. Sayers was crouched on all fours, with several of the floorboards beside him and a torch clasped in his hand probing one of the gaps that had been created. Even as she stood there, she heard his grunt of satisfaction and saw him reach into the gap to carefully lift something out.

Glimpsing the light switch on the left-hand wall just inside the door, she snapped it on and cleared her throat. 'Having fun, Daniel,' she said quietly.

He moved with surprising speed, springing to his feet and whirling round towards her, an ugly-looking claw-hammer he had snatched from somewhere gripped menacingly in one hand.

'You interfering cow,' he snarled and advanced towards her, the hammer held up on at shoulder-height in his hand. 'This is where you get yours.'

'Oh, I don't think so,' she replied, and producing a small aerosol container from her pocket sent a lethal spray of CS Gas droplets into his face.

The effect was instantaneous. In seconds he was on his knees, his hammer clattering to the floor as he swayed from side to side in front of her, clawing at his streaming eyes and dissolving in a fit of panic-stricken coughing, choking and retching as his diaphragm went into temporary lock-down and he desperately tried to breathe.

Bending down to pick up the claw-hammer as Ann Jones joined her in the room, Kate gave a grim smile. Like all serving officers, having personally experienced the effects of CS gas during training she knew exactly what Sayers was going through, but conscious of what he had done to his own mother and what he had been prepared to do to her, she felt little sympathy for him.

With the assistance of Ann Jones, who displayed surprising strength when Sayers tried to resist, slamming him face-down on the floor, she forced his arms up behind his back and snapped on a pair of handcuffs.

'You are nicked,' she breathed in his ear. 'Burglary and attempted assault on police. And maybe even multiple murder?'

Cautioning him and leaving him lying where he was under the watchful eye of her colleague, she contacted police control on her radio and called for uniform back-up. Then, stepping over his quivering body to see what he had produced from the gap in the floorboards, she found a tin box about 12ins x 10ins x 8ins lying on the floor by the cavity.

'Well, what have we here, Daniel?' she murmured, bending down for closer scrutiny, but taking care not to touch the box. 'I think we'd best get our SOCO team to give this the once over before we take a look, don't you?'

But Sayers was still suffering from the effects of the CS gas and merely groaned in his misery.

It was a good 20 minutes before the big police Transit van pulled up at the back of The Scarlet Dancer and two burly constables carted the now very subdued prisoner away. Kate crouched for several minutes beside the tin box, probing the cavity in which it had been hidden with the aid of her pocket torch. But she saw nothing but cobwebs and the bare ceiling board of the room beneath.

'Maybe it's a deed box,' Jones commented tongue in cheek from just behind her, 'you know, Dibble's last will and testament?'

Kate emitted a short laugh. 'If it is, I hardly think Sayers will have been named as a beneficiary,' she retorted. 'Anyway, the box was obviously of enough importance to our thuggish friend and the mystery man Sayers' mum overheard him talking to on the phone for him to risk being caught getting hold of it.'

Jones was plainly puzzled. 'But if it was that important, why wasn't the job done sooner?'

Kate shrugged. 'Maybe Sayers' phone conflab was with an accomplice who was suddenly getting anxious about things? On the other hand he himself might have deliberately delayed making his move until he was sure the police had finished with the crime scene and it was safe to go ahead?'

Jones sighed. 'Whatever the reason,' she replied, 'I have to admit, I can hardly wait to see what Pandora has got hidden inside her nice tin box, can you?'

They didn't have to wait long either and as it turned out, the wait was well worth it.

* * *

Kate had anticipated another stormy encounter with Roscoe when she returned to Highbridge police station with Ann Jones – not so much because of her arrest of Sayers for burglary, which he could hardly have criticised, but due to the circumstances of her involvement in the first place.

She was relieved to discover that the DI was out, however – apparently on route to the incident room at Bridgwater and after that to Lenny Stallard's post mortem, which he had managed to get slotted in for that afternoon.

At least this gave her a few hours grace and she did her level best to make the most of it. Fortunately, for the second time, SOCO worked a lot faster than usual and within an hour of booking Sayers into the custody sergeant's tender care, Kate and Ann Jones returned to the CID office to find the SOCO supervisor, Samantha Lindslade, waiting for her with the tin box now open and available for inspection.

'All printed and photographed,' Lindslade said with a grin and placing the box on Kate's desk, she left the two detectives to it, parting with the comment: 'Enjoy.'

They realised what she meant the moment they lifted the lid. Packed inside the box were separate bundles of £50, £20 and £10 notes, secured with elastic bands.

'Strewth!' Jones breathed, 'There must be a fortune here.'

Kate nodded gravely after checking three of the bundles at random. 'I make it ten bundles and if each one totals the same as the three I have just counted, that is to say a nice round 500, we are talking £5000 – hardly a fortune, but a lot of dosh for a down-and-out publican – particularly as he has probably already laundered several loads already.'

'No wonder Sayers was so keen to get his hands on it.'

Kate stacked the notes to one side of the box and shook her head. 'I don't think it was just the money,' she said and lifted a small hardback book out of the box, which had been hidden underneath the notes. 'I wouldn't be surprised if it wasn't this that he was really after.'

Flicking through the pages of the book she whistled. 'It's a ledger,' she said, scanning the handwritten entries, and she placed the book open on the desk in front of her colleague. 'See, each page is ruled in four columns, a date in the first column, a name in the second, a sum of money in the third and some sort of symbol in the fourth – either a diamond, a star, a square or a triangle. Each symbol obviously has some sort of coded significance and though I haven't the faintest idea what that could be, it's clear that all the entries in the register relate to individual payments for something. Furthermore, if you look, not one of the sums listed is below three figures.'

Jones peered at the page. 'Booze and or cigarettes?' she suggested. 'Dibble ran a smuggling business, after all. These could be payments on account.'

Kate shook her head. 'I don't think that's it,' she replied. 'My gut feeling is that this ledger is a record of something altogether different – probably something a lot more sinister and no doubt particularly unsavoury, going by Dibble's interest in child internet porn. The sums are all more or less uniform and there are no fractions, just whole figures, with each amount much too large to be attributed to individual purchases of illicit alcohol or cigarettes.'

She stared at her. 'But more important, look at the names listed.'

Jones did so and gulped, raising her gaze to meet hers. 'Some of these are well-known personalities,' she exclaimed and pointed at one entry. 'That's—'

But Kate cut her off, placing a finger over her lips and glancing quickly around the office where a couple of colleagues were sitting at their desks.

'I know, but no names,' she said. 'Not here.'

'But he's a government minister and this one …' Jones pointed '… is in films.'

Kate nodded. 'This ledger is dynamite and whoever sent Sayers to retrieve it knew that only too well and was desperate to get hold of it before we found it. I don't know how, but I am convinced that what we have here is linked in some way to four murders, plus the attempted murder of Hayden and myself.'

'So much for a straightforward investigation,' Jones breathed.

Kate closed the ledger and returned it and the money to the tin box, finally shutting the lid and leaning on the top of it for a few seconds.

'Multiple murder is never straightforward,' she said. 'And I'll tell you something else – I don't know whether you noticed it or not, but when our friend, Sayers, went for me with the claw-hammer, he was holding the hammer in his left hand!'

CHAPTER 22

Roscoe was so subdued that for a moment Kate thought he was going down with something. He hardly raised his head from behind his desk when she entered his office after a brief knock.

'Got Daniel Sayers downstairs, Guv,' she said, hiccupping on the cheese sandwich she had just bolted after a ten-minute trip to the canteen. 'Just nicked him for burglary.'

Roscoe grunted and raised his gaze from contemplating the desk top to meet hers.

'Caught him red-handed breaking into The Scarlet Dancer,' she went on.

He nodded, but seemed too preoccupied with his own thoughts to assimilate the information.

'Bastard went for me with a claw-hammer,' she added quickly, more in an attempt to shake him out of his reverie than anything else.

He sat back in his swivel chair to stare at her. 'I'm going to get done,' he said, his voice empty of feeling. 'I've just had forms served on me. For smoking fags in the nick. Have you ever heard of anything so bloody petty?'

Kate winced. 'Well, I had nothing to do with it!' she snapped defensively.

He waved a weary hand in front of her. 'I know that now,' he cut in. 'Seems one of the plods downstairs shopped me.' He emitted a hard bitter laugh. 'Job's coming to something, isn't it, when one of your own stabs you in the back like that?'

Then he seemed to inwardly shake himself and straightened in his chair. 'Okay,' he said in a more business-like tone, 'you'd better tell me all about Sayers.'

So Kate did exactly that, leaving nothing out except who had put her on to things in the first place. Strangely enough, he didn't ask either, but uncharacteristically listened without interrupting her until she had finished.

Then, with a wicked grin, he produced a packet of cigarettes and lit one up. 'In for a penny,' he said. 'They'll probably hang me out to dry on this one anyway – been looking for an excuse for years.' His eyes hardened. 'Now, about Sayers. Where is he now?'

'Interview Room 2,' she said.

He took a long grateful pull on his cigarette and nodded. 'Then go and interview the arsehole,' he said, 'and take Jones with you.'

As she turned for the door, however, he abruptly snapped his fingers, so that she swung back towards him.

'Oh by the way, Stallard's death *was* sus,' he added. 'Pathologist found bruising on the back of his neck, previously hidden by the blood. She maintains this is unrelated to his fall and is entirely consistent with a heavy blow with a blunt instrument of some sort prior to his death. She thinks he was smacked with something from behind, then pitched off the walkway. So we're back in the shit. The only saving grace is that the press don't appear to have got wind of Stallard's death yet – force press office have told me that there's nothing about it in any of the papers or on the broadcasting networks, which gives us some time in hand at any rate.'

Kate couldn't resist a gloat. 'So I was right then?'

He scowled. 'You're always bloody right, Lewis – that's what pisses me off!'

She treated him to a thin smile, realising that it actually did serve as a Roscoe-type apology this time, but before she could think of a suitable reply, he had literally disappeared behind a cloud of smoke and the loud eruption of beery wind which then issued from within it signified that the conversation was over.

* * *

Daniel Sayers had no intention of playing ball. Sitting on the other side of the interview room table to Kate and Ann Jones, with his rotund, florid-faced solicitor beside him, he refused to answer any questions whatsoever. He couldn't deny the burglary at The Scarlet Dancer – obviously left with no option but to accept that he had been caught bang to rights – but he would not say anything about the tin box or the ledger, why he had raided the pub in the first place, or who he had been speaking to on his mobile before the burglary. Instead, he simply scowled at them, broke wind noisily and occasionally picked his nose to demonstrate his total disinterest in the proceedings.

The only brief change in his demeanour came when Kate revealed that Lenny Stallard had been murdered. The shock in his expression could not have been manufactured, but whether his reaction was due to the death itself or the fact that Stallard's demise had been established as murder rather than the unfortunate accident someone had tried to make it look like, Kate was unable to decide. In any event, he quickly recovered and became just as sullen and uncommunicative as before, restricting his responses to angry denials when it was suggested that he was a multiple murderer.

Finally forced to admit defeat, Kate had him returned to his cell before stomping back to the CID office in a frustrated, truculent mood.

'Nothing?' Roscoe said with an almost triumphant grin.

She grimaced. 'Bastard wouldn't say a bloody word,' she replied.

He shrugged. 'Well, at least you've got him for aggravated burglary after he went for you with the hammer, and that's a result in itself.'

She snorted. 'But not the result our multiple murder inquiry needs. Despite Sayers' arrest, we're still no closer to finding the connection between the goings-on at The Scarlet Dancer and four brutal murders.'

'Maybe there isn't one?'

'There has to be. I don't believe in coincidences, Guv, and neither do you. Sayers is up to his neck in something – something so dire that it has necessitated the deaths of four people to cover it up, but what, that's the point?'

Roscoe sighed and sat back in his chair. 'So you think Sayers is behind it all?'

She shook her head and adopted her usual stance, leaning against the door frame of his office. 'He's too thick – imbued with a primitive cunning, I'll give you that, but thick nevertheless.'

'He could still have been our killer.'

'If he was, someone was pulling his strings.'

'The mystery character you told me about – the one he was chatting to on his mobile?'

She nodded. 'More than likely. After all, it was straight after that call that he screwed The Scarlet Dancer to retrieve the ledger. But he's not letting on who it was.'

'Have you interrogated his phone?'

'First thing we did when we came back, but he'd already deleted the number – his calls log is completely empty.'

'So check with the phone company and get them to try and retrieve the number, if that's possible.'

'Already in hand – I've got Ann Jones on it – but that will take time and going by past experience, she'll have to jump through quite a few hoops with the network supplier before she gets there.'

He nodded and took a noisy sip from a cup of coffee on his desk. He seemed tired – preoccupied – his usual fire gone and replaced by something akin to disinterest. Kate suspected that the disciplinary inquiry hanging over his head had hit him hard – especially the fact that he had been shopped by one of his own colleagues, which in his book of old-school principles, was the worst transgression any police officer could commit. He couldn't come to terms with the fact that times had changed and loyalty and comradeship in the brave new policing world – where everyone was encouraged by the hierarchy to "snitch" on each other – could no longer be relied upon. Kate felt almost sorry for him.

'We'll just have to wait for that then, won't we?' he said. 'There's no real hurry – Sayers isn't going anywhere, is he? And in the meantime, you might as well nip over to see the Slaters and put them in the picture.'

He made a bitter grimace. 'Give you something to do until the next stiff turns up, eh?'

* * *

All three cars were parked in front of the house when Kate arrived at Sycamore Lodge – the late Colonel's big Volvo in the far corner and the flashy red Jaguar and MGC sports car belonging to Carol and Charles Slater a few yards from the front door. It was early evening and the lights blazing in the lower windows of the house gleamed on the bodywork of the Jaguar and MGC as Kate parked the CID car alongside them, then threaded her way between the two cars to the front door. Charles Slater greeted her on the doorstep and he looked both surprised and delighted to see her, his gaze blatantly stripping her naked where she stood.

'To what do we owe this undoubted pleasure, Sergeant?' he drawled smoothly, showing her into the sitting room. 'Unfortunately Carol is in the shower at the moment.'

Kate nodded and sat on the edge of the proffered armchair, feeling distinctly uncomfortable under his devouring stare.

'I don't need to see her specifically, Mr Slater,' she said. 'I just popped by to give you some news. Lenny Stallard has been found dead in a derelict warehouse.'

'Dead?' he exclaimed, his eyes widening. 'Wow! That's a shock. When was this?'

'Yesterday afternoon.'

'Good lord! Accident, was it?'

'What makes you think that?'

He made a face. 'Well, I just assumed – are you saying it wasn't an accident?'

She frowned. ''Fraid not. We believe he was murdered, which means we're now looking for someone else.'

'Murdered? But … but why would anyone want to kill *him*? After all, he was the dastardly villain in the first place.'

She shrugged. 'No idea, but we have a suspect in custody at the moment.'

'A suspect? Does he have a name?'

'I'm sorry, I can't say.'

Before he could press her further, the door opened and Carol Slater walked into the room, barefoot and clad in black trousers and a fawn sweater. Her hair seemed damp and needing a thorough brush, and she was not wearing any make-up. She stopped dead when she saw Kate sitting in the chair, obviously surprised by her presence, but then she forced a smile.

'Sergeant,' she acknowledged coolly. 'Has something happened?'

Her brother turned towards her. 'Lenny Stallard has been found dead at that damned cider farm, Sis,' he said. 'Sergeant Lewis says they have a man in custody on suspicion of murder, but won't say who it is.'

'It isn't a case of "won't say", Mr Slater,' Kate corrected. 'I can't say.'

'Stallard – dead?' his sister gasped. 'But how—?'

'I can't tell you that either,' Kate interjected.

The shocked woman dropped into an armchair opposite, as if she had had all the wind knocked out of her. 'But … but surely, as victims, we have a right to know the details?'

'Sadly, not, Miss Slater. We do not release details of police investigations whilst they are still ongoing.'

'But are you sure Stallard was actually murdered? Could his death have simply been an accident?'

Kate gave a grim smile. 'That's what it was made to look like, but no, it was definitely not an accident.'

'So what led you to believe it was murder? After all, anyone can lose their footing.'

'Again, I can't tell you that either.'

'At least tell us whether you believe Stallard was responsible for the murder of my father and the others – that would serve to reassure us that we are not at risk from some other psychotic thug.'

'Personally, Miss Slater, I don't think you have anything else to fear now, but as to the rest, we don't have any answers at the moment. We are still investigating Stallard's death. I have just called by to keep you up to date.'

'This changes everything,' Charles Slater put in, his frustration showing. 'Throws everything into confusion.'

Kate frowned heavily, hardly hearing him. Something was bothering her, though she couldn't put her finger on what it was. She was uneasy, tingling with a nervous energy that she could not satisfy. Her inbuilt antenna had picked up important information, yet she couldn't for the life of her determine what it was. For a few seconds she just sat there, trying to extract the information, but her weary brain refused to release it, throwing up mental blocks as her thought processes tried to penetrate the cerebral passages leading to the depths of her clouded subconscious.

Then, suddenly aware that both the Slaters were studying her with a curious, puzzled intensity, she shook herself out of her reverie and smiled. 'Sorry, I went off on one there. Long day. Tired, I suppose. What did you say?'

'Nothing much,' Charles Slater said, smiling back, 'I was just wondering what the next move of the police will be over this?'

Kate hesitated. 'That will depend on what forensics turn up for us from the scene,' she prevaricated. 'Analysis of forensic evidence takes time, I'm afraid.'

'You have got a lot of it then, have you?' Carol Slater asked, then gave a wry smile. 'But you can't tell us that either, of course?' she added with more than a hint of sarcasm.

For some reason, the comment got under Kate's skin, but before she could come up with a suitable response, her personal mobile activated. Startled and considerably embarrassed by the interruption – she hadn't expected it as she'd left her police radio/phone in the car – she stood up and fumbled for the phone which had somehow become tangled in the lining of one of her pockets.

'Sorry,' she said, 'I really have to take this.'

Charles Slater extended a hand towards the door. 'Please,' he said. 'It's not a problem.'

But it was when Kate stepped out into the hallway and swiped the phone to answer it, for a familiar voice greeted her. It was Bradley Jakes.

'*You're a dark one*,' the journalist said.

'How did you get my personal mobile number?' she snapped back at him.

A hard chuckle. '*I thought we were partners?*' Jakes said.

'What are you on about?' she demanded. 'I'm busy.'

'*Stallard*,' he went on, irritation creeping into his tone. '*You never told me about his sudden demise. Found out today from one of our stringers.*'

She snorted. 'I don't answer to the press, Jakes. If you miss a story, that's your problem.'

'*Is it true, though? That he's snuffed it?*'

'That's for me to know and you to find out,' she replied.

He sighed. '*I must admit, when I heard about more police activity at Yardley's, I thought it was to do with the ongoing investigation into the assault on your hubby, but an hour ago I was told that your prime suspect had croaked. Why didn't you tell me about that, Kate?*'

'I don't have to tell you anything. If you were a good enough journalist, you would have found out about Stallard yourself.'

'*True, but I missed getting the story on to the front page today – as did the rest of my colleagues – and because of your rather deceitful reticence, the public have been kept completely in the dark about the development. Several editors are on the warpath, I warn you. You'll be savaged for this.*'

'You mean no one got the story at all?' Kate mocked. 'Oh, what a tragedy. I feel so sorry for you.' Then, with her finger poised to cut him off, she stiffened in her seat, an icy shard slicing through her brain.

'*How did he die?*' Jakes continued, ignoring her rude retort. '*Was it an accident or was it murder?*'

But Kate was no longer listening to him. She was concentrating on the voice in her brain instead. Something had triggered a response from her subconscious, reactivating her short-term memory, which had begun regurgitating information like a silent tic-a-tape machine.

Then, as realisation dawned on her, she cut Jakes off in mid-stream and stood there, leaning against the wall in a state of shock. What was it they had said during her advanced detective training course? Listen, assimilate and evaluate? She had done none of those things effectively during this multiple murder investigation. She had allowed herself to be influenced by her own pre-conceptions and constantly distracted and diverted from her core purpose by red herrings cast in the way. As a result, she had failed to consider the wider perspective and had only tumbled to the truth after receiving pointers unwittingly provided by a resentful interfering journalist – pointers incidentally, that Roscoe had already supplied and which her closed mind had not picked up on. She had been deaf as well as blind!

Then she froze as a hand reached out from the doorway behind her and took hold of her phone.

‘I think I’d better have that,’ Charles Slater drawled, levering it out of her grasp. ‘Now why don’t you come back into the sitting room and join us?’

His invitation was polite enough, but the large knife in his hand indicated that refusal was not an option.

CHAPTER 23

'Well now, this is cosy, isn't it?' Charles Slater said quietly after Kate had obediently sat herself down in the chair she had previously occupied. 'Sorry I eavesdropped on your conversation, but you see, I realised, even before you took the phone call, that you had probably twigged my inadvertent faux pas. Am I right?'

Kate felt Carol Slater's eyes boring into her from the chair opposite and grimaced. 'Not entirely. I had sussed something was wrong, but wasn't able to nail it down until—'

'Your journalist pal came up with the goods? I guessed as much from your comments.'

Kate nodded. 'I told you Stallard had been found dead in a warehouse. I didn't mention Yardley's. Yet you told your sister it was the cider farm, despite the fact that nothing on the murder had been put out in the newspapers or via the broadcasting networks.'

He tutted. 'So I did rather drop myself in it then?'

Kate shrugged. 'No more than your sister did when she said anyone can lose their footing. I never revealed how Stallard had died, so how would she have known unless—'

'She was privy to his death, eh?' He tutted again and glanced across at Carol Slater. 'Naughty girl, Sis. You should be given 40 lashes for that.'

Carol Slater tossed her head angrily at the frivolity, and treated Kate to a baleful glare. 'The evil bastard deserved to die anyway. He killed mummy.'

'No, he didn't,' Kate contradicted. 'Stallard was set up, I realise that now. Your brother was actually responsible for her death, wasn't he? Then you both put the blame on Stallard – which you tried to do again this time, with the murders of Dibble, Jacobs and your own father.'

She glanced at Charles Slater. 'You probably used your father's old commando knife too, Mr Slater – which I suspect was the twin of the one you are holding now. It fits the pathologist's description to a T.'

Carol Slater's eyes narrowed, but her brother's smile broadened. 'Full marks,' he said. 'Do you think we're having that Agatha Christie moment – you know, when the great detective explains how she detected the crime?'

Kate ignored the mocking question. 'The only thing I can't work out is why?'

'Of course,' he agreed, 'the all-important motive. That is a little bit more complicated, though, isn't it, Sis?'

'Something to do with The Scarlet Dancer and Dibble's illegal activities, I would think,' Kate suggested.

'Ah, the inimitable Mr Dibble,' he murmured. 'But let me correct you on one point, Sergeant. The activities you are no doubt referring to were initially set up and financed by us – they weren't Dibble's, they were ours. He just provided the premises and managed the joint enterprises for us.'

'Joint enterprises? You mean bootlegging and prostitution, don't you?'

He shrugged in unashamed acquiescence. 'There's good money to be made in both undertakings, Sergeant, but particularly when you can supply attractive rent boys for the sexual gratification of certain pillars of our society – well-heeled clients who will pay handsomely for the privilege of absolute discretion where their identities are concerned.'

He propped himself on the arm of Kate's chair and manufactured a sigh. 'Both our businesses were doing so well too, but then Daphne found out what was going on and blew a gasket. A dedicated Christian, she threatened to tell our father everything if we didn't pack it all in.'

'So you murdered her – your own mother?'

'She wasn't our real mother,' Carol Slater snapped. 'She was our stepmother.'

'Which made it easier, did it?' Kate retorted .

Charles Slater shrugged. 'Yes, I suppose it did,' he agreed. 'And anyway, she had to go. If the old man had found out, he would have stopped our future inheritance. We couldn't have that – a lot of money was at stake.'

Kate nodded. Things were becoming even clearer now. 'So you hired some woman, professing to be a cleaner, to seduce and con Lenny Stallard into breaking into the house, so he could be tied to the scene, before you offed Daphne Slater?'

In response, both the Slaters snorted with laughter. Then, seeing her puzzlement, Carol Slater stood up and bowed theatrically. 'Your cleaner,' she said.

'You?' Kate gasped.

Carol Slater's face broke into a sneer. 'Why not?' she mocked. 'I'm a hairdresser and beautician with a cupboard full of wigs – playing the part was easy. As Stallard had never met me, he hadn't a clue he was being conned, and all I had to do was keep out of the way during the court case, just in case he recognised me.'

'A perfect plan, in fact,' Charles Slater put in. He made a face. 'But then our patsy managed to break out of prison, just two years after being put there, and that sent us into a spin—'

'Until,' Carol Slater resumed, 'we realised that it presented us with a golden opportunity.'

'To murder your father?' Kate said, the disgust very evident in her tone.

Charles Slater sighed again and stroked her hair, forcing her to draw away from him.

'We had a bit of a cash-flow problem, you see,' he said. 'Expensive tastes and all that. We had tried to get the old man to sell up and move into a smaller place – we'd have made a nice bundle on a property like this – but he refused.'

He shrugged again. 'That left us no choice but to claim our inheritance early. We had planned to do the business when he went on one of his bird-watching expeditions to the hide. But a hitch occurred, which nearly scuppered the whole thing. His leg had nasty shrapnel damage from his army service and on the day we had selected, it was playing him up so badly that he could hardly walk. So, to persuade him that a trip to the hide was necessary, I told him I had seen Stallard down by the lake. That was enough of an incentive and grabbing his shotgun – which I later returned to the house – he let me drive him over there in his Volvo.'

'So that's why his shoes were so clean?'

He frowned. 'Shoes?'

'Yes, the soles of his shoes were unmarked, which meant he could not possibly have walked to the bird hide – he must have driven or been driven there – which raised the question, where was the car?'

He raised his eyebrows appreciatively. 'Clever girl. I must admit, I'm impressed. I didn't think about that.'

'It's not the only thing you didn't think about either.'

'Oh?'

'Yes, binoculars. It's a bit unusual for someone to go bird-watching without them.'

He made a face. 'Oops! Seems I made a right a hash of things,' he said.

'Oh, I don't know,' Kate replied with bitter sarcasm, 'you still succeeded in murdering an innocent, defenceless old man. How did you manage to get him to turn his back on you?'

'He trusted me,' he said simply, and without a trace of guilt in his voice or expression. 'I persuaded him to sit down while I scouted around outside with the shotgun, ostensibly looking for Stallard—'

'Then crept up behind him and plunged the knife in his back like the true Judas you are?'

He shook his head, unaffected by her words or the venom in her tone. 'I didn't need to,' he said. 'Sis was already there, weren't you, Sis?'

Kate threw a quick horrified glance at Carol Slater's sneering face and felt sick. 'You?' she choked. '*You* murdered your father?'

Carol Slater gave an extravagant wink. 'And Jacobs and Dibble too,' she admitted with what seemed like a perverse sense of pride before pouring herself a glass of wine from a half-full bottle on the coffee table beside her. 'Although I have to say that poor little Daphne will always be my most memorable termination. She was what you might call my first blood.'

She sipped her wine for a moment, before continuing. 'Having said that, the whole thing certainly took some organising. Timing was crucial, you see, and we impressed on Lenny that he had to carry out his break-in dead on midnight. By then Chas and I knew that Daphne would be in bed and have finished reading her book, as usual – she was a stickler for routine. All I had to do was close down my salon party at 11.40 and drive to the house, entering via a back door and hiding in the attic room where I could watch for Lenny's arrival. Chas had arranged to take daddy out for a drink at a local pub which was only five minutes away and as soon as our burglar arrived I called his mobile, which he had on vibrate, to let him know. He didn't pick up, but cancelled the call without Daddy ever knowing the phone had rung—'

'And he and the Colonel arrived just as Stallard was leaving?' Kate interjected, tiring of Carol Slater's long self-indulgent explanation which was obviously feeding her warped ego, '… giving you time to creep downstairs and stab a poor elderly woman to death?'

There was a spark of irritation in Carol Slater's eyes at the interruption. 'Exactly as planned,' she said with emphasis. 'And as Chas made his pretend pursuit of Stallard and Daddy limped slowly up the stairs to Daphne's room, I slipped away, returning via the front door a convenient half hour later to express my horror at the dastardly crime. Brilliant, eh?'

For a moment, Kate just stared at her, a new understanding dawning.

Carol Slater was about 5ft 4ins in height, stocky and muscular and obviously very fit – the evil cow worked out, for goodness sake, and she was no doubt as strong as any man. She therefore fitted the profile of the killer to a tee and it was now apparent why both Dibble and Jacobs had suffered the initial stab wounds to the lower back. Both were tall men and had obviously been standing upright or walking when attacked; Carol Slater's much shorter stature meant that the lower trunks of her victims were a much easier target to aim for.

As an experienced detective, Kate couldn't help asking herself how on earth she could have missed all the pointers that were so glaringly obvious and why it had not occurred to her before that the person she was looking for could be a woman? And there was another thing too: it was obvious now that the strong smell Hayden had detected when he had been attacked in the warehouse had not been aftershave or deodorant at all, but perfume – Carol Slater had reeked of it as much as Daniel Sayers had stank of deodorant – but she had failed to pick this up. And even as she'd been sitting there, lost in bitter recriminations, the final piece of evidence had been delivered right in front of her. Carol Slater had poured her wine – using her left hand!

'Run out of questions, Sergeant?' Carol Slater cut in on her reverie, the sneer back in her tone.

Kate got a grip on herself. 'Not quite,' she retorted as calmly as she could manage, even though her throat was drying up and she was conscious of a tell-tale tremble developing in her legs. She was only too well aware of the fact that –

as would have been the case with Ronnie Dibble if he had not been interrupted – once she ran out of questions and the Slaters' egos had been fully satisfied, her life expectancy would be measurable in terms of minutes at the most.

'I did wonder why you simply belted my husband at Yardley's instead of finishing him on the spot. Bit of a slip-up there, wasn't it? After all, you then had to try again at the hospital, didn't you? And I can't think why you tried to waste me by tampering with the brakes on my car as I wasn't even close to suspecting your involvement in the murders, so I was no threat to you.'

Carol Slater made a face and shook her head. 'I hate to disappoint you, Sergeant,' she replied, 'but I can assure you that neither Chas nor I know anything about the attack on your husband. We were nowhere near Yardley's when that happened, so it must have been someone else.'

She smirked. 'Maybe a jilted lover, eh? As for your car being tampered with, that's news to us and as you have already said, why would we bother? Until now, you were not a problem for us – you didn't have a clue that we were behind the murders until a few minutes ago. Perhaps it was the jilted lover again?'

'I don't believe you.'

'As if I care – but it happens to be true. Why would I lie to you – especially in your current predicament?'

'So I suppose you also deny that you stiffed Lenny Stallard at the cider farm?'

Carol Slater gave another shrug. 'Not at all, but Chas and I were left with no choice. When Stallard broke out of clink, he phoned me at home to reveal that he had found out I was the one who had set him up over Daphne's murder. He said he wanted money as the price of his silence – an extortionate amount of it – so he could disappear abroad, and he demanded that we met up at Yardley's or he would go to the newspapers and force a retrial. Silencing him therefore became a real priority.'

'But not as much of a priority as fitting him up for the murders you had planned, was it? Neither you nor your brother actually saw him in the grounds of this house, did you? You just dreamed that up to colour the situation and establish Stallard as the escaped con on the revenge trail.'

Carol Slater smirked. 'Spot on, Sergeant! It was easy disposing of him too. I agreed to meet him at his former hideaway to sort things out and while we were talking, I made out I had heard a noise downstairs in the warehouse. When he went out on to the walkway to look, I hit him from behind with a little steak-hammer I'd brought with me in my handbag and he tumbled over.'

Kate grimaced again. 'And to further tie him into the murders of Jacobs, Dibble and your father, you planted the knife you'd used on them in his doss, knowing full well that police forensics would match the DNA from the blood deposits deliberately left on the blade to that of at least one of his victims.'

'You've got to give it to her, Sis,' Charles Slater chortled, 'she really is very good.'

Kate ignored him. 'Except that Dibble and Jacobs weren't stiffed just to frame Stallard, were they?'

Carol Slater nodded slowly. 'How very perceptive of you, Sergeant,' she admitted. 'Their murders were a necessary element in the vengeance motive we had created for Stallard, of course, and they also provided an excellent smoke-screen for the planned demise of dear old Daddy. But on top of this, both Dibble and Jacobs had it coming anyway; Lenny's break-out had just given us the opportunity. You see, Dibble was creaming off an increasing percentage of the business profits, stashing it away to satisfy his own greed when he thought we weren't looking.' She shook her head disapprovingly. 'He had to be punished for that, of course …'

Her expression twisted into an evil mask, as her true self showed through the thin veneer that had so far concealed the cold-blooded psychopath living inside her.

'… As for Jacobs, that bent bastard had had us over a barrel ever since I'd wasted Daphne. You see, he sussed what had really happened at the original murder scene very soon after turning up at the house. Unfortunately we made a few minor mistakes and that was fatal where an observant prick like Jacobs was concerned. His price for overlooking the evidence was a partnership in our joint business ventures, with a nice lump sum paid to him in cash on a quarterly basis. Blackmail is a despicable business, Sergeant – worse than murder, in fact – and I have to say, fewer things in life have given me greater pleasure than dispatching that particular excuse for a man.'

Kate felt her skin crawl under her cobra-like gaze. 'It hasn't stopped you from going for a bit of extortion on your own account, though, has it?' she accused. 'The names in the ledger you sent Daniel Sayers to retrieve from The Scarlet Dancer could have netted you even more than the money you were making from your other two businesses.'

'Ah!' Charles Slater left the arm of the chair and crossed the room to reach for the bottle of wine beside his sister. Kate thought about making a run for it while she had the chance, but then dismissed the idea as a non-starter, realising that she would never even reach the front door before he or his sister got to her. 'So, as it appears you know all about the ledger,' he said, pouring wine into another glass, 'I assume that the suspect you have in custody is Master Sayers, eh?'

Kate nodded. 'And he'll be singing his heart out to my team right now.'

He chuckled again. 'Oh, I doubt that. He has too much to lose. The fact is, he was working for Dibble as a casual barman to start with, but after being taken on as a bit of muscle for our twin business ventures, he was actually the one who came up with Stallard's name when we were looking for a suitable patsy for our burglary. He knew nothing about the plan to waste poor Daphne, of course – he just thought we wanted someone to screw the house so we could claim on the insurance afterwards. Even when our mother actually departed this world, he still thought his old mate had done the job in a moment of panic. It wasn't until Stallard broke out and we decided to remove Dibble and Jacobs that he began to put two and two together – not exactly "Brain of Britain" you see – but by then he was in too deep to extricate himself and just had to do as he was told.'

He drained his wine glass and returning it to the coffee table, he sauntered back to her chair and propped himself on the arm, as before.

'Naturally, he was also due for the chop as soon as he had handed the ledger over, but that can always come later – police custody suite, prison cell or whatever – and I have every confidence of his silence in the meantime …' he smiled at her again '… as I have in yours, Sergeant, which will soon be profound.'

Caroline Slater snorted angrily. 'Let's just get this over with, Chas,' she rasped, setting down her empty wine glass and standing up. 'We need to get rid of her before she is missed.'

'Quite agree, Sis,' he replied slowly, his brows now wrinkled in thought. 'Not in here, though. No sense in ruining the carpet – it's Persian, after all. What we need is a nice little accident …' His voice trailed off and then abruptly his smile broadened. '… and I think I have just the scenario.'

He stroked Kate's hair again, this time with the edge of the knife as he stared into her face. 'Sorry about this, Sergeant, but I'm sure you understand, we really don't have any choice—'

'Killing me won't get you off the hook,' Kate blurted, cutting him off. 'My colleagues know I came here to see you. It's the first place they will look when I don't call in.'

He made a "so be it" motion with his other hand. 'We shall just tell them you went off somewhere else. How could we be expected to know where you were going after you left here?'

'You've forgotten about the CID car.'

He shook his head. 'No I haven't, Sergeant. It will form the basis of your unfortunate accident. River levels are quite high at the moment and it would be quite conceivable for you to be driving a little too fast in the dark and end up in the Huntspill river. He held out his free hand. So, ignition keys please.'

Kate fumbled in her pocket, then handed them over, commenting drily: 'So what would I be doing there after calling on you?'

He shrugged. 'Who knows? Maybe you were following up on another enquiry? You know, the dedicated officer, exhausted after such long hours, misjudging things and careering off the road. All very tragic—'

Caroline Slater cut him off this time. 'Sounds good to me!' she snapped. 'Let's get her out to the car.'

Briefly turning her back on them as her brother stood up and jerked Kate roughly to her feet by one arm, she strode to the three-seater settee across the room and reached down behind it. When she turned round again she had her father's shotgun in her hands.

'Still not in a gun cabinet then?' Kate observed tightly, thinking of the day she had castigated the Colonel when he had produced the weapon from the self-same spot.

Caroline Slater sniggered – not a pleasant sound – and raised the shotgun so that it was aimed at Kate's chest.

'We'll just have to have this offence – to use the official parlance – taken into consideration with all our other offences, eh? The gun is loaded this time too,' she said, 'and it would make a nice big hole in you at this close range.'

'Pack it in, Sis!' her brother snapped nervously. 'I said not in here.'

He slipped the knife into the belt of his trousers and tapped Kate on the hip. 'Are you carrying cuffs?'

'Cuffs?'

'Don't prevaricate!' he snarled, his affected charm vanishing in a second. 'Give them to me.'

Conscious of the twin barrels of the shotgun covering her and the eager gleam in Carol Slater's eyes, Kate carefully reached under her coat to unclip the handcuffs she always carried in a pouch attached to her belt and handed them to him.

'And the keys to these as well.'

She gave him her bunch of keys and waited.

'Okay, you know what I want you to do,' he said. 'Put the bracelets on – both wrists.'

She hesitated and the knife, which was now back in his hand, pricked her side through the material of her coat.

'Do it!' he said, his voice now harsh and uncompromising.

With a sinking feeling in the pit of her stomach, she again did as she was told, even though she realised that with the cuffs on her chances of making a break for it had reduced to just above zero.

'Good girl,' he acknowledged, his false smile back with a vengeance. 'Now, go ahead of me into the hall. I know a nice little place by the river where we can finish our conversation.'

Feeling the sharp point of the knife in the small of her back, she had no option but to do as he said, but as she stepped through the doorway she was acutely conscious of the fact that, unless she could think of her way out of her present predicament PDQ, the conversation he had referred to would be the last one she ever had …

CHAPTER 24

Kate felt very much like the condemned prisoner on route to the gallows or the firing squad as she headed slowly back along the hallway, thinking that less than an hour before she had entered the house with absolutely no idea what she was walking into. Had it not been for Bradley Jakes' phone call, she would probably already have left again – safe and sound in her ignorance – and the cruel irony was that, while she had finally got most of the answers to the questions she had been seeking throughout the inquiry, they would be of no use to her or her colleagues now as she was likely to be taking them with her to her grave.

But then her morbid reflections were abruptly cut short by Charles Slater's sharp command: 'Stop there for a moment!'

She was just two to three feet from the front door and at first she thought that he was going to step past her to open it, but the next instant she saw out of the corner of her eye that Carol Slater had stopped halfway through the sitting room door and was bending down just inside the hallway. Turning her head very slightly, she saw that the woman had rested the shotgun against the wall and was in the process of pulling on a pair of gumboots. Of course! She was barefoot and the area outside the front door was surfaced with sharp bits of gravel – no fun if you have no shoes on.

Kate reacted to the situation almost without thinking. Charles Slater had half-turned towards his sister, waiting for her to pull her boots on, and had involuntarily lowered his knife at the same moment.

It was a big mistake. Handcuffs are designed to severely restrict a prisoner's movements, but their tough unyielding steel and angular edges can also make an excellent weapon. Lurching round suddenly, Kate slammed both clenched fists and her steel encased wrists into the side of Charles Slater's head with all the desperate force she could summon.

The result was predictable. Caught totally unawares, he stumbled backwards with a wild, agonised cry, blood streaming from a deep gash in his temple from the cuffs, and crashed into his sister, also knocking her off balance.

'Bitch!' he screamed, lashing out at Kate with the knife, but the blade scythed empty air, for she had already lunged away from him to the front door. As Slater staggered unsteadily towards her, she wrenched the door open and bounded through, flinching once as the roar of Carol Slater's shotgun followed her into the gathering dusk.

Luckily the blast missed her and then, stumbling across the gravel forecourt, she had jerked to a halt at the back of the Slaters' Volvo, panting heavily in the comparative safety of the deep shadow cast by the big, heavy vehicle.

Throwing wild panicky glances around her while she tried to make up her mind which way to run, she flinched as the forecourt's security floodlights blazed into life and peering round the rear wing of the Volvo, she saw both Carol and Charles Slater standing, apparently undecided, a few feet out from the front door. It seemed that neither of them had seen where she had taken temporary refuge, but with only four cars parked within a few yards of where they were standing and no other cover for several square yards, she knew it wouldn't take them long to pin-point her position.

She drew back to the other side of the car and crept towards the front, pausing just level with the edge of the front wing. Obviously the Slaters had not expected her to get as far as the Volvo, for they were checking round the other cars first. She had just seconds to make another run for it, but with her would-be assassins between her and the main entrance and a 7ft-high wall enclosing the front of the property otherwise, the only possible avenue of escape was the side gate accessing the grounds at the rear.

Taking a deep breath, she launched herself across the intervening space just as Charles Slater turned away from the other cars and headed towards the Volvo, the commando knife in his hand glinting in the security lights. Hampered by the constricting handcuffs, which threw her off balance, Kate could not have been at more of a disadvantage, but fear and desperation are powerful drivers and she made the gate a split second ahead of his shout.

The shotgun blasted as Kate jerked the gate open, tearing a massive hole in the wicker fencing, but she was already through and lurching along the path towards the familiar rose arch. She got to the edge of the lawn as Charles Slater burst through the gate behind her. She tripped over a border of low-level shrubs and almost fell, but then she felt soft wet grass beneath her feet and stumbled and slithered through emerging moonlight towards the safety of the woods.

Once again the bark of the shotgun followed her. Shit! Carol Slater must have got hold of a fresh supply of cartridges. But the aim was too hurried and instead the blast took a chunk out of a stone statue gracing a dried up fountain in the centre of the lawn.

And then Kate was among the trees, a shadow merging with other shadows, crashing through the sodden undergrowth with total disregard for the low branches whipping across her face and the higher boughs tearing at her scalp like the claws of swooping birds of prey.

At which point she fell and fell heavily, her cuffed hands unable to break her fall and twisting under her as she slammed into the ground, air exploding from her lungs in a loud painful gasp.

The Slaters must have picked up on the sound and they were close, too close – she could hear them pushing through the undergrowth just yards away. She hugged the ground, gritted her teeth and lay perfectly still.

'She's around here somewhere,' Charles Slater exclaimed breathlessly from a point that seemed just feet from her. 'Ought to have brought a bloody torch.'

'Your fault,' his sister complained. 'You should have kept your eyes on her in the first place.'

'Shut it!' he snarled back, his voice further away now, the sounds of the undergrowth being trampled underfoot also starting to fade. 'Let's just find the bitch. If she gets out of here, we're stuffed.'

After a few more minutes, there was silence and Kate moved a leg experimentally. It was obviously badly bruised but she was sure she could stand on it. As for her wrists and one arm, which had been trapped under her body, numbness was starting to give way to a throbbing ache and in addition, she felt sure that the handcuffs on her wrists had cut into her flesh. Morbidly, she wondered what her police colleagues would make of the marks if the Slaters managed to recapture her and put Charles Slater's murderous accidental drowning plan into effect. Obviously her killers would remove the cuffs before the CID car was pushed into the river with her insensible body inside it, but the marks would be very evident, even if only slight, and they would become a lot more pronounced several hours after her death. Would SOCO or the forensic pathologist suspect she had been handcuffed prior to her death and initiate another murder inquiry, or would someone like Roscoe file the whole thing to avoid another costly investigation?

Tightly gritting her teeth again to stop herself crying out, she dug her elbows into the soft ground and gradually drawing her legs up under her a bit at a time, managed to get up on to her knees. Then, leaning one shoulder against the trunk of a nearby tree for support, she slowly straightened, first one and then the other leg to push herself upright. For a few minutes she stood there, swaying drunkenly, her senses swimming while she tried to maintain her balance and shake off a sudden attack of debilitating nausea.

More crashing noises way over to her left. They were still hunting for her. She now knew how a fox or a deer felt when pursued by the hunt.

Slivers of moonlight penetrated the autumnal remains of the canopy above her head and she groped her way forward, listening carefully to ensure that the sound of her pursuers did not get any closer as she advanced.

But then suddenly there was silence again, save for the steady dripping of moisture from the boughs above her head after recent rain. She froze. Where had they gone? Not given up, surely? No, they couldn't afford to. Maybe they had decided to stop and listen in an effort to track her movements in the same way as she tried to track theirs?

She took extra care, feeling her way with the toe of her boot, the perspiration glistening on her forehead and the various pains in her body seeming to fuse into one single fiery, throbbing agony.

She was almost on her last legs, she knew that, but she had no option but to keep going. Somehow she had to get out of this place and alert her colleagues. And it was at this point that it began to rain once more.

Moments later, the woodland gave way to marsh and she stiffened when she saw the wooden shed crouching among the reeds on the edge of the lake, rain striking the moonlit water with long slanting rods. The bird hide! She had actually cut diagonally through the woodland to the very spot where Colonel Slater had been murdered by his psychotic, avaricious offspring.

So now what? She was obviously a long way from the road, but to try and retrace her steps back to the house would be the height of folly. The odds on her making it out of the grounds via the main entrance without running into the

Slaters again were so poor that they were not even worth entertaining. She felt sure that the possibility of her trying to double back would already have occurred to the pair of them and one of them at least would very likely be lying in wait along the way. Yet staying where she was certainly wasn't an option.

She studied the rough ground between the edge of the woods and the lake in both directions, the moon's eerie light, bright and constant, despite the rain. There was no sign of anyone. A bird squawked from the lake shore, followed by the sound of wings beating feverishly on the water. Apart from that, there was only the noise of the rain. She raised both hands to wipe her sodden hair out of her eyes with one wrist and frowned. So, where the hell were the Slaters? Hiding somewhere – maybe in the shadows of the hide – waiting for her to emerge from the trees? Or could they have headed back to the house, thinking she might have returned there to try and phone for help while they were scouring the woods for her?

A fox padded out from among the trees to her right, sniffed the air, then swung away from her towards the drove which struck out across the moor 20–30 yards beyond the hide. Even from where she crouched she could see the police crime scene tape stretched taut between two posts – seemingly mocking her, challenging her to break through. The drove was her only hope. She had to get beyond that tape, get beyond it and run like hell.

She took a deep breath and stepped out from cover. Then, casting a further quick nervous glance around her, she stumbled towards the drove, rain cutting into her face, plastering her hair over one eye and splashing up over the tops of her boots as she slithered through puddles that had formed in the already saturated marshy ground.

The single strand of crime scene tape stood out in the moonlight like the gaunt finishing line of a marathon race, drawing her on, and she was actually within feet of it when the sinister figure materialised directly in front of her, legs apart for stability and shotgun levelled directly at her chest from shoulder-height. Carol Slater must have been hiding among the trees just yards away from her – just as she'd feared – and at such close range, there was not the slightest chance of the psychotic killer missing her.

But as Kate slithered to a stop, tensing her body instinctively for the blast that she felt sure would come, strong hands gripped her hair from behind, jerking her head back with painful force against a sodden shoulder as the sneering voice of Charles Slater breathed in her ear: 'Well, how nice to see you again, Sergeant. We thought you would try to leave us by the back door.'

Kate made no effort to struggle. There was no point. Even if she managed to break free of Slater's grip she knew his sister would simply blow her away with the shotgun – besides which, she had no idea whether he was still armed with the knife. So she simply went limp in his grasp, which seemed to surprise him.

'What's up, Kate?' he said. 'Finally give up, do you?'

He chuckled and tightened his grip on hair, making her wince. 'Still, you won't have to worry about it all much longer, sweetheart. You see, you've actually helped us out. Now we won't have to snuff out your lights in the Huntspill. We can do that here in our own little lake before we dump you and your car in the river. It will be a lot easier transporting a corpse than a living, breathing police detective.'

Out of the corner of her eye, Kate saw Carol Slater approach them, the shotgun now held in one hand, pointing at the ground – at once presenting her with an opportunity to try to turn the tables. With Charles Slater so close to his captive, his sister couldn't afford to use the shotgun during the struggle. But even as Kate raised her foot with the intention of raking her captor's shin with her heel, as she'd done with Bradley Jakes, she dismissed the idea as suicidal. Even if she managed to break free, she was still several yards from the cover of the adjoining woodland and despite the Slaters' original plan to make her death look like an accident, there was no doubt in her mind that the shotgun would be turned on her the moment she made a run for it – that was if Charles Slater's knife did not plunge into her body first.

Then the opportunity was lost to her anyway and her hair was nearly ripped out by the roots as Slater hauled her sideways, dragging her across the marshy ground towards the hide with one hand. She fell once, but he did not falter in his stride, pulling her upright even as she went over on to one knee. She felt trembling wooden planks beneath her feet and the next moment found herself at the end of the hide's rickety jetty, staring down into inky water in which rain-spattered moonlight was reflected in constantly changing kaleidoscopic patterns.

Carol Slater was beside them now and as Kate tried to pull back from the jetty's edge, her tormentor laughed. 'Beautiful, isn't it?' she sneered. 'Just right for a nice baptism.'

Out of the corner of her eye, Kate saw her step back briefly to rest the shotgun against the side of the hide, then she tensed as the woman seized her right arm in a powerful grip. At the same moment, Charles Slater's hand ploughed deeper into her hair, securing an even tighter grip while his other hand took hold of her left arm. Despite her frantic struggles and her attempts to kick out at the legs of her captors, she was forced down on to her knees and as the stagnant breath of the lake rose up to greet her, the stark realisation hit her with a cold numbing certainty that, after a career littered with close-calls, this time she was actually going to die.

'Au revoir, Sergeant,' Charles Slater mocked close to her ear and then she was tipped over the edge.

CHAPTER 25

The moonlight caressing the surface of the lake parted with an eruption of fluorescence, plunging Kate into a heavy, suffocating blackness that pounded through her eardrums with agonising force and burned her eyes as it enveloped her in a crushing vice. Icy, foul-tasting water blasted into her lungs, locking her diaphragm, and rapidly anaesthetising her brain. At first she tried to resist, tried to pull herself free of the lake's deathly embrace, but her cuffed wrists and the unrelenting pressure from the hands pressing down on her head from above, prevented her from pushing upwards towards the dancing white light through which she had plummeted. Then the blackness was in her head and she didn't care anymore. Instead, she felt a growing sense of peace – a desire to succumb and sink deeper into the now comforting darkness.

But in the midst of the tranquility, sudden muffled thuds from somewhere above her head and violent turmoil as the darkness itself seemed to boil around her. Excruciating pain in her head and chest and she felt herself being hauled out of her new-found nirvana, upwards towards the light. The lake did its utmost to hold on to her, only releasing its prize with a gurgling snarl of chagrin as the strong arms grasping the collar of her coat won the day and hauled her to safety.

For several minutes she lay face down on the wooden jetty, gasping and choking on the vomit and mucus that jettisoned from her stomach and lungs under the pressure of the same hands that had pulled her from the lake. Then, as she began to regain her senses, it became apparent that her "saviour" was no longer performing artificial respiration, but had got up from a crouched position and was now standing over her.

Her brain was mushy and confused, unable to properly comprehend how what was happening had actually happened. Who had pulled her out of the lake? Where had they come from? And most important of all, how had they managed to get past the Slaters with their shotgun?

She tried to get up, but at first exhaustion from her near drowning, coupled with the intense chill that had deadened much of the feeling in her body – particularly her handcuffed wrists – left her too weak even to get to her knees. But then the burning mist that had formed in front of her eyes from exposure to the bitterly cold water dispersed and she was able to focus on her surroundings – at which point she discovered precisely why the Slaters had not been a problem for her rescuer. It had stopped raining now and in the brilliance of a full moon, the grisly evidence was exposed in all its macabre detail.

Charles Slater was dead, that fact was beyond doubt. He was lying in a grotesque heap a few feet from where she herself was lying. His head was turned towards her, one glassy eye fixed on her, unseeing. The other was just a ragged cavity where the bullet had entered his skull, leaving an even bigger hole when it had exited and depositing glistening mucus-like brain matter over part of the jetty.

Turning her horrified gaze towards the bank, she saw Carol Slater. She had obviously been shot too, but was still alive and crawling snail-like along the jetty, leaving a bloody trail behind her, heading towards the shotgun, which was leaning against the hide where she had left it.

The figure in the black hooded coat standing beside Kate had swung round and was watching the woman's progress with what seemed like a sort of detached curiosity – just like a cat which allows its prey to creep away a short distance before it pounces on it again. Then, sauntering unhurriedly after the stricken woman, as if there was all the time in the world, the figure bent over her, a large automatic pistol in one hand, and coldly shot her in the back of the head.

Kate at last managed to struggle up on to her knees, using the wall of the hide for support, but froze again when the killer turned back towards her, face invisible behind some sort of mask in the blackness of the hood, pistol pointing directly at her head. She stared at the wicked-looking weapon with a sort of horrible fascination, terrified, yet confused as to why her rescuer had bothered to save her from drowning if the plan was now to summarily execute her; wondering in a perverse sort of way – as she had before when faced with Dibble's shotgun – whether she would actually be aware of the shot or the brief muzzle flash before the bullet blew out her brains.

But instead of pulling the trigger, the assassin lowered the weapon slightly, gave her a brief salute with the barrel, then wheeled round and strode off along the jetty. Within a couple of minutes the dark figure had crossed the broad expanse of open ground and disappeared into the woodland, a shadow lost among a multitude of other shadows.

* * *

Kate didn't go after the killer. She didn't want to chance her luck and in any event, shocked, handcuffed, soaking wet and unarmed, what could she have achieved anyway? So instead, she forced herself to go through Charles Slater's pockets until she found the keys he had taken from her, then tried to unlock the cuffs. But despite a determined effort, she was unable to twist her hands into the right position to insert the key in the small hole. In the end she abandoned the attempt altogether and steeled herself to go for a second option. Slater's mobile phone was in another pocket, but he was lying on top of it and it was necessary to roll him over on to his back in order to reach it. That was no mean feat with the handcuffs on, but she finally managed it, shuddering as he seemed to stir slightly when she tugged the phone free.

She dropped the mobile twice before she succeeded in dialling the emergency number and although she received the promise of immediate assistance from the headquarters operations room, it was a good 20 minutes before the flashing strobes of two police cars and an ambulance bumped along the drove towards the hide and a further half hour before Roscoe turned up, dishevelled as usual and smelling of beer.

He glared accusingly at Kate as she sat shivering on the upper step of the hide, with handcuffs now removed and her quivering body wrapped in the woollen blanket one of the uniform patrols had produced from the boot of his car. It was as if Roscoe considered her to be directly responsible for the two corpses lying on the jetty. Soaked to the skin, with water still squelching around inside her boots, she couldn't have felt more wretched, but if she'd expected an expression of sympathy from him after her ordeal, she was disappointed.

Instead, he concentrated on grilling her over the circumstances that had resulted in a further double murder for him to investigate, regardless of her exhausted sodden state or whether she had suffered any physical injury or mental trauma from the incident. It was only after he had extracted every morsel of information from her that he grudgingly agreed that she could stand down, callously instructing her to furnish him with a written statement once she had tidied herself up.

She stumbled back through the woods to the CID car she had left at the front of the house just as Lydia Summers, the forensic pathologist, arrived. And an hour later, after returning the police car to an almost deserted Highbridge police station and driving home to Burtle in her hated yellow Fiat 500, she was in a hot bath with a double whisky cupped in her hands – lost in steam and her own tangled thoughts.

Her wrists were red and puffy with a nasty cut to one where the handcuffs had chafed the skin and she could already see bruises coming out in ugly bluish patches on her arms and thighs. She had been very lucky, she knew that, and the irony was that she owed her life to a ruthless killer who had materialised from nowhere and for some reason had decided to rescue her, yet had executed both the Slaters in cold blood. Who was he and why had he specifically targeted the Slaters?

Furthermore, where the hell had he come from? His presence at the scene could not have been coincidental; armed and masked as he was, the murders must have been premeditated – even if he had originally intended carrying them out at the house and had then followed the pair through the woods to the hide. Maybe her arrival at Sycamore Lodge had frustrated that original plan?

But on top of it all, something else was bugging her, something about the killer she had picked up at the scene that she sensed was highly relevant. It had awakened a sort of recognition in her brain but a recognition of what? In her present state of confusion, she was unable to home in on it. Yet a strident voice in her head persisted in telling her it was there; all she needed to do was tease it out. All!

Finally climbing out of the bath, she drained her whisky glass and dried herself down with a vigour prompted by angry frustration. What the hell had she seen? What was it that was blocking her memory? The voice in her head was taunting her now, telling her: "I have what you want, but I'm not going to release it." Damnation!

She dressed in clean clothes and after washing her tangled hair, spent half an hour combing it out. The face in the bathroom mirror staring back at her was drawn and haunted, with mauve smudges under the eyes and abnormally pale lips. Grimacing, she applied some lipstick, eye make-up and a little rouge to make her look a bit more presentable for visiting Hayden in hospital. Then, reaching for her perfume spray, she grimaced again when she noticed that several of her fingernails had been broken in her struggles with Charles Slater. What a state she had got herself into!

And it was then, as if the mere application of make-up had in some way acted as a catalyst to memory recovery, that the wall which had been thrown up around her subconscious began to crumble and the information she had been trying so hard to extract, rushed out at her like the water bursting from a breached dam.

Then she simply stood there, gaping into the mirror, her whole being rebelling against the enormity of what her own thoughts were suggesting, but knowing in her heart of hearts that the data her subconscious had reluctantly parted with provided an exact fit.

* * *

There was a light on behind the drawn curtains of the ground-floor flat and a dark blue Land Rover was parked outside, half on and half off the pavement.

Kate checked the radiator grill of the vehicle and glancing at her watch, was not surprised to find the radiator was cold. It was at least two and a half hours since the double murder at Sycamore Lodge, so the engine of the 4x4 would have had plenty of time to cool down. The beam of her torch did reveal a substantial amount of mud coating the tyres, but that in itself didn't prove anything, since the roads across the Levels were pretty mucky at this time of the year anyway.

The floor in front of the driver's seat was a different matter, however. Just glancing through the window, Kate could see in the torchlight that it was filthy, with clay-like lumps attached to the rubber mat and the brake pedal. 'Seems like you've been somewhere very muddy tonight,' she murmured.

Checking further, she found more supportive "evidence" in the form of a pair of heavily muddied walking boots dumped on the mat in the front passenger well, but there was no sign of a pistol of any sort. Well, there wouldn't be, would there, she mused? Someone who sets out to murder two people would hardly leave the weapon on show in their car afterwards, would they?

She hesitated for a few moments, then, deciding on a direct approach, walked up the short path to the front door and knocked. There was no answer. She tried the handle and found the door was unlocked. She took a deep breath, opened it and stepped through into a short hallway.

Light streamed through an open doorway to her left – the front room – but peering inside, she saw that it was empty. There was a further open doorway on the same side of the hallway a pace or two beyond, which she could see was in darkness – the bathroom and toilet, as she later found out – and at the far end of the hall, a third door facing her, which was closed this time although she could see a bar of light at the bottom.

As she stood there, she heard the clink of a glass and a chair scraped suddenly on the floor. She approached the closed door and knocked. There was no reply, so she pushed it open. The room was a small kitchen. A figure was sitting on the far side of a bare wooden table with a bottle of wine and two half-full glass in front of them. The figure treated her to a smile as she entered the room.

'Hi, Kate,' Jonah said quietly. 'Take a seat – I've already poured you a drink.'

Kate stared at her for a moment. The TDC was wearing a blue roll-neck sweater and what appeared to be blue jeans. A black hooded coat had been draped over a chair in the corner of the room and even from where she stood, Kate could see the mud stains on it.

'I don't want a seat or a drink,' Kate replied grimly. 'I want an explanation.'

Jones smiled again and dropping one hand into her lap, she produced an automatic pistol which she pointed directly at Kate's chest.

'Oh, but I insist,' she said. 'So why don't you just sit down anyway?'

* * *

'How did you find out?' Ann Jones queried ruefully, lowering the gun, then placing it on the table in front of her as Kate sat down opposite. 'Was I that obvious?'

Kate shook her head. 'Not until I got home tonight and put on some perfume. That jolted my memory and provided the first hint. Chanel No. 5 has quite a distinctive smell and it is one of the perfumes I have at home. In fact, it was the Chanel that I chose to use tonight and which I suddenly realised the killer of Charles and Carol Slater was wearing.'

Jones raised an eyebrow. 'I should have been more careful after your obsession with perfumes and aftershave during the Stallard investigation, shouldn't I?' she said. 'Still, I hardly think the fact that both the killer and myself happen to wear Chanel No. 5 would have been enough to convict me of murder.'

'Not on its own, no, but after I was pulled out of the lake, I noticed something else – my rescuer had lost part of the second finger of their right hand—'

Jones tutted. 'Silly me. Should have kept my gloves on. But I've never liked wearing gloves when I'm handling a firearm and I didn't expect to come across someone as observant as you anyway.'

'Not observant enough, it seems,' Kate retorted. 'I've just noticed something that should have been apparent to me long before now. You appear to be left-handed, just like Carol Slater, and you are currently holding the pistol in your left hand, as you were when you shot her. But I never picked up on this before and I should have done. After all, I have seen you using a pen and drinking from a glass, yet I failed to notice that you favoured your left hand.'

Jones gave a short laugh. 'Ironic, isn't it – both your female killers being left-handers? Actually, I'm ambidextrous and always have been, but since the loss of my finger, I have tended to favour my left hand for key tasks, like handling firearms—'

'And belting my husband over the head?' Kate cut in. 'That was you, wasn't it?'

Jones flinched slightly. 'Yes, but it was an accident,' she said. 'I didn't mean to hit him so hard. I was just trying to get away.'

Kate's mouth tightened. 'Is that so? Then why try to waste him at the hospital afterwards? Frightened he might have been able to identify you later, were you?'

Jones shook her head vigorously. 'That's not true. Yes, I did go there, but to see how he was doing, nothing more. I felt very guilty and wanted to satisfy myself that I hadn't killed him.'

Kate snorted. 'Tell that to the marines.'

'But it's the gospel truth. The staff nurse saw me bending over his bed and assumed I was trying to interfere with the equipment, but I was actually checking on him, that's all.'

'So why not ask to visit him in the normal way and why run off when spotted?'

'Oh come on, Kate. I hardly knew him, so it would have looked mighty suspicious if I'd asked to see him, wouldn't it? As for running away, if I'd stayed, I'd have had a bit of explaining to do, wouldn't I?'

Kate was obviously still unconvinced. 'So what were you doing at Yardley's in the first place? Just out for a bloody stroll?'

'I went there to see Stallard.'

'To see him? How did you know he would be dossing there? There's nothing on his file about that.'

'He told me.' Jones sighed and took a long pull on her glass of wine before continuing. 'Listen, I need to explain something to you. Do you remember me telling you I had been trying to find my real mother and that when I finally managed to trace her, I learned she had died? Well, what I didn't tell you was that my mother had turned out to be Daphne Slater.'

'Slater?'

Jones nodded. 'Her maiden name was Armstrong, but as I told you before, she wasn't married when she fell pregnant with me and my father died shortly afterwards.'

She hesitated, as if reluctant to put into words what she had to say. 'When I left the military, I joined the Met, as you know, and it was a couple of years after that before I managed to trace my mother. Then, within days of this, I read about her murder in the press and later learned that Lenny Stallard had been sent down for the crime. I felt cheated and also for some reason compelled to visit him in prison to find out why he had killed a defenceless old woman. I'd already gained a law degree before joining the army, so it was easy to persuade the Met to let me enrol on a mickey-mouse psychology course, examining the causes of offending, part of which involved visiting a prison to interview offenders.'

She shrugged. 'Naturally, I chose the prison Stallard had been sent to and interviewed him at length, though he had no idea I was a police officer. He consistently protested his innocence and although he was plainly a very unpleasant man, it wasn't long before I began to doubt the evidence on which he'd been convicted.

"I decided the case needed a bit of unofficial reviewing and the best way of achieving that was to be on the spot to do it. So I applied for a transfer to this force and asked to be posted to the Bridgwater area on the grounds that I had already purchased a flat locally. Your Personnel Department was very accommodating too, actually sending me to Highbridge, and it came as a real bonus to me when my request for the CID attachment was approved. As a result, I ended up on the spot and right where I wanted to be—'

'Yeah,' Kate interrupted drily. 'On the spot and ready and willing to organise Stallard's break-out.'

Jones frowned. 'I had nothing to do with his escape. The idiot did that all on his own, completely out of the blue, but he rang me on my mobile afterwards and asked me to meet him at Yardley's as he had discovered something very important – something that had been the catalyst for his escape.'

'Which was what?'

'An old pre-recorded programme he had watched on the television in his cell about conservation in Somerset. It had shown the artificial lake the Slaters had created some years ago at Sycamore Lodge and had included an interview with Colonel Slater.'

'How was that significant?'

Jones smiled grimly. 'The interview took place in the sitting room of the house, with Carol Slater sitting in the background, and Stallard got quite a shock, for he immediately recognised her as the woman who had conned him into breaking into the house, albeit that she'd then had blonde hair.

'When I met up with him at Yardley's, he was very excited and said he intended confronting Carol Slater about it, but before I could dissuade him from this, you and your husband turned up on a building search and he scarpered. I never saw or had contact with him after that, until I saw his corpse at the cider farm several days later.'

'So why didn't you follow up on his accusation – or at least suggest something to me to point me in the right direction?'

Jones snorted. 'With what evidence? The Slaters would have laughed in our faces.'

'So you decided to become judge, jury and executioner yourself?'

'Not immediately, no, but as the inquiries you and I carried out continued, I became more and more certain that Stallard had been right. Finally, I decided to confront the late Colonel's offspring myself this evening. But after parking my car in a gateway nearby and walking in on foot, I heard Carol Slater's shotgun go off and from the cover of the strip of woodland bordering the drive, I was just in time to see you running through the side gate with the Slaters in pursuit.'

Jones held up her hands in a gesture of "c'est la vie". 'I followed you all through the woods to the hide and you know the rest.'

Kate looked even paler than she had after returning from the murder scene as she tried to digest all that she had been told. 'For someone who professed to be such a shrinking violet at post mortems and crime scenes,' she commented, 'you showed little compunction in carrying out premeditated murder.'

Jones gave an apologetic smile. 'Yes, sorry about that, but see, I wanted to present myself as rather weak and squeamish to avoid attracting any sort of attention or suspicion and on top of that, I have a bowel problem and was genuinely feeling sick.'

'So all that about being a non-combatant Redcap who had only seen service in Gibraltar, Germany and Aldershot was total crap?'

'Not entirely. I was a Redcap, but I actually served in Iraq and Afghanistan. I lost my finger and got the scar on my face – as well as some other hidden injuries – in an action against insurgents in Helmand province. I got sent back to Aldershot afterwards and was demobbed a few months later.'

She stared at the pistol lying on the table in front of her and stroked the cold steel with two fingers almost affectionately. 'I sort of "borrowed" this Browning from the armoury when I left the mob.'

'So you are no stranger to killing then?' Kate observed sarcastically.

Jones studied her for a moment. 'The Slaters deserved to die after what they did,' she said quietly, without answering the question.'

Kate frowned. 'Did I deserve to die too?' she asked. 'I assume it was you who cut the brake pipes on my car?'

Jones made a face. 'I only did that to frighten you,' she replied. 'You wouldn't give up on the investigation and I feared that you might discover the truth before I had completed my own inquiries and could act on them.'

She shrugged. 'I had intended cutting the pipes right through, so that the fluid would have drained away completely by the time you got up in the morning, when you would have found you had no brakes before you set off for work. Unfortunately you caught me at it and I wasn't able to finish the job – I can only say sorry.'

'Sorry? You think that's enough? I could have been killed.'

Jones nodded. 'I realise that, but what's done is done, I can't do anything about that now and anyway, my own time is fast approaching.'

Kate frowned. 'Your own time?' she echoed. 'What do you mean?'

Jones gave another shrug. 'Two to three months at the most, I've been told,' she replied. 'Bowel cancer, the aggressive kind. Nothing they can do apparently.'

Kate couldn't think of anything to say for a moment. Then she blurted. 'But you could get treatment.'

Jones shook her head sadly. 'Been all through that, Kate,' she said. 'It's terminal and I've had to accept that.'

'So … so what will you do now?'

'Do?' Jones echoed. 'What can I do?'

Then she abruptly picked up the pistol and before Kate could stop her, inserted it in her mouth and pulled the trigger.

AFTER THE FACT

Hayden Lewis stretched luxuriantly in the big double bed and stared at the sunlight creeping into the room through the slats of the newly installed vertical blinds. Then, with a smirk, he picked up the little bell from the cabinet beside the bed and shook it several times.

Kate appeared in the doorway after the third shake. 'Yes?' she queried drily.

Hayden beamed. 'Nice cup of tea, I thought?' he said.

'Did you?'

Kate walked into the room and pulled the blinds right back, causing Hayden to wince in the glare. 'Well,' she said, 'seeing as I have two days off and you are rehabilitating at home for another week, I thought it would be a very good idea if we got some fresh air.'

Hayden looked apprehensive. 'Fresh … er … air?'

'Yes, the stuff that seeps around the cottage.'

'Ah, that fresh air.'

Kate approached the bed and he jumped as she jerked back the covers. 'And since it is now ten o'clock in the morning and it is a fine dry day, I think it would be excellent rehab for you to concentrate on the garden.'

He gaped. 'The garden?'

'Yes, there are leaves to rake up off the lawn, pruning to do and a nice crop of weeds to pull out of the gravel path.'

'But … but I'm ill.'

'Were ill,' she corrected, 'and if you remember, the doc said you were overweight and needed to get plenty of exercise, now that your wound is more or less healed.'

She reached forward and grabbed his foot, hauling him down the mattress. 'So, up, you lazy sod, and get weaving!'

Hayden sighed and sat up on the edge of the bed, in no hurry to do anything and searching for excuses to delay the inevitable.

'How's poor old Roscoe since he was caught lighting up a fag?' he asked. 'Given up the old weed now, has he?'

Kate finished digging out pants, socks and a pair of jeans from the chest of drawers and opened a wardrobe to pick out a shirt for him.

'Official caution,' she replied. She tossed the clothes on to the bed beside him. 'But old habits die hard and I can't see him packing the fags in at his time of life.'

'Missing me, is he?' Hayden chuckled.

Kate stared at him critically. 'Hardly. He thinks you're a complete waste of a skin and I'm beginning to agree with him.'

Hayden feigned a hurt expression. 'That's not a very nice thing to say,' he said. 'Now I know how Bradley Jakes must have felt. Fancy dropping him in the cart with Traffic on a drink-driving after all the good info you said he put your way on the Stallard business.'

Kate grimaced. 'I didn't drop him in the cart,' she replied, rising to the bait. 'He was just unlucky enough to be caught twice over the limit, that's all.'

'Well, someone shopped him.'

Kate nodded. 'Well, it wasn't me, but at least it will keep him out of my hair for a while.'

He grinned. 'Probably for good. A reporter disqualified from driving is no good to his paper at all. Can't really see him hanging on to his job after that. Such a *nice* fellow too.'

She snorted and headed for the door. 'He's an arsehole and you know it. Now, when you've finished prevaricating, get yourself in gear.'

He frowned suddenly. 'I reckon that commendation you got from the chief constable over the Stallard affair has gone to your head,' he grumbled. 'You'll be expecting to meet the Queen next.'

'Jealousy will get you nowhere,' she retorted. 'Now move it!'

'But what about breakfast?'

'If you're a really good boy, I'll knock up some bacon and eggs for you once you've had a shower.'

'A shower? Wouldn't it be better to shower after the gardening when I'm hot and sweaty?'

'You are hot and sweaty now, fat man. So get on with it.'

Hayden was still muttering as he headed for the bathroom, but he had only just stepped into the cubicle and turned on the hot jets when the door opened and Kate's naked body squeezed in beside him.

He gulped. 'What about breakfast?' he exclaimed.

She handed him a bar of soap. 'Sod breakfast,' she said.

THE END

The Detective Kate Hamblin mystery series

Book 1: MURDER ON THE LEVELS
Book 2: REVENGE ON THE LEVELS
Book 3: FEAR ON THE LEVELS
Book 4: KILLER ON THE LEVELS
Book 5: SECRETS ON THE LEVELS

Please join our mailing list for updates on DETECTIVE KATE HAMBLIN, free Kindle crime thriller, detective, mystery books and new releases.

http://www.joffebooks.com/contact/

Thank you for reading this book. If you enjoyed it please leave feedback on Amazon, and if there is anything we missed or you have a question about then please get in touch. The author and publishing team appreciate your feedback and time reading this book.

Please join our mailing list for free kindle crime thriller, detective, mystery, and romance books and new releases. http://www.joffebooks.com/contact/

Our email is office@joffebooks.com

http://joffebooks.com

We hate typos but sometimes they slip through.
Please send any errors you find to
corrections@joffebooks.com

We'll get them fixed ASAP. We're very grateful to eagle-eyed readers who take the time to contact us.

Printed in Great Britain
by Amazon

36249811R00148